Alice E. Bartlett

A New Aristocracy

Alice E. Bartlett

A New Aristocracy

ISBN/EAN: 9783337101039

Printed in Europe, USA, Canada, Australia, Japan

Cover: Foto ©Andreas Hilbeck / pixelio.de

More available books at **www.hansebooks.com**

BY

"BIRCH ARNOLD,"

Author of "Until the Daybreak."

——— ——

BARTLETT PUBLISHING COMPANY.

NEW YORK : 30 AND 32 WEST THIRTEENTH ST.
DETROIT, MICH.: 44 WEST LARNED ST.

———

1891.

ELECTROTYPED AND PRINTED BY
THE PUBLISHERS' PRINTING COMPANY
30 & 32 WEST 13TH STREET
NEW YORK

"Talk about questions of the day. There is but one question and that is the Gospel. It can and will correct everything that needs correction. . . . My only hope for the world is in bringing the human mind into contact with Divine Revelation.

"WM. E. GLADSTONE."

INTRODUCTION.

"WRITE ye for art," the critics cry,
  "And give your best endeavor,
That down the aisles of length'ning time
  Your fame may speed forever!"

"Write ye for truth," my heart replies,
  "And prove that generous giving,
May help some blinded eyes to find
  The noblest way of living."

The simple story, plainly told,
  May bear its own conviction,
And words alive with buoyant hope
  May supersede their diction.

Give me the horny-handed clasp
  Of some good honest neighbor,
Who finds within the words I speak
  A strength for earnest labor.

Give me the lifted, grateful smile
  Of some poor fainting woman,
Who knows that I regard her soul
  As something dear and human.

Give me the fervent, heartfelt prayer
   Of just the toiling masses;
To be remembered with their love
   Your boasted art surpasses.

And this be mine, whate'er the fault
   Of manner, not of matter,
Along the rocky ways of life
   Some living truths to scatter.

BIRCH ARNOLD.

A NEW ARISTOCRACY.

CHAPTER I.

MR. MURCHISON was dead. The villagers announced the fact to each other with bated breath as they gazed with reverent awe at the crape on the door.

"Poor man," they sighed, vaguely sympathetic; "it's well enough with him now, but there's the children."

"Ay, there's the children," more than one responded feelingly.

Mr. Murchison had been the rector of the small parish of Barnley, distant perhaps a hundred miles from the city of C——, the great commercial center of the West, and having attended faithfully to his duties for a series of years, had been stricken at last with the dread pangs of consumption. Two years of painful waiting had passed away, and now the release had come. Devout, patient, and faithful, who could doubt that it was well with him?

"God tempers the wind to the shorn lamb," tremblingly spoke the clergyman who had been summoned to conduct the burial service. "Surely He will so influence the hearts of His people that these bereft ones, these fatherless and motherless children, shall not suffer from contact with the cold and bitter side of life."

Comforting words truly.; words that fell, as rain falls on parched fields, upon the benumbed senses of those who wept for their dead; words that touched the hearts of the little band of parishioners, and made each one wonder for the time being what he could do for them; words that resulted in offerings of flowers and fruit for one week and—so soon do good impulses die—in comment and unsought advice for another.

It was a well-known fact that aside from his library and household belongings Mr. Murchison had left nothing. A student and a biblist of rare discernment, he was happiest when deep in abstruse research, and many a dollar of his meagre salary had gone for volumes whose undoubted antiquity might help him to the completion of some vexed problem. Sometimes, looking up from his treatise or his sermon, he would glance at Margaret, his eldest daughter and careful housekeeper for the last five lonely years of his life, and think painfully of the time, the dread sometime, that was sure to leave his darlings unprotected. He wished, good man, that he might have money; not that he coveted the dross of earth, but that it might be the Lord's will to shield his loved ones from contact with bleak and bitter poverty. Many a prayer was rounded with that earnest supplication, to which he supplemented, always in complete resignation, "Thy will, not mine, be done." But he never saw the earthly realization of his hopes. He always grew poorer; his clothing just a trifle shabbier, the table a

little plainer, and Margaret daily more and more put
to her wit's ends in the difficult problem of making
something out of nothing. But who shall say the
faith of a life-time met with no recompense? Who can
declare, with certainty, the blinded eyes saw not afterward with clearer vision that he had left each of his
darlings God's highest riches, a brave human intelligence?

Margaret Murchison, the eldest of the three children, was too strongly built, physically and mentally,
to be beautiful. It is indisputably true that where
nature puts strength she also puts hard lines, and every
feature of Margaret's face bespoke the positive nature;
quick to comprehend and fearless to execute. Yet
hers was by no means a masculine or an ugly face.
Though strongly marked, there was still an indefinable
attraction in the warm depths of her blue eyes and
the smile of her mobile and sympathetic mouth. She
was, withal, strangely wholesome to look upon; one
of those rare beings, as it came afterward to be said
of her, whose faces rest you as calm waters and green
fields rest eyes that are blinded with the dust and tur-
moil of the city's streets. In figure she was tall, with
that breadth of shoulder and hip which indicates endurance, free and graceful in her movements, apt in
her utterances, and unusually keen in her intuitions.
At the time of her father's death she was twenty-four
years of age, thoughtful even beyond her years. Hers
had been a hard school. Poverty prematurely sharpens
wits and generates ambition, and ever since her earliest
recollection she had witnessed the daily pinchings and

privations of stern necessity. Questioning often with wondering eyes and grave thought, she had early learned to strive against this oppressor of her household; but the best of effort had only kept the lean wolf of hunger from the door. The father, wedded to abstruse speculation and erudite research, had not that talent for money-getting which is expected of the "working parsons" of country villages; and though the mother had been possessed of uncommon tact, meagreness in every detail of Margaret's physical growth had always confronted her. Not so intellect-ually, however. The bond of sympathy between parents and children had always been strong, and in the communion of thought the barren home life was lifted into realms of peace and plenty. Nobody re-membered how Margaret learned to read. The faculty seemed to come with her growth, like her teeth, and almost as soon as she had mastered the rudiments of reading, her father delighted to feed the grave little head with as much of the mental pabulum upon which he feasted as the infantile brain could digest. Her capacity proved something like that of the sponge, growing receptive in proportion as it was fed, and when at eighteen she was vouchsafed a year of school life at a church institution, she astonished both faculty and pupils by disclosing such an odd mixture of knowledge as no other pupil had ever brought to the school. Latin and Greek were far more familiar to her than fractions, and the geography of the Holy Land an open page beside the study of her own state and its form of government. Her aptitude for language was wonderful, and her ability for philosophical reasoning much beyond her years. She achieved marvels of learning in the one short year, only at its expiration to be called away by the sad announcement of her mother's mortal sickness. She reached home in time to comfort the anxious heart with the promise to keep always a home for the loved ones left behind. For five years she had faithfully fulfilled this promise, and now death had come again to take her last and only support. In the moment of her bereavement she did not realize how largely she had been not only self-dependent, but had been the mainstay of the little household. Love makes even the strongest natures yield to its silken leading-strings, and the tie between father and daughter had been no common one. But it was she who had been the prop that upheld the fabric of his life in these weary later years. It was on her brave heart he had leaned more and more; but she had no thought of what she had given. She had received, ah! who shall count the memories and pledges that loyal love has in its keeping?

But the prosaic side of life confronted Margaret one morning a week after she had laid her dead away, and roused her from the apathy of grief that follows even the wildest tempest of tears.

"Not even time to mourn," she said wearily. "Death comes; but life goes on, and it must be fed and comforted. I must work to drive the cobwebs from my brain and this strange inertia from my limbs. Something to do, some duty that must not be evaded, will heal and strengthen anew."

These reflections had been induced by a visit Margaret had just received from one of the vestrymen of the church at Barnley, who had called with words of condolence and inquiry. He desired to know, if it was not impertinent, what course Miss Murchison had decided upon relative to her future and her family.

"I have made no decision as yet," answered Margaret wearily; "I have been too absorbed in other things. Why do you ask, Mr. Dempster?"

"Well—ahem!—my wife and I had a talk about your—your prospects, and we thought that if—if—that is, we would like to help you, seein' as you're one of our pastor's family."

"You are very kind," said Margaret gently.

"Well, you see," began Mr. Dempster hurriedly, "we've always kind o' liked your folks, and my wife and I was sayin' that seein' as you'd be pretty likely to have a hard time, we'd like to help you out a bit. Now, there's Elsie: she's young, you know, and real bright and smart, and we thought maybe you'd be willin' we should take her and bring her up. She'd have a fust-rate home, you know."

"Mr. Dempster," said Margaret, ignoring the half-boastful tone in which the last assertion had been made, "do you think I could give away one of these children over whom I've watched for five years, and whom I promised never to leave as long as they needed a home? No, sir. My life has been hard, as you say; it may be harder yet; but as long as I have life and health I shall keep my promise. Besides, you forget that Elsie has not yet finished school."

" I know; but they was a-talkin' it over in the vestry last evenin', and they said they didn't see as you could afford to keep the children in school any more, as your father's salary is, of course, discontinued. You see, it takes money for clothes and incidentals."

" I am fully aware of that fact, but I have strong hands and a stout heart; because we are poor and cast down now, I see no reason why we should always be so. Do you, Mr. Dempster ? "

" No, no, of course not," hastily asented Mr. Dempster.

" Is it the opinion of the vestry that Elsie and Gilbert need no further education ? "

" Oh, no. They was only a-sayin', as they was talkin' about ways and means, that if you couldn't take care of 'em we—that's Mr. Dodd and me—would take 'em off your hands."

" I've no doubt that you meant kindly ; but I intend to teach them to take care of themselves, and there is no care equal to that. The parish of Barnley has been very kind ; but I assure you, sir, there is no happiness like being independent, and that, with God's help, I mean to teach my brother and sister to be."

" Then you mean to say you refuse our offers of help, Miss Murchison ? " said Mr. Dempster, bristling a little.

" Not at all. Indeed, I shall be glad of any assistance you can give me in the way of work. You know before my father's health failed I used to make your wife's dresses. I'm a little out of practice now, but I think I could soon get back the old deftness."

"Why—yes—but Mrs. Dempster sends to C——
now for her work. She says she gets better styles,
and takin' all things into consideration, it don't cost
such a dreadful sight more."

Margaret smiled involuntarily. She knew how the
Dempsters, from greatest to least, counted the cost
of everything, and she knew the offer to take Elsie—
dear, sunny-hearted Elsie—off her hands had not been
so much a question of philanthropy as gain. Could
she so have disposed her heart as to give Elsie away,
the bare thought of the drudgery which would have
been her portion as maid-of-all-work in that household
would have been sufficient to deter her.

"Well, I must be goin'," said Mr. Dempster as
Margaret remained silent. "You know they've hired
a new parson and he will be here this week," he added
from the doorway.

"So soon!" exclaimed Margaret with a start. "And
—and—you will want the parsonage right away?"

"Well, there ain't no particular hurry, I suppose;
but the folks thought it best to give you a week's
notice to quit," and having delivered this parting shot,
Mr. Dempster said "good-day" hastily and walked
out of the gate.

So soon! so soon! to leave the dear home that
spoke so tenderly of those who had gone away! To
leave the cozy corner where stood her mother's arm-
chair, as it had stood for years, often bringing its
memories of the sweet face and gentle hands which
had presided over the hearthstone so long ago. To
leave the sacred room where stood her father's desk,

from which not a paper had been removed since the nerveless hand had dropped the pen in the midst of a sentence of his last sermon; the room where stood his well-filled book-cases and his shabby furniture, and go—where—oh, where? asked Margaret's heart in utter anguish. She grew suddenly weak with the rush of memory and regret, and slipped down upon the floor in an abandon of grief.

The outer door swept open and a young girl, entering hastily, cried sharply as she knelt beside the prostrate form: "O Meg! dear, brave Meg! what has happened?"

"Nothing, Elsie dear. I have only been bewildered of late, and had forgotten that this is no longer home."

"Must we leave soon?"

"Within a week."

"It is sudden; but I knew it must come sooner or later. I am not sorry, either, Meg; for we will go out into the world to work for each other and make a new home."

Meg shook her head. "You are brave, Elsie, with the ignorance of youth. You do not know what gulfs lie between your hope and its accomplishment. While I——"

"You, Meg," interrupted Elsie, "are wearied with the weight of your burdens, and I must take them off your shoulders and rest you good and long."

"Oh, confident youth! What a sweet comfort this little rose is to me," and Margaret took the bright face between her hands and kissed it fondly. It was a rose indeed that Margaret raised to her lips. Bril-

liant with the rich coloring of the brunette, lit up by
a pair of dark velvety eyes, a full, red-lipped, delicately-
curved mouth, and framed in a mass of black, lustrous,
curling hair, Elsie's face was undeniably beautiful.
Somewhat petite in form, she was the embodiment of
grace in every movement.   Naturally hopeful and
sweet-tempered, she had been all her life a source of
comfort to Margaret.   If she felt that she had greater
patience, she found encouragement in Elsie's greater
hopefulness.   If she felt in herself greater power to
conquer adverse circumstances, she relied equally upon
Elsie's faculty of throwing the best light upon everything, and taking trouble as little to heart as possible.
Unlike, yet like.   Margaret's strength was born of
conviction and experience, and duty, her imperial mistress, held her firmly to her course.   Elsie's courage
and cheerfulness were as inherent a part of herself as
her rippling black hair or her daintily-fashioned foot,
and love was the governing impulse of her life.   She
would do for love's sake what no amount of cogent
reasoning could convince her ought to be done for
duty's.   She "hated the name of duty," she had been
heard to declare with an imperious stamp of her little
foot.

"If one was good, because love prompted her to do
all these nice things for other people, wasn't that
enough?   And as for 'doing good to those who de-
spitefully use you,' she believed the Lord wasn't very
angry if you only just didn't do them any harm!
And she felt sure that He would forgive her if she
couldn't and *wouldn't* like the Dempsters."

All this had happened long ago, and now it came back to them as Meg told Elsie of Mr. Dempster's offer.

"The old—gentleman!" exclaimed Elsie as Margaret glanced up apprehensively. "I was only going to say 'heathen,' anyway," she added mischievously. "Do you think it is my duty, Meg, to accept the offer, and learn under their guidance to be a meek and quiet Christian?"

"My poor Elsie, you will never be a meek Christian, I am sure. Let us hope Mr. Dempster meant well, and so forget all about it."

"With all my heart, since I am not going to him. So long as my dear old Meg commands I obey. He needn't have troubled himself about the school, for I don't intend to go back."

"Indeed you must. I shall write to Dr. Ely to-day and ask a place for you and Gilbert. You know what our prospects are, dear, that it must be head and hands for each of us, and it behooves us to put as much into our heads as time and circumstance will allow."

"And you, dear?" asked Elsie wistfully.

"I shall find something for my hands to do. They are good strong hands, and they must put bread into that little mouth."

"What can your hands find to do here? There is nothing better than sewing or dish-washing. You are fitted for better work."

"I hope I am; but it does not follow that I must refuse to do what I can find to do, because I cannot find what I want. If nothing better offers I shall even try the dish-washing."

2

"O Meg! I couldn't bear to see you so lowered."

"You misuse the word, Elsie. I should feel that I lowered myself more in refusing the work at hand, in the vain hope of finding something pleasing and gen-teel. Dear little girl, your solemn old Meg wants to disclose to you the prosaic rule by which she means to measure her life. It will seem dry and hard to you in your youth and bloom; but you must learn some time, and if the bitter tonic is taken early nothing seems quite so bitter afterward. Shall I tell you?"

"Y-yes," answered Elsie hesitatingly, "only — only——"

"I know. You dislike even to be told that life is uncompromising. Well, then, we'll say no more about it. I see I cannot learn for you."

"It is not that," exclaimed Elsie. "I am only just beginning to see how you had to forego your youth and bloom to learn for all of us. Tell me all about it, and teach me to be your helper. I am such a lover of pleasure, I never can be strong like you. Tell me how you learned it, Meg."

"I did not learn to be less than happy. I only learned to do well what lay nearest me, and in that there is happiness. There is the whole dread secret, Rosebud, and if you want me to be epigrammatic and terse here is the formula: Aim high; mind is the greatest of God's forces. Be honest; a clean con-science is the best bed-fellow at night. Do cheerfully what lies nearest you; fortune surprises the faithful."

"Diogenes in petticoats!" exclaimed Elsie, all her cheerfulness returning. "Make a dictionary, Meg,

on the plan that A stands for Apple, and Gilbert and
I will not need to go to school."

"No, I've tried philosophy enough on you; you
laugh at it."

"Not for worlds! Trust me, Meg, to learn it all
somewhere on the road to threescore and ten. It is a
'sair' lesson for one of my temperament; but if it
'maun be' it 'maun be.'"

"I hope your prosy Meg may live long enough to
see you safely conning it; for I feel as if I were born to
keep your wings from singeing."

"What a heroine you are, Margaret Murchison!
I am fain to fall at your feet and worship you."

"That would be foolish. Wait to see at least how I
bear the burden and heat of the day. You may have
to reverse your opinion."

"Never! Even if you sit with idle hands the rest
of your days. But to go back to our muttons. What
are we to do?"

"Write to Dr. Ely," answered Meg, rising to her
feet. "Bring me my writing-desk, Elsie."

"On one condition," said Elsie, placing a hand on
either side of Meg's face and looking pleadingly up
into her eyes: "write please for Gilbert. Let me stay
with you."

"No, Elsie. Education will be worth everything to
you. You cannot be successful without it."

"Then teach me yourself. Dr. Ely said you had a
wonderful mind."

"Good friable soil for seed; nothing more. I have
but a handful of knowledge and that would soon

be exhausted.   I cannot consent to your leaving
school."

"I'll not *leave*—I'll never go back," said stubborn
Elsie. " Don't look so reproachful! This much I am
decided upon : while you drudge I drudge, so that's
said, and I isn't a-gwine to unsaid it, nuther," she added
roguishly, imitating the negro dialect and attitude.

"Obstinate little girl! I perceive I must bring my
desk myself."

"No, no, Meg," and Elsie sprang to the door.
" Only promise!"

"It is your good I seek, child."

"I know it; but let me be unselfish this once. It
may be my only chance of redemption."

"You shall have your way," said Margaret with
eyes suffused with tears.

"Dear, good Meg," exclaimed impulsive Elsie,
throwing her arms round her sister's neck. "We'll
cling together. You shall be the oak to hold me up,
and I'll be the ivy to keep you warm—and green!"

CHAPTER II.

"MEG, I've an idea!" exclaimed Elsie several morn-ings later, as Margaret returned from an unsuccessful search for a house, as well as work at the hands of Mrs. Dempster and several other ladies of the parish.

"I'm glad to hear it. Ideas are good things to have," said Margaret, wearily dropping into a chair.

"Of course you haven't found work, or anything else but advice, have you? Well, this is my idea: let us go away from Barnley."

"O Elsie!"

"I know it's hard; but we'll starve on advice. It's cheaper than beefsteak, of course; but it is somewhat weakening after one has breakfasted, dined, and supped on it. Let's go away and dig for a living. See what I found this morning," and Elsie drew from her pocket a newspaper clipping of late date, and read aloud an advertisement:

"For Rent: A small house at Idlewild, with three acres of ground well supplied with small fruits. Only thirty minutes' ride on dummy to city market. Rent cheap, or will sell at reasonable price. Call at Harris & Smith's, cor. Vine and Tenth Sts., C——."

"Meg, let's go and see it."

"Why, Elsie, child, how is it possible?"

"This way. Maybe I'm visionary, but I've an idea that we can make enough money out of the place to pay the rent and keep us. See here: 'only thirty minutes' ride on dummy to city market.' Now, three acres of ground, if good for anything, ought to raise potatoes."

"Admitted. Go on with your proposition."

"Potatoes *with* salt constitute a very fair living for a hungry man; *without* salt they keep starve to death away—ergo, let's plant potatoes! To be serious— I've thought of this. It is now February, and we'll need to make haste. We've raised our own potatoes in the parsonage garden for years, and good ones, too. Why not raise double the quantity somewhere else and sell the surplus? The small fruits advertised may be worth cultivating, too. You are a splendid amateur gardener—everybody says so; and there's Gilbert—to be sure, only a boy; but a boy is good for some things sometimes—and I consider myself capable of being taught. Now, I've sketched the outlines of Eutopia, and you must fill in the shading."

"Outlines are easily drawn; the skill lies in the filling in."

"Therefore I left it for you. I feel as if we might dig our living out of the soil easier than out of the oftentimes ungracious favor of humanity. Suppose we look this place up to-morrow?"

"I cannot see my way clear yet. Where is all the money to come from to start us in this venture? It takes money for spades, you know."

"I realize it. Can't we sell something?"

"What—our old clothes?"

"To the rag-man perhaps. Seriously, have we nothing of value we can spare?"

"I can think of nothing."

"I can. O Meg, the hardest part of my suggestion is yet to come. Dr. Ely said when I named some of the books in poor father's library that they were of undoubted value, as many were out of print. He spoke especially of the two Caxton copies, Plantin's 'Biblia Polyglotta,' and Sparks' 'Life of Washington.' Dear Meg, the question is: Shall we keep our treasures and starve, or in letting them go find a chance of outgrowing our poverty? I am tired of this grinding life that takes the color out of your cheeks and puts wrinkles where dimples ought to be. Much as I love the dear old books, I love hope for you and for all of us better. O Meg! it is no sacrilege to say that if our father could speak to us he would tell us to sell them. The heritage is precious; how precious to us few can guess. But, my sweet sister, your hopes and happiness are dearer to him, I know. Don't sob so, Meg; you will break my heart. Forgive me for suggesting it. It really seems best."

"I know it, Rosebud," said Margaret after a long silence. "I must think about it. I cannot decide yet."

As Margaret spoke she raised Elsie's tearful face and kissed it tenderly. It was more difficult for Margaret to give up the books than Elsie had dreamed. They were not to her, as to Margaret, the great mine of wealth from which she had drawn the intellectual riches that were already hers, and from which she had hoped to glean a far greater abundance. Dear as they were for the associations' sake, many of them having been successively her grandfather's and father's, and hallowed as they were by the thought of the dear eyes which had once delighted in their pages, this relinquishment of her ambitions seemed the most cruel hurt of all. She knew that Elsie's suggestion was practicable; that it opened a way out of their present difficulties; but it was the slipping of the cable that bound her to the old life which, despite its hardships, had seemed so idyllic in its visions and mental attainments. If she gave up her books, what could she hope for beyond the barren drudgery of mere existence? With her books she could revel in an ideal world where the hard facts of her daily struggles could not intrude. They were indeed a heaven of remembrance and a heaven of hope to her. Where, oh, where else could she find the oasis of rest, the one little gleam of personal happiness which she had hoped might be allowed her? And yet duty, even from the mouth of Elsie, whom she had hitherto regarded as a mere child, said all too plainly that the cherished books must go. There seemed to be no other solution of the vexed question of subsistence. It was a very pale face that Margaret raised to Elsie's anxious glance several moments later; but it was determined and calm.

"You are right, Elsie; you excel me in practicability even now. I will write at once to Dr. Ely."

"Meg, I was cruel to you."

"As facts are sometimes cruel. Now let us cata-

logue the books, that Dr. Ely may judge of them.
Not another tear, Rosebud, but forward."

A reassuring smile and a fond kiss calmed the rising
storm of regret in Elsie's heart. With protean quickness the smile so natural to her face came back, and
hastily mounting the small step-ladder, she took down
the books and gave title, name of author, and date of
issue to Margaret to jot down. There were perhaps
some eight hundred books, of which only a small portion would in these days of reprints possess an unusual interest for the bibliophilist. Among the latter
were: Smellie's " Philosophy;" Plantin's " Biblia Polyglotta " in eight folio volumes, published in the sixteenth
century; Dunton's "Life and Errors," 1659-1733; Caxton's books, mostly translations from the French;
Nicholl's " Literary Anecdotes;" Sotheby's " Handwrit-
ing of Melancthon and Luther;" Davy's "System of
Divinity," twenty-six volumes; Dolby's "Shakespearean
Dictionary;" Ainsworth's " Historical Novels;" Hone's
" Early Life and Conversion;" Timperly's " Encyclo-
pedia of Literary Anecdote;" " The Bay Psalm Book;"
Adelung's "Historical Sketch of Sanscrit Literature,"
translated by Talboys; Krummacher's " Elisha." Aside
from these somewhat rare books, the library took a wide
range in history, poetry, fiction, and travels. Margaret
could scarcely repress the desire to cry out once more
against the sacrilege. Here was information for a life-
time; here forgetfulness of the past, elysium for the
future! Why must this grief be superadded to all she
had borne? But with heroic effort she choked back the
tears and went calmly on with her work. By the time

she had finished the list and written a letter to Dr. Ely, of the Episcopal school at A——, she had put aside regret and was once more ready to look facts squarely in the face. "The first step that costs" had been taken, and never afterward to Margaret did any sorrow seem like the wrench of this one. It was with alacrity, amounting almost to cheerfulness, that she went about her task of packing the household goods, and though sometimes tears would for a moment dim her eyes and tender memories paralyze her hands, yet the serene conviction that her decision had been wisely taken seemed to hover like a nimbus of light above the sadness of the slowly-moving hours.

One morning as Margaret, with her brown locks shrouded in a wide-frilled sweeping cap, her dress hidden by a high-necked calico apron of nondescript make, stood upon a step-ladder, engaged in removing the dimity curtains from the sitting-room windows, a peremptory knock at the open door behind her caused her to turn so suddenly that the ladder tipped and threw her, with unexpected suddenness, into the arms of a dignified gentleman who stood upon the threshold. Quickly disengaging herself, she exclaimed with a laugh:

"My greeting is unusually fervent, Dr. Ely; but you perceive that circumstances——"

"Were too many for you," he interrupted, as Margaret paused for breath. "I hope you were not hurt?"

"Not in the least; but a trifle confused. Will you walk in and be seated? I did not look for a personal answer to my letter, otherwise I should have deferred my packing."

"I decided to come only at the last moment, and so could not write you. I am not at all sorry that I surprised you; in fact, I found it rather pleasant."

Margaret glanced up apprehensively, a new wonder growing in her eyes, which the doctor was quick to note and interpret. "I felt that it would be much easier to adjust the prices of the books and come to a satisfactory arrangement of matters through a personal interview. Therefore I am here."

"And quite welcome; but you must pardon the incoherent state of things."

"With all my heart, so long as you remain rational. And now I wish you would tell me what you propose doing."

"I? Working for a living."

"At what?"

"Anything I can find. Just now Elsie has me under control. She is bent on making a market gardener of me. Please look at this advertisement. We have already made appointment to visit the place, and if satisfactory and the books are disposed of, to take immediate possession. What do you think of the plan?"

"H-m. It might be good, but how about the children's education?"

"That was what worried me greatly at first; but both of them say so long as I work for a living they shall help too. We have decided to give an hour each evening, after it is too dark to work, to a little home culture. After all, it is the practical application of knowledge that makes one educated."

"Quite true, Miss Margaret," answered the doctor as he gravely regarded her. "Give me a few more details of your plan, and let me see how practicable it is."

As Margaret proceeded with an animated recital of the schemes which she and Elsie had lain awake nights to concoct, Dr. Ely sat so intently watching her that she flushed and grew uneasy under his scrutiny. He, however, was not aware of it; for his mind was borne in upon itself, and he was tracing step by step the years of his life that had brought him to this present moment. He was a dignified man nearing the forties, with a grave manner that was often thought austere, but which was only the outward covering of a nature too keenly sympathetic and appreciative to risk the disapproval of an obtuse world. Like all delicate and sensitive things in nature, he wrapped himself in a husk, and only those who penetrated the outward covering knew how beautiful was the inner temple of his soul, how genial its warmth, and how playful the fancy that tended the altar of his imaginings. His sudden encounter with Margaret this morning had brought to the surface a slight hint of its existence, but the quick wonder of her eyes had sent it again into hiding. He had been for some ten years the president of the school at A——, and stood entirely alone in the world. For twenty years he had cherished the memory of a fair girl wife who had been companion and helpmeet but three short months, when death claimed her. In her

grave he had thought to bury love, and live henceforth
a solitary worker, with no dreams to entice again beyond the prosaic outlines of his daily duties. But
Margaret Murchison's year at the school had affected
him strangely. He had watched the girl's development with uncommon interest; had been touched
more than once by the clearness and unusual candor
of her nature, and grew to have a profound admiration
for the strength and purpose which upheld her. When
she had been so suddenly called home by her mother's
death, he had missed her more than he liked to own
even to himself. Despite the disparity in their years,
he felt that hers was a nature to draw from its ob-
scurity all that was highest of attainment in his own.
He was but too conscious that, struggle as he might,
he somehow fell short of his desires. His most earnest
efforts seemed to fall half-heartedly upon those around
him. The fault must be his; the long loneliness of his
life—with neither father, mother, sister, brother, wife,
to share a single aspiration or make vivid a single
heart-glow—had unwittingly isolated him from mankind. When the light of this love fully dawned upon
him, his soul felt the glow of a new purpose, and it
became to him the symbol of a wider sympathy and
charity, because of which Divinity long ago found need
to send a sign to all mankind. His school was not
slow to feel the change, and when the time became
ripe for him to speak, he felt that he was no longer
offering Margaret, in all her freshness, the remnant of
a heart and life, but the first fruits of a living soul.
He hastened to Barnley, strong in his purpose to lift

her at once from the toil and privation of poverty. He had watched her career as best he could, in the occasional letters received from her father, who never failed to comment upon her strength and growth of character, and his love had grown with the subtileness of fancy until he had never stopped to consider the effect it might have upon Margaret. Surely to be sheltered and loved—ah! how he would prove his love to her—ought to be reason enough for any woman so bereft and friendless. So he had reasoned until he caught the apprehensive glance of Margaret's eyes, and then he knew that his dream had not been hers, and that love with her would not be made at once answerable even to the most passionate appeals. All these musings ran swiftly through his mind, the while his intent glance remained upon Margaret's face, unconsciously drinking in its variable play of expression. At last she ceased her recital, and said in a slightly constrained voice: "I think I have told you all our plans for the present, Dr. Ely."

But the intent eyes never left her face as the doctor asked wistfully: "Are you sure you've strength for so much?"

"I have faith that it will be given me."

"Yes, yes, it will," he replied fervently, as he roused himself with an effort. "And now let us take a look at the books."

He followed Margaret into the study and stood long in silent contemplation before the shelves. He was evidently making a careful computation of the value of the books. "How much money will you need for this undertaking?" he asked, suddenly turning to Margaret.

"I have very little idea. I can scarcely tell until we have seen the place."

"Ah, yes, I had forgotten. Of course you are not sure of anything as yet. When did you say you had appointed an interview with the agent?"

"We had expected to go this afternoon, if we had a satisfactory letter from you in time. If not, the interview was to be postponed until to-morrow."

"And you have not had that satisfactory letter yet. Well, you shall have it now. The books are even more valuable than I thought. They number, I think you said, some eight hundred volumes. Now, I wish to propose a plan of my own. Suppose I advance you the sum of four hundred dollars on the books to begin with, allowing you to select such as in your home culture club you will doubtless need, and reserve the balance—I will not place an exact price on them now —to be drawn upon in case of further demand for money. Then, when you have made your fortune, you are to have the books back at the price I paid for them."

The doctor waited some time for Margaret's answer; but she stood with head slightly averted and was silent. At last he could wait no longer, but bending forward, glanced down at her face. Tears stood on the long lashes and trembled on her cheeks. "Margaret," he cried sharply, "what have I said that is wrong?"

"Nothing!" she exclaimed, suddenly extending both hands to him. "Your goodness is so unexpected that I am not strong enough for it."

He caught her hands in his own as he said impulsively: "Listen, Margaret. It is not goodness—it is rather pure selfishness. I came here this morning intent on offering you not the worth of the books, but something I was foolish enough to fancy of more value —myself. No, don't start; but hear me out. Man-like, I fancied that I had but to speak and you would let me take you away from all the toil and privation; but now I know you——"

Margaret gently drew her hands away, and interrupted him: "I never dreamed of such a thing. It is impossible."

"If I loved you, Margaret, had loved you for years —don't look so incredulous—ever, since you were a school-girl, and had waited patiently until the time was right, hoping that my love might win its response even as the flowers respond to the warmth and light of the sun—if I offered all this and a life-long devotion, would it then be impossible?"

Margaret glanced up wonderingly, appealingly, into the eager face above her.

"It is all so strange, so confusing; but I cannot— it would indeed be impossible; for—forgive me, I do not want to hurt you—I do not love you, Dr. Ely, and I——"

"Say no more," he said gently, "I knew it even before I spoke; but I am glad you understand me. I have been a lonely man all my life, and you can perhaps imagine how, even old as I am, I find delight in the companionship of one who is quick to understand

and appreciate all that interests me. I love you, dear child, with the one love of my life; but I shall never again obtrude it upon you. I must, however, claim one favor. I am willing to sink all that I had hoped to the calm basis of friendship; do not deny me that. Let me help you, even as I had meant to before I spoke, and I promise faithfully never to claim anything more at your hands than the just consideration of one friend for another. You stand alone and inexperienced—put aside what has passed and let my age and experience help you."

Margaret, watching him as he spoke, could not fail to be touched by the sincerity and unselfishness of his words. For reply she placed her hand in his and said softly, "I will."

"One word more. If the time ever comes—mind, I do not expect it, I do not even beg it—but if the time does come when your heart can respond fully to the love that shall be yours as long as life lasts, you have only to say 'come,' and I will obey you though it be to the uttermost parts of the earth. May I ask this too?"

"It is not much to promise," said Margaret gently, "but it may be too much to hope for. I have never had time for anything but immediate duties, and I am afraid I shall never find time for anything else. I have always felt that I belonged to these children. If, however—and I can discern but the faintest hope—if such a time *should* come, you may be sure that the word will not be uttered half-heartedly."

3

A blush stole up to Margaret's cheek as she spoke, making her whole face glow and soften with an unwonted beauty that the doctor's observant eyes did not fail to note. They were suspiciously misty as he raised her hand to his lips and said fervently:

"Amen. Now let's to business."

CHAPTER III.

"OH, I think it is delightful," exclaimed Elsie as she, Margaret, and Dr. Ely stopped in the late glow of the afternoon sun before the gate of the place at Idlewild. "Such a charming tangle of briers to get scratched on while hunting for very stray berries."

"There is something to be done here before one could hope for returns," assented the doctor. "But let us explore the house, and see whether it is possible to exist in it."

The house, by courtesy a cottage, had four rooms, so called. Elsie suggested boxes as a better name, but found consolation in the fact that four rooms for three people left a breathing-room that each could occupy in turn. The rooms were black with smoke and slippery with filth, and even Margaret felt something very like despair as she exclaimed piteously: "The muscle and soap it will take to cleanse it."

"Is it habitable otherwise?" asked the doctor as he rattled windows, examined hinges and locks, and poked into chimneys and cupboards. "Fairly good. White-wash, paint, soap, and muscle, and you won't know it, Miss Margaret. Now let us see what the garden is like. Wants underdraining badly. Soil clayey and cold, but admirably situated for outlet of drain. A few muck-heaps and this garden will blossom like the rose."

"But you frighten me," exclaimed Margaret aghast. "I haven't the slightest idea how to drain it, and I am sure it will cost more than we can afford."

"We are only examining possibilities. 'Small fruits,' a dozen ragged currant bushes, some straggling strawberry vines, grapes that have run riot, and a 'delightful tangle,' as Elsie says, of raspberry bushes. Common, too—no, Gregg if I am not mistaken. Ah! that is better. 'Three acres of land'—not more than two and one-half that can yield anything. Now, Miss Margaret, if you and Elsie are ready we'll interview the agent."

"The place will not pay for the outlay upon it, I am afraid," said Margaret despondently, as they went out of the gate.

"Not this season, certainly; but we can tell better when we have seen the agent and found out what we can do with him."

"Well, if you had not insisted on coming with us I should have turned back in dismay. Somehow, when I can see a way through I am ready enough to act; but I become frightened when the wall is so high I cannot see over."

"That is natural enough. Very few women have the courage to scale precipices; but those who undertake the problem of self-support must encounter all of a man's difficulties. We are a chivalrous people here in America, but that chivalry usually consists in giving a woman a fair field and no quarter. If you seek to be one with us in opportunities, you must be one with us in conditions."

"If I might always be sure of such fair considera-tion I shall not complain. A woman, however, cannot insure her own incompetency against the greed of those who are chivalrous enough to take advantage of it. She must always be more or less a victim."

"So long as she remains incompetent. Experience, however, is the great moulder in her case as well as that of her brother. She demonstrates her capacity in proportion as she learns the same hard lessons. One of the first of these lessons is not to ask any more of the world because of her sex. When women cease clamoring for a man's rights and a woman's pre-emi-nence at one and the same time, then will the dogged opposition of those to whom she appeals be less notice-able."

"Yet it is quite natural for the weak to ask a little extra standing-room of their more fortunate brothers."

"It is one thing to ask by virtue of a common sympathy, and another to demand as a right. Man-kind is a good deal like the pig that Paddy tried to drive to market. 'Shure if ye iver git 'im there, ye must head 'im t'other way.' It might be well to try the scheme on the agent of this place."

As Margaret glanced up and caught the humorous twinkle of the doctor's eyes, she said quietly: "I leave the settlement of the matter in your hands, while I watch your effort in getting the pig to market. I shall have need to learn all I can."

Mr. Smith, of the real estate firm of Harris & Smith,

was a portly, self-satisfied man, who regarded the applicants for the little place at Idlewild with a somewhat lofty stare over the rim of his gold eye-glasses. It was quite evident from his manner that so small a transaction as this was not considered worth any extra amount of civility. But the pompous manner neither abashed nor diverted Dr. Ely from his purpose. With a man's decision and firmness he stated his wishes, met objections, overcame difficulties, and obtained satisfactory results, with such facility that Margaret felt herself well-nigh overwhelmed in the dismal swamp of her own incapacity.

When the contract for the specific performance of each had been duly drawn and signed, and Dr. Ely, Margaret, and Elsie had once more regained the sidewalk, the doctor asked: "Well, Miss Margaret, did I get my pig to market?"

"As I should never have dared to do."

"I knew it," and the doctor's face grew suddenly grave. "It is a big undertaking for a slender untried woman."

"No," said Margaret gently, "not when I have such an adviser."

"Well, I intend to see you safely settled before I leave. There is a great deal in getting started right."

"I haven't a demur to make—not even an expostulation as to the trouble you are making yourself. The time to assert my independence will be when I am monarch of all I survey."

"You'll have nothing to do now for three years to come but develop your skill as a gardener. I fancy you will not find altogether easy work or satisfactory returns."

" I do not expect to. I have my apprenticeship yet to learn; but it seems to promise more than any other available thing. Besides, I shall count even mistakes as so much marketable goods in the future, if I am only wise enough to profit by them."

" He is wise indeed who always succeeds in doing it."

The doctor at once set himself to supervising the laying in of the drain, the painting and papering of the little house, and the trimming and pruning of the tangle of vines and bushes in the garden. With the aid of Gilbert, a bright lad of sixteen, the untidy place soon came to assume an air of neatness and thrift which at once impressed Mr. Smith with the idea that his tenants were people on whom it might be worth while to expend a little civility.

It was the first of March, raw, cold, and inhospitable, when, with their household belongings, the little party was set down at the door of the new home. It was late in the afternoon and all were cold, tired, and somewhat dispirited. Even the doctor's equanimity was beginning to give way before the settled obstinacy of a refractory stove-pipe, when a brisk knock at the door of the sitting-room interrupted operations for a moment. Margaret opened the door, to be greeted with the cheery voice of a little black-eyed woman who stepped in without waiting for an invitation. " Good-efening to you all," she cried. " I am Lizzette Minaud. I lif ze next door, and I haf prepared ze souper for you. Do not say 'Non!' I take it so amiss. You look so blue, so tired, so ready to cry, pauvre child," and she laid her hand warmly upon Margaret's arm as she spoke.

"You are very kind, but——" and Margaret glanced apprehensively at the doctor.

"Oh, your — your — ze gentilhomme will go, I am sure. I haf known how ze tired comes in mofing, and you sall work so mooch ze better when you haf supped. I keep you only so long as you sall need ze rest and refreshment."

"A thousand thanks," said the doctor heartily. "To be sure we will go. Gilbert, you and I can have a good deal more patience with this unruly stove-pipe after we have partaken of this lady's supper, eh?"

"I can't answer for you, sir, but I know I am hungry as a wolf."

"So mooch ze better. Hunger ces ze sauce piquante to black bread."

"Did you ever feed a boy?" interposed Elsie, glancing roguishly at Gilbert. "If not, I warn you beforehand."

"Non, non. I do not need ze warning. Lizzette Minaud's table ees nefer empty."

"We are taxing your kindness, I fear," said Margaret, as they prepared for the visit.

"Non, eet ees ze plaisir. I—I like your face," and the impulsive little woman again grasped Margaret's hand. "We must be friends, and friends take no thought of ze trouble of serving each ozair."

"You have given the true meaning of friendship," replied Margaret earnestly.

Lizzette Minaud's house was a "box" indeed, not even as large as the one which seemed so small to Margaret and Elsie; but it was a marvel of neatness and taste. The oak floor of the salon, as in grandiose style Lizzette designated her sitting-room, was like a mirror in its capacity to reflect objects, and nearly as dangerous to walk upon. Here and there bright-colored rugs, knit by the expert fingers of the mistress, lay before couch, stove, and tables. The walls were a delicate cream tint, with dado and frieze composed of crimson, brown, and golden maple leaves delicately veined and shaded, each one the particular work of Lizzette. In response to the delighted exclamation of her visitors, she explained in perfect frankness that having little money and some skill, she had determined to decorate her home—bought with the savings of years—in as tasteful a design as she could achieve. She was rewarded with gratifying success, for the grouping of the leaves was so artistic and the coloring so perfect that nature seemed to be rivalled in the reproduction.

"You are an artist!" enthusiastically exclaimed Margaret.

"Non, non—only a Frenchwoman and a cook," she answered with a characteristic shrug. "I haf all my life been cook for ze great families. In France first, in America many year since. I marry twelve year since, and my husband he go away when my Antoine but two year old. He ees here in zis room, and he will be so charmed to meet you." As she finished speaking, she turned toward a little alcove and presented to view, what at first seemed a little child propped up on a couch. A second look, and it was at once discovered that the child was a hunch-backed lad of some ten years, with dwarfed and misshapen limbs that refused to support him. With that appealing gaze so often noted in the suffering and unfortunate, his dark eyes looked out from beneath a brow broad, smooth, and white. Rings of jet-black curls, a straight, delicate nose, and a mouth with lips thin and bloodless and downward curved, completed the cast of his features. But it would be impossible to reproduce in words the innate beauty of the smile that lit up his face or the sublimity of spirit which looked out of the dark eyes. Impulsive Elsie was on her knees beside him in a moment.

"You dear angel!" she exclaimed, picking up one of the thin, white hands and kissing it. "I shall love you, I know."

"Everybody does. Everybody is so good," said the lad simply. "You are good to come. I wanted to see you."

"Eet ees true," said Lizzette, "he would not rest until I had tried to make ze welcome. He ees sometimes lonesome when I go about ze work, but he ees always patient and always so kind. He ees un grand scholair, too. See, he read zis," and Lizzette held up in triumph a well-thumbed copy of Shakespeare. "It is ze Anglais. He learn so fast, and he read Santine et Racine tres bien. I go to school to mon enfant soon," and the little mother patted the boy's pale cheek in an effusion of pride and fondness. The lad glanced up lovingly and said quickly:

"Non, non. Ma mère has quicker eyes and more wisdom than Antoine. Is the supper ready? I am very hungry and want my wheel chair."

The mother turned to get it, but Gilbert was before her, and gently lifting the lad into it, he started it toward the little kitchen where stood the supper-table.

"Ma mère is a famous cook," said the lad with a bright smile. "She makes appetite when it has forgotten to grow."

"So he say," said Lizzette with a shrug. "I only follow ze way of my art."

The doctor, who had long been silent, glanced up as they seated themselves at the table, and asked: "Do you indeed think cookery an art?"

"Oui, oui, sir. Ze grand art, sir. Ze grain of ze man ees as ze food he eat; if it be coarse, he coarse too. Strong, may be, but not ze fine gentilhomme who eferywhere see ze lectle beauties of life, and so rest you wiz ze gracefulness of his way."

"Perhaps you are right, madam," said the doctor gravely, "although I confess I had never looked at it in that light."

"Eet ees like ze art of ozair sings. Ze leetle touch zat makes ze picture, and as Antoine say, ze poetry of Shakespeàre. Will it please you to speak ze grace?"

Lizzette's supper-table was a sight to tempt less weary and hungry wayfarers than our dispirited quartette. It was simplicity itself, the principal dish being a salad so crisp in its delicate ravigote of finely-flavored herbs that Elsie declared it "a mortgage on the summer, since it had stolen all its sweetest flavors."

Lobster rissoles, a mushroom omelette, with cold bread, a soupçon of preserved plums, black coffee, and tea served from the depths of a Japanese cosey, completed the menu.

"The salad, Miss Elsie, ees made of ze weeds of ze wayside," said Lizzette. "Vous Anglais despise ze sings ze French live by. I make zis salad of ze herb you call dandelion; I find it growing eferywhere. I mix it wiz ze cressom—you call it water-cress—growing by ze brooks, toss it up wiz ze ravigote of tarragon, chervil et bumet, and behold you have, as you say, 'ze summer in mortgage to ze winter.'"

"Count me a pupil to the economy of these versatile French," exclaimed Elsie rapturously. "I know now what I was born for. Madam Minaud shall make an artist of me. I am positively inspired with ambition."

"Or Madam Minaud's supper," observed Gilbert.

"We Americans long ago accepted the gospel of plain 'boiled and fried,' and your dispensation is only just beginning to be felt among those who have lived abroad. It is certainly a much-needed lesson," said the doctor as he complacently accepted Lizzette's offer of a second omelette.

"Ze French nevaire trow away like ze Anglais. Zey save ze leetle sings, and so zey grow reech where ze Anglais—il a de quoi vivre mais bien maigrement."

"Our lines have fallen in pleasant places," cried Elsie enthusiastically. "Antoine shall teach me French, and Madam Minaud shall bestow upon me the art of converting wayside weeds into meat and drink for the fleshly tabernacle."

"You are making the bargain all for yourself, Elsie. What compensation do you propose in return?" asked Margaret with an amused glance at the girl's flushed cheeks and sparkling eyes.

"Compensation?" exclaimed Antoine quickly "Everything! herself, love—ah, we shall be more than paid. I shall have the companion I have longed for, and ma mère will see the rose come back to my cheeks and be glad. Is it not so?" and the child's hand sought Elsie's as it rested on the back of his chair.

"Yes, yes," said Elsie eagerly. "You shall have all the comfort I can give you, dear child."

As she spoke she pushed back the jetty curls and left the warm touch of her lips upon the lad's white forehead. In an instant the thin arms were around her neck, and he cried excitedly: "I love you so, and I shall never be unhappy again."

Grave Dr. Ely turned away from this scene with quivering lip, and his voice was not altogether steady as he said: "Well, Gilbert, that stove-pipe does not look half so formidable as it did before Madam Minaud's delicious supper."

"Indeed, no, sir. I feel like a Hercules."

"All right. Let us see how soon we can slay the giant disorder. In view of the circumstances, madam will excuse a hasty departure."

"Certainment. Work ees master in our leetle world."

"Work and love, ma mère," exclaimed Antoine.

"Antoine is right," said Margaret. "These are the soul and body of existence; to toil is the Divine command—to love the Divine purpose."

"We must perforce obey the command," exclaimed Elsie, patting Antoine's cheek. "The purpose we will leave to its own solution."

"I've already solved it," answered Antoine with a ripple of laughter that brought a happy light to Lizzette's eyes as she answered the "good-nights" of the little party.

CHAPTER IV.

IT did not take long to settle the little four-roomed house, for Dr. Ely proved himself an every-day worker. The week that had passed since he had left his school had been full of business. The purpose which he saw in Margaret and Elsie had awakened a new interest in his life, and to see that their feet were firmly fixed in the way they had marked out for themselves seemed to him the task, as well as the pleasure, of an elder brother. Looking upon life as the vast field from which should spring all that is highest of development and achievement in humanity, he was touched with the hope of being a factor in the ambitious purposes of these inexperienced and well-nigh friendless girls. He believed fully in allowing to each individual soul the opportunities for measuring its own power, and while a certain sense of loss came upon him when he realized that the expectation of taking Margaret into his own life could not be fulfilled, he felt ennobled and strengthened by the desire to be one with her in her efforts of self-advancement. "Not now, not now; but some time, perhaps," he said to his heart, and during his week of early and late work not one word or look of his had disturbed the serenity of Margaret's mind. He had been solely and simply the elder brother on whose experience and friendly aid she could rely. Now, however, the little home was in order; the tiny sitting-room with its painted and polished floor, its bright rugs, its gayly-cushioned Boston rockers, its hassocks that served the double duty of seats and boot-boxes, and last, but not least, its revolving book-case with the few of the well-known volumes which Margaret had selected from her father's library and which Dr. Ely had supplemented with some contributions of his own. These were principally works on art and the intellect, by Ruskin, Hammerton, and others, and a few books of poetry by Dante Rossetti, Keats, Tennyson, and a superb *édition de luxe* of "Aurora Leigh." They were all seated in this room surveying its finishing touches the evening previous to Dr. Ely's departure for A——.

"Well, it is pleasant," he exclaimed. "I shall carry its memory with me when I go, and in imagination behold you seated every evening around the open stove, feasting on the contents of this handy little book-case. I shall remember how white the curtains are, how dainty the table scarfs and the head-rests of the chairs, and how really fine those oleographs and photogravures on the wall appear in the glow of the fire-light, and I shall fancy you are all taking on flesh and good spirits under the inspiration of Elsie's cooking."

"You are very kind not to insinuate one word about dyspepsia," answered Elsie demurely. "But I am really enthusiastic over my promised lessons in that grand art, as madam so grandiloquently calls it. You know some people are born great, and I really feel that I am destined to achieve my highest expression in an apostleship to the pots and pans of the kitchen. Like the starvelling poet of the story-books, I shall doubtless astonish the world when the flame of my soul has burst into a dish fit to set before a king.

"You are somewhat mixed as to metaphor," exclaimed Margaret with a laugh.

"Well, I hope to mix more than metaphors by-and-by. But tell me, Dr. Ely, are you conscious of either an aching void or an aching fulness, whichever dyspepsia happens to be, since you sat under my dispensation?"

"I haven't had such an appetite in years. I don't in the least question your genius for cookery, and when you have learned to make something out of nothing with a ravishing French name and taste, you can count on achieving a world-wide fame."

"Fame? a bauble! I look only to the expression of my art," and Elsie rolled up her eyes and shrugged her shapely shoulders with an abandon of French mannerism that was as startling as it was amusing. Something in Margaret's apprehensive glance caught the doctor's quick eye. What wonderful fire and keenness lay in the little girl's mobile face. Ah, well, Margaret was right; there was work for her here. With an abruptness that seemed almost harsh he spoke:

"He 'jests at scars that never felt a wound.' Art, Miss Elsie, in its entirety is deep, and high, and long, and men have sought it, and with palsied finger on the pulse of time have died unanswered."

The laughing eyes of Elsie grew suddenly grave.

4

"Dear me, one can't be enthusiastic nowadays without finding a wet blanket thrown over her at the first step. Nevertheless I don't intend to wear cap and spectacles until long after my humble divinity has crowned me mistress. My ambition is such a simple one—just to tickle the palates of my little world. Now, doctor, don't discourage me."

"Not for the world. Epicurus, if he were here, would doubtless pronounce a benediction on your ambition, and I am not sure that your purpose does not already deserve a laurel leaf, for it has been more than once reiterated that the crying need of the day is good cookery."

"Thanks. I am glad that my mission has the support of the public mind, or palate. Either will do, I suppose. But how is it with you, Meg? I haven't heard you declare as yet for any reform."

"I am not so sure of my mission as you are of yours, nor so confident of being born to greatness."

"That's bad. One surely ought to believe in herself if she expects to get on. Perhaps the doctor can help your indecision."

There was a mischievous twinkle in Elsie's eyes that was not lost on the doctor, but with the utmost gravity he replied: "Well, yes, I think I can. It will be a mission worth while to learn the problem of self-support and self-education under adverse circumstances. It will need something more than enthusiasm."

A patience and a finesse of which I am not sure I am master. I am only mutely feeling my way now. Indeed, the doctor has lifted so much responsibility

from my shoulders in this new venture that I hardly
know what I can do."

"You will know when the opportunity comes to act.
Just now you needed the little friendly direction I am
very glad I was able to offer.   There are times when
even the strongest are not wholly self-reliant."

Tears stood in Margaret's eyes as she answered:
"How unblessed is he who can make no claim on loyal
friendship.   May I always prove myself worthy of it."

"We'll not question that now, nor in the future,"
said the doctor, a glow of light in his eyes that watching Elsie did not fail to note.   "Now, tell me your
plan for making use of this mine," he added, touching the book-case at his right hand.

"I've been thinking we must get at the nuggets
with as little delay as possible, for we haven't time to
bore through worthless drifts of scoria, even though
at the bottom may be a mine of wealth.   We must
make practical and immediate use of what we learn."

"True," interposed the doctor as Margaret looked
up interrogatively.   "I am deeply interested."

"This, then, is what I've been thinking: every
thought of other minds from which we can draw sus-
tenance must be drained of its nutriment before we
seek another, and that thought must be made to bear
relatively upon our own.   In other words, it must
father a new growth in our own minds, for in that way
only can education have any practical bearing upon
life and action."

"Excellent!" exclaimed the doctor warmly.   "Go
on, please."

Margaret's cheek flushed as she complied. ."It is my purpose, then, in this home symposium to bring no thought that we cannot healthfully digest. Occult research is only for the man of leisure. This is the first principle that shall govern our intellectual feast. The second shall be the democracy of our purpose, or, in other words, the hand-to-hand start we shall make in our race for knowledge. No one shall be debarred because he has not learned the alphabet of reason; we will give him the chance to learn it. The third requirement will be only good moral character," and Margaret finished with a laugh.

"Regardless of social position, remember, doctor," exclaimed Elsie. "In short, Margaret has sketched the outlines of a new aristocracy, wherein moral worth and purpose count first, with brain and healthy digestion a good second, and where wealth doesn't stand any show at all."

"You forget that is the goal toward which the first two tend," said Margaret eagerly. "An aristocracy founded on those principles could not be an insecure one—could it, doctor?"

"It is admirable as a dream, and as a dream impracticable, I fear."

· "By no means," said Elsie as she noticed the shadow that crossed Margaret's face at the doctor's words. "You forget that it concerns only three people. We shall reform the world chiefly by beginning to reform ourselves. Nothing could so suit our Eutopian ideas as to call it 'A New Aristocracy.'"

"An aristocracy of potato diggers!" exclaimed Gilbert, looking up from his book.

"Exactly. We have a right to a kingdom of our own within these walls. Our fame and our pride need not go beyond them."

"Safe enough on that score," said Gilbert ironically. .

"Well," said the doctor merrily, "I shall count myself one of the aristocrats even when miles away."

"But I haven't told you all my plan yet," said Margaret. "It concerns this very potato-digging that to Gilbert seems so incongruous with our high purposes. On the principle that everything we have is the product of the earth, there is nothing out of proportion in even potato diggers striving for the highest development, and as our impressions all come to us from our contact with every-day things, we shall find an astonishing philosophy grow out of potato-digging if we look for it. In my endeavors to carry out the behests underlying the propagation of plants, I expect to find questions that will lead me into as yet unexplored paths, and I shall endeavor to treasure up these questions and their answers if they can be found. I shall exact the same process of reasoning from all the members of our circle, and shall expect every evening to be regaled by Elsie with a philosophical monologue on the amount of nutriment there is in an egg or the exhilaration to be derived from the dish-pan."

"Then you will be disappointed. My ideas are not perennial; but if I chance to evolve some flavor that a Frenchman would doubtless call 'heavenly,' you may look for a harangue."

"A practical school of philosophy it seems to shadow forth; but the proof of the pudding is in the eating, you know," said the doctor with a smile.

"I don't underrate the difficulties in the way; but I think we three ought to be able to do something with ourselves on that basis," said Margaret.

"Certainly," replied the doctor. "And I shall endeavor to remodel my own work from the same standpoint. I have been a dreamer and an enthusiast, and it has remained for an untried girl to show the practical application of my dreams. I shall go home a wiser man."

"You frighten me, doctor, with the seriousness of that statement. It is all untried as yet," exclaimed Margaret in evident distress.

"True; but I can see its first steps. After these the way may open wider and clearer. It is certainly worth trying."

With this indorsement Margaret felt satisfied, and there was color in her cheeks and brilliancy in her eyes as she and the doctor talked long and animatedly until late in the evening. Gilbert had stolen away to bed and Elsie was deep in a novel of Antoine's.

"I shall have to shake myself well together when I get home," said the doctor, when they discovered the lateness of the hour. "I've been living a new life and the old one will seem strange."

It was hard for Margaret to acknowledge even to herself after the doctor's departure that she felt lonely and uneasy; but somehow she missed the careful forethought that had been as new as it had been unexpected. It was a strange experience in her barren life, and scold herself as she might, she could not find it unpleasant. But for the present she would not, she might not indulge in dreams. A work that might stretch into years lay before her. That done—well, how strong is faith? A new beauty, however, stole into her face; its somewhat stern lines relaxed, and tender, almost pathetic, little curves grew about the corners of the firmly-set lips. It was quite apparent to those who knew her that the calm reliance of her nature had been disturbed by something strange and sweet, yet not even Elsie guessed its full meaning.

CHAPTER V.

It was the middle of April. Already in sheltered corners the thin blades of grass were fringing the walks and telling mutely of the stir at their roots. The sky had an unwonted tint of blue, and occasional breezes came up from the Southland laden with the balm and spice of the new-born earth. Hooded in their green cloaks, the dandelions lifted their yellow heads and took a sly peep from their enveloping fringes. The crocuses were just ready to laugh, and the purple bells of the wild hyacinth were tinkling un-heard in the soft air. The robins were hilarious in the intoxication of hope, and Elsie and Antoine were endeavoring to rival them in the ever-recurring joy and promise of the spring. They were in the garden at Idlewild; Antoine in his wheel chair, and Elsie pre-tending to wield a trowel around the roots of a few straggling rose bushes. She was an indifferent worker, however, for every now and then Antoine would catch the bursting refrain of some over-joyous robin, and throwing back his handsome head, would imitate it so closely as to call forth rapturous applause from Elsie and a chorus of answers from neighboring trees. Presently Elsie began to purse her red lips in a wild attempt to rival Antoine and the birds. Each attempt was followed by gay bursts of laughter such as can issue only from the lips of children and the utterly care-free.

"It is no use," said Elsie after awhile. "I never can be a bird."

"Then you can't fly away from me," said Antoine gravely, laying a thin hand upon Elsie's cotton-gloved ones.

"Would it grieve you if I should?"

"It has been heaven since you came," said the lad simply.

"I don't believe you know what heaven is, if a madcap girl like me can make it for you."

"I've read somewhere that 'heaven lies in a woman's eyes;' but I suppose that was meant for full-grown men, not for little chaps like me. It is heaven all the same to find a companion—one who can laugh before I do. Ma mère always laughs *after*."

"Did you laugh a great deal before I came?"

"No, I only laughed when ma mère was looking. I had to do it to keep the tears out of her voice. Oh, I've been so lonely, always thinking, thinking, and I wanted not to think."

"Dear child, don't let us begin now. At least we'll put sad thoughts away. Have you found your blossom for the home circle to-night?"

"Not yet. Miss Margaret said it must grow from the soil of our daily life, and nothing seems to grow in my soil."

"Listen, Antoine. You say I make heaven for you because I can bring you laughter. Has not that thought grown in the barren soil you complain of? Now make a blossom out of the root and stalk."

"I am too dull. You will not let me enter the circle if I show you how little I can make a thought. I only live when I forget myself and everything around me in somebody else. I am such a useless lad."

"No, no, you must not allow yourself to think such things. See what a comfort you are to your mother; and how I delight in that odd little head of yours. I neglect my work to talk to you, and shall have Margaret scolding presently," answered Elsie, picking up her trowel and giving one or two energetic digs at the sod about a rose bush.

"Miss Margaret never scolds, I am sure," said Antoine emphatically. "But oh, if I could run and leap and work!" The words ended in a half-sob.

"We all have our appointed tasks, Antoine," said Elsie softly. "Some are made to do and some are made to bear."

"Mine always to bear!" exclaimed the lad bitterly. "Never to be a man with a man's hopes and ambitions. Just a little dried-up mummy——"

"There, there!" interrupted Elsie, taking the flushed face between her hands and kissing it. "Not very much of a mummy with such a vehement tongue as that. Dear child, let us put the inevitable away. Heavy as the cross is, love lightens it, and love will always be yours. No one can look at you without loving you."

"For what?" asked the lad eagerly. "For my misfortune, or what other reason?"

"For the spirit in those dark eyes and the atmosphere of love that radiates from you. The spirit is greater than the body, and life need not be useless to you nor you to life."

"And is there more to hope for than the pity that says 'poor child' when it looks at me?"

Breathlessly Antoine asked the question, and as breathlessly seemed to hang on Elsie's words: "Men crippled like you, Antoine, have made the world pause to wonder at their powers, and hail in reverent acclaim the genius that is immeasurably above mere physical perfection."

"But I haven't any genius," said Antoine with a disappointed sigh. "I have only one intense longing."

"For what? Tell me."

"You will laugh at me."

"Not for the world."

"Well, then," and Antoine's pale face flushed with the energy of desire, "for music. To pour out my soul in wordless utterances like the birds; to rise, to float on waves of song, away above everybody."

The little thin hands were clasped together in an ecstasy of feeling, and the bent body was restlessly swaying back and forth among the cushions.

"Have you ever tried?" asked Elsie simply.

"No; ma mère doesn't even know it. She says I whistle like a bird, and that is all she knows. She is too poor to buy me anything to make music with."

"What would you like?"

"I think I could play the violin best, for that doesn't need anything but arms to bring out the ex-

pression. Ah, what joy it would be to make something talk for me, to me. I *know*, Elsie, I could teach
it to say the things in here that are so dumb now because they have no way to speak," and the restless
hands clutched his breast as he spoke.

"Wait a moment," exclaimed Elsie, jumping up
quickly and running into the house. She was back in
less than a moment with an old violin case in her
hand.

"Ah!" she exclaimed, seeing the light of eager expectancy spring into Antoine's eyes. "Don't be too
sure of anything. I found this in the rubbish when
we moved. I don't think it was poor father's. I never
heard him play it. By the way, I believe it was left at
our house by some stranger. Indeed, Antoine, we
never had any gayety in our home. It was only just
the serenity of well-performed duty, unless I whirled
into a storm for a change. But now, Antoine, if this
fiddle can sing, we'll have a little gayety, won't we?"

"Oh, won't we!" echoed Antoine, as Elsie busied
herself with removing the sack in which the violin had
been carefully tied. Alas! the violin had but one
string, and not a shadow of any other to be found in
sack or case.

"Well, it's evidently whole," said Elsie, thumping
the back, "and strings can be bought. Take the bow,
Antoine, and wake the echoes with one string. We'll
make a noise, at any rate."

Antoine took the old violin and examined it carefully, thumping the one bass string with the gravity
of discovery. Once or twice he adjusted it under his

chin, and made a motion as if to draw the bow across the string. Suddenly he stopped.

"No," he said decidedly, "until there is a voice I cannot speak, and even then, Elsie, how do I know I shall not fail? I know I shall with you watching me. Some time when the strings are on the violin and I am all alone, and I feel the song bird here in my breast, I will try. Something tells me I shall succeed—that it is my life, my hope; but I do not know, after all," and over the dark eyes stole the cloud of despair that so often makes the bravest genius fearful of its own weakness.

"We will make it hope for you because we will work for it, dear," answered Elsie. "Even genius is nothing without work."

Antoine did not answer, and Elsie, noticing the cloud still hovering over the lad's face, pushed his chair to the other end of the garden, where Margaret, Lizzette, and Gilbert were busied over cold frames and garden beds. Looking over the low paling that separated Margaret's garden from that of Lizzette, they could already see the tender green of early vegetables showing through the glass plates of the hot beds. Lizzete eyed them approvingly.

"Next year you sall rival me," she said, laying a brown hand on Margaret's shoulder. "But nefer fear —zere ees room for bof in zis world. We nezair of us grow reech, c'est vrai; but we lif and zat ees somesing. Ah, Gilbeart, you lose von goot foot zere. Now put it zis way and see your frame couvair so mooch more ground. Eet ees ze inch saved zat makes ze foot gained in ze market garden. See! Can you find von inch to spare in zat leetle space of mine? Eet all yields, and yet Lizzette Minaud ees une tres pauvre femme."

"Poverty is a relative term, you know. Enough to eat, to wear, and to grow on are all that any one needs. It is in the enough, however, that lies the division of opinion," said Margaret as she helped Gilbert adjust the frame to Lizzette's satisfaction.

"Zat ees true; but as ze world look at us we haf very leetle."

"But if we have contentment therewith, we have everything," answered Margaret. At this juncture Elsie, who had wheeled Antoine into the path beside her sister, broke out impetuously:

"Margaret Murchison, do you mean to say that you are perfectly contented? I don't believe one word of it. You are not contented, for if you were you wouldn't be striving with might and main to earn the wherewithal to make a gentleman of Gilbert and a lady of me. You'd let us remain clodhoppers to the end of our days. It is all nonsense to preach contentment when your actions give the lie to your words."

Margaret glanced up quickly at the vehement assertion.

"There is a difference between the contentment that has only stagnation in it, and that which is satisfied to grow under the conditions which environ it until the time ripens for wider growth and leafage. If I am contented it is because I am willing to work step by step and inch by inch as the way unfolds. There is only disaster in trying to reach the height at a single bound. Order is subverted and reason impeded in such attempts."

"My wise sister, put on my harness and teach me to trot soberly by your side. I do so want to jump the gates for a wild run, and forget harness, duty, and all the unpleasant things of life. Antoine and I have been trying to be birds this morning."

"You didn't succeed, I conclude."

"Well, no; at least I didn't. Wings will never grow for me, but Antoine is going to rival the birds some day. See here! I found this among the rubbish in father's study, and Gilbert when next he goes to the city shall get the strings, and when Antoine has learned to mirror his soul in music I'll——"

"What will you do?" asked Margaret soberly, as Elsie paused for breath.

"Dance my way into fame! Now don't look so horrified, or I shall think you are going to be a 'Miss Prunes and Prisms' instead of the good wholesome 'sister' Dr. Ely thinks you are."

Elsie watched with sparkling eyes the pink flush on Margaret's cheek, and a moment later mischievously intensified it by saying: "I wonder how the staid Dr. Ely would relish hearing the world say that the sister of——"

"Elsie!" exclaimed Margaret apprehensively.

"I was merely going to say—of the lady he admires so much was premier danseuse at the Standard?"

Elsie was half-way to the house by the time she had explained herself.

"Oh, cet Elsie!" exclaimed Lizzette with a laugh. "What fire, what verve zere ees under zàt pretty head."

"She's a great puzzle to me," said Margaret somewhat sadly. "I really fear she'll burn her wings yet. I hope I can keep her out of the candle."

"She'll keep herself out," exclaimed Antoine energetically. "She's got a heap of good sense; but she's just like some wild bird, made to be gay and beautiful all her life."

"She's been dropped in a sorry corner of the world, if that is her destiny. There is little hope of anything but the daily drill of duty in this household," answered Margaret.

"She'll never drill under any other captain than love," said Antoine with a smile up into Margaret's grave face.

"And he'll have to be a pretty lively fellow to keep up with her antics, too," said Gilbert as he leaned his hoe against the fence and took up the fiddle to examine it.

Margaret's face grew thoughtful as she heaped the earth about the frame. "Love, love," said she to herself. "After all, it is like the sun, the vivifying influence of the world, and duty sounds cold beside it. I must find out what it is that is trying to burst its bonds in my little girl's bosom. It may be I am too slow and dull for the gay spring-time that is budding there."

"Antoine," she exclaimed presently, "Gilbert shall fix up the old fiddle and you shall learn to wake us up. I believe we've been too sleepy for Elsie."

"O Miss Margaret! she is so lovely and so are you," he added naïvely.

"The old fiddle, Antoine," said Margaret, responsively patting the boy's hand, "the old fiddle has a history. Some eight or nine years ago my father took into his house a sick man, who came apparently from nowhere and was apparently journeying to the same place. He was very ill when he came to the house, and begged for a night's lodging and supper. My father never turned any one who was hungry from his door, and so he came among us, and sat all the evening a silent figure in the chimney corner until bed-time. He had nothing with him but a bundle tied up in a red handkerchief and the fiddle. My father, with a delicacy which was characteristic of him, did not even ask the man his name, and so we never knew who he was, nor where his friends were, if he had any. About midnight we were all awakened by strains of the weirdest music; sometimes so sad and wailing that it seemed like a human being in agonies of pain, again as gay and glad as any chansonette, with here and there bird notes so sweet and clear one could almost hear the forest echoes, and then the maddest, wildest, most rollicking melodies breaking in upon it all. At last it stopped with a discordant crash of the bow across the strings, and father stepped to the door of the sick man's chamber, to find him lying across the bed raving in delirium. We nursed him through a two-days' illness, and then he died without having told us a word of himself. There was nothing to indicate who or what he was in his little bundle, and so

5

that and the violin were put away and nearly forgotten until we came across them in moving. I am glad Antoine is going to have the violin. My grave father had no use for it."

During the recital of Margaret's story, Lizzette Minaud had stood a rapt listener, her brown face working with some unwonted emotion. When Margaret had finished she said huskily, " Ze violin for Antoine, Miss Margaret ? C'est très-bon. I tank you so mooch. Now Antoine will pour out his soul; he ees so like son père, mon pauvre Jacques—ah Dieu! où est-il ? "

" Is he not dead ? " asked Margaret in surprise.

" Non. When Antoine two year old, he go look for work. He promise me to come back soon; mais le temps—c'est long, long. I nevair hear von word. I know notings if he be living or dead. But ze violin eet bring back ze memories. Mon Jacques he love eet so, and play très-bien."

" Ma mère ! ma mère ! " cried Antoine, throwing up his arms at sight of Lizzette's agitated face.

" Chut ! chut ! " answered Lizzette, bending down to kiss him. " C'est passé, mon garçon. Now we will be gay like ze birds, and happy ze livelong day."

Margaret had slipped away during the little colloquy between Lizzette and Antoine, and presently returned with a small bundle carefully tied up in an old bandana handkerchief. Untying the knot, she spread its contents open to view.

" Mon Dieu! mon Dieu ! " cried the voluble Frenchwoman, clutching the handkerchief and falling in a paroxysm of weeping at Margaret's feet. "Ze cushion I made for him; ze hair comb; ze neccessaire—I know all, all. Mon pauvre Jacques! And you, Miss Margaret, ze angel, ze comforter of his last hours? Plut à Dieu! cet I too might have been wiz him. Ze violin, celui de votre père, Antoine. Le bon Dieu! Zese friends, ze violin, ze kind care de mon pauvre Jacques, votre père—ah! my heart ees bursting wiv ze—ze—gratefulness. I weep my eyes away," and the affectionate creature clung to Margaret's skirts in a bewilderment of grief, wonder, and joy.

"It seems like a miracle," said Margaret, stooping to raise Lizzette from the ground. "But it only shows how small the world is and how interdependent we are. We shall be still warmer friends after this."

Antoine, a mute but agitated witness of the scene, reached out a hand to Elsie, who had stolen quietly beside his chair.

"How strange, how dear, how beautiful it all is!" he exclaimed.

CHAPTER VI.

THAT evening, gathered in the little sitting-room at Idlewild, were the five people who made up the Home Circle Club which Margaret had organized, and who, Elsie laughingly said, "represented the bone and sinew of the 'new aristocracy' which was to revolutionize the world."

"Only think," she exclaimed before Margaret had gravely called the meeting to order. "Only think of the greatness concentrated here! In my grave sister I recognize the 'Morning Star' of the new reformation; a second Wickliffe with the mantle of peace and gentleness bravely wrapped about her slight form. In Gilbert another Sir Isaac Newton, who shall discover a new law of gravitation, which shall make the gold of the miser fall of its own volition into the outstretched hands of the philanthropist. In Antoine a later Corelli, who shall render all these aspirations into a new classic for the benefit of future generations; and in ma mère an Archestratus, who shall, in verifying Voltaire's enthusiasm, 'qu'un cuisinier est un mortel divin,' solidify this band of enthusiasts with the material offering of something good to eat."

"And you?" asked Margaret.

"The unfortunate mortal upon whom you will all practice."

"I should like to begin by subjecting you to the law of *gravity*," exclaimed Gilbert.

"Never fear," said Margaret. "Time will bring gravity soon enough, and Elsie can't throw stones at us without endangering her own enthusiasms. Her next new dish will be our opportunity, Gilbert."

"Unless I put a guard over it."

"Will the meeting please come to order?" said Margaret soberly. Elsie subsided into her corner and Antoine lay back among his cushions, and listened with interest to Margaret's statement of the purposes of the little home club. "The first part of our plan is to develop thought, and we have decided that such thought must come to us in response to our daily needs or grow out of our daily work. We therefore expect each member to bring what we will call a blossom for the wreath of every-day living; this blossom may be perhaps a wayside weed or a cherished bloom of some inner chamber of the heart. Nothing is too small or simple for this wreath, so that out of it we may extract some consolation, hope, or purpose. Upon these thoughts that are thrown together, and which shall be kept in a record book, will depend the evening's reading. In this way we think the demands of our mental and moral needs will be best satisfied. Elsie, what have you to offer?"

The mischief had apparently died out of Elsie's face as she answered: "A good many things have come to me to-day; but the most pronounced thought has been the despair of enthusiasm and the futility of the most earnest effort. I burned with the desire of a Fran-

catelli to achieve an omelette; but having no eggs the
earnestness of purpose failed me."

A ripple of laughter greeted Elsie's announcement.

"Wanted," exclaimed Gilbert, "a new invention for
making hens lay; otherwise the foundation of our cas-
tle in Spain will not be equal to its walls."

"Now, Antoine," said Margaret, "let us hear from
you."

"The day has been good to me," replied the lad,
"for in it I have learned how sweet it is to hope."

"And I," said Lizzette, "haf found zat friendship
haf no price."

"While I," asserted Gilbert, "have found a boy's
back can ache a great deal harder at work than at play."

"Now, Margaret," asked Elsie, "how are you going
to philosophize over the want of eggs and a boy's
back? These incorrigible facts take the poetry out
of our plan, I am afraid."

"Not in the least. It is the very thing we are endeavoring to do, make our philosophy fit our material
wants. It may be that the world wouldn't call our
reasoning by so dignified a name; but we don't care
for that. This is our world, and into it we are striving to bring as much of both earthly and divine sus-
tenance as will best fit us to receive the greatest
amount of happiness. Therefore, since eggs will con-
tribute to the mental balance and physical well-being
of Elsie, to say nothing of the rest of us, we must look
up some information regarding henneries. The garden planted, Gilbert must exercise his ingenuity in
building one, while the rest of us——"

"Devise some means of making a hen lay two eggs a day," interposed Elsie.

"Elsie, I am ashamed of you," exclaimed Margaret with forced severity. "To think that already you develop the greed of a monopolist."

"Well, what is Eutopia good for, if it doesn't make all doors swing back with the 'open sesame' of good wishes?"

"Good to hope for," said Gilbert dryly.

"And to work for," added Margaret quietly.

"And ze hope and ze work keep ze world moving. But ze boy's back, Mees Margaret, zat is a question not yet answered."

"A good game of base-ball would cure that, eh, Gilbert?"

"I protest," exclaimed Elsie, "against any more nonsense this evening. On our first grand opening to be found on such a lamentably low plane is belittling to our great aims. There has not been a word said yet about the crying need of our country, the deplorable condition of labor, the injustice of our government, etc., etc. Will not our serene presidentess inform her breathless audience how we are to strike at the roots of these evils at once?"

"Chiefly by attending to our own business. In the breast of each individual lies the power of bettering himself, and as we better ourselves intellectually and morally, as well as materially, by so much we better the world."

"It sounds easy," said Elsie dubiously.

"It *is* easy," said Margaret firmly. "Grind out of

our hearts the selfish love of ease that creates the un-
holy desire to build up ourselves by pulling others
down, and bravely resolve to shirk no plain duty, and
the battle is half-won. Now let us turn to the real
business of the evening. I have laid out a line of history work for the first half-hour; for the second, belles-
lettres and poetry; for the third, discussion; and for
the last, music."

" From Antoine's violin ? "

"Yes, and from an organ to accompany him."

" Has the organ materialized ? " asked Elsie, gazing
incredulously around the room.

" It shall to-morrow. We can obtain one by monthly
payments, and only a little plainer living, fewer
clothes, and the thing can be managed. I'll agree to
wear calico all the time, even Sundays if need be."

"And I won't even *think* of a ribbon," exclaimed
Elsie, with a mischievous twinkle shining through eyes
that were suspiciously misty.

"Amen," said Gilbert. " I'll wear patches and play
' bones.' "

Lizzette and Antoine said nothing; but a look of
intelligence passed between them, which told of a purpose they did not care to mention just then. And so
the little Home Circle Club was arranged. Three
evenings.in the week the programme came to be suc-
cessfully carried out. Margaret kept a record of all
the proceedings, carefully noting down the doubts and
difficulties that beset them, and as carefully adding
all truths that came to help them. The music of the
violin and organ was not a startling success at first,

for the empty purse prevented all thought of tuition
except that furnished by self-teaching manuals; but
as exceptional genius lay beneath Antoine's curly
locks, and Elsie was an uncommonly bright scholar,
it was not long before the two young heads had
solved the puzzling rudiments of music, and were on
their way toward a tolerable amount of proficiency.
Antoine was a new being. His mother affirmed that
the music would cure him. A faint color tinged the
hitherto pale cheeks, and an unusual sparkle lit up the
dark eyes. It would have been hard to find a happier
group of people than the five at Idlewild. They
were like one family in their interests and efforts.
Lizzette flitted in and out of both domiciles, intent
now on Elsie's cooking, now on Antoine's music,
which came to her ears at all hours of the day and
night—for the violin had grown to be like a living
companion to the crippled lad—now helping Gilbert
and Margaret in the garden or gravely puzzling over
some of the English books on Margaret's table. They
were all busy, cheerful, and conscious that they were
making progress, intellectually and materially. Lizzette's experience had been the safeguard over Margaret's efforts in the garden. It was prospering finely,
and already Lizzette had sold at her stall in the market
at C—— enough to make Margaret feel that her hard
days of work with hoe and spade were sometimes sure
to be well rewarded. As the season progressed the
work in the garden required additional help. In an
old negro woman, known to everybody in the neighborhood as "Aunt Liza," together with her son Eph,

Margaret found the needed assistance. Often she worked beside them, finding as acquaintance progressed a perpetual source of annoyance in the aimless and half-hearted way in which they worked. Irresponsibility seemed to be with them the predominating characteristic, and strive as she would against it, she frequently found her efforts not much more successful than so much writing in water. They would both listen to her instructions with serious but blank faces, and relapse at once into that indolent method which was a continual thorn in Margaret's New England thrift. It was her first serious stumbling-block on the way to that high plane of achievement whereon she had made no allowance for the thriftless, the ignorant, and the irresponsible. To her well-regulated mind, all people *ought* to be industrious, patient, and ambitious, and it was a keen thrust against her composure to be brought into contact with the unpromising side of human nature. It was not so much that the two did not earn the wages she paid them, as that she saw failure, suffering, misfortune before the two unthinking mortals. She felt a moral responsibility in endeavoring to set their feet aright, and so tried in numberless little ways to impress upon them a faint idea of the requirements of life. She found in the little hut where they lived a deplorable poverty, and undertook to question Liza, who in the summer, together with Eph, earned fairly good wages, how it happened that they were so poor.

"Dunno, Miss Margaret," answered Liza with a grin. "Spec somehow me an' Eph ain't got no way of sabin'. In the summer time we has 'nough ter eat, and we firgits about de cold, and so when de winter comes, folks 'bout here is mighty good, and don't let us go hungry, and that's jes' de way we gits thru."

"But wouldn't you rather save a part of your wages in the summer and fix up the cabin good and warm, and be able to feed yourself and have people respect you?"

"Spec 'twould seem better to have de old cabin fixed up; but as for folks 'spectin' ole Aunt Liza and nigger Eph—yah! yah! I reckon, Miss Margaret, yer ain't lived long o' niggers much."

Liza's fat sides shook with unctuous laughter as she looked up into Margaret's face.

"No," said Margaret, "but I think every one is entitled to respect who earns it, whether he is black or white."

"P'raps that's so," assented Liza, "but niggers ain't white folks, nohow. They's a pore down-trodden race fo' suah," she added, catching the whine of some clap-trap orator. "Dey jes' don't know how to be any better."

"They can learn."

"Mighty hard work teach a nigger; dey's got dreffel thick skulls. Niggers is the comicalest folks too; jes' gib 'em a chicken bone and a watermillion and dey don't care fo' nuffin' else," and Aunt Liza stopped work long enough to chuckle over her own wit.

"But they ought to; because chicken bones and watermelons don't grow on every bush. They ought to learn how to take care of their money, and buy little homes of their own, and grow into citizens that are honest and self-respecting."

"Specs it take mighty long while to do dat, Miss Margaret. Niggers don't have nuffin' mo'n a few pennies at a time, and dey's sartin suah to git away jes' soon as dey turns roun'."

"Did you ever count up how much money there would be in saving five cents a day for a year, or even a summer?"

"No, don't know 'nuff; but Eph hyah's been to school. Eph, you jes' count 'em up."

"Cain't do it. Hain't got that fur. Ye see," said he, glad of a chance to rise from his cramped position, with the ostensible object of explaining himself, "I's only jes' larned de A B abs and hain't got no time to go no mo'. I's got to hire out all de time."

"Well, five cents a day for six days in a week make thirty cents; that sum for fifty-two weeks in a year makes the sum of $15.60."

"Ooeeh!" exclaimed Eph. "Dat's mo' money 'n I ever seed at a time. Jes' five cents' yer say? How much ef it's only thru de summer dat we sabes it?"

"That depends upon how many months you work. If you work from April to November, say a period of twenty-six weeks, there will be seven dollars and eighty cents. Would not that go a good way in helping to clothe and feed you in the winter?"

"Golly, yes," exclaimed Eph. "I never has no clothes when the col' spells come on. I's allus shiverin' 'roun' in de winter and hopin' fo' spring."

"Eph," said Aunt Liza, roused by Margaret's arithmetic into an unusual interest, "jes' s'posin' we 'uns tries dat little specolation. Five cents hain't a drefful sight ter sabe a day, but it do heap up 'mazin' fast, dat's so. Jes' let's make Miss Margaret hold de money fo' us; fo' dar ain't no use o' us tryin' ter sabe it. It jes' burn holes in our pockets fo' shuah."

"I's agreed," answered Eph, getting up again and making an elaborate bow to Margaret. "Specs Miss Margaret tryin' a little mission on us; but lawsee! reckon dar's need 'nuff of it, and I's putty shuah dar ain't nobody nicerer to be banker fo' us."

Having delivered this speech, Eph leaned up against the fence with the air of having supplied a long-felt want. Margaret smiled and began, "I am afraid——"

"Heah, you Eph!" interrupted Aunt Liza, picking up a clod and hurling it at Eph's head, "you lazy nigger! go to work, or yer don't git no five cents to sabe."

Eph cleverly dodged the clod and leisurely sank to his knees. "Specs Miss Margaret hain't no 'bjections ter actin' as ouah banker," he resumed with the utmost complacency.

"I don't believe that's the best plan. Can't you lay it up yourselves, and resolve not to touch it till cold weather comes?"

"Shuah fo' sartin, Miss Margaret, a nigger don't know how to sabe a cent. It jes' gits away, dat's all. Onless you's our banker, like Eph say, we don't git rich by time col' weather's settlin' down."

Aunt Liza, unmindful of the reproof she had just administered to Eph, sat up in the path, and with numerous gesticulations proceeded to emphasize her statement. "It's mighty good o' yer, Miss Margaret, to take a likin' to us no-'count niggers, and I's jes' goin' to try and see ef dar ain't some good in ouah ole bones aftah all. Ef you'll jes' keep ouah sabin's I'll make dat Eph work every day in de week and go huntin' Sundays."

"Well," said Margaret, with difficulty repressing a smile, " I'll try it. Now let's see if these two rows can't be finished by noon."

"Meg," said Elsie, as Margaret came wearily into the house at the noon hour, "what have you been trying to do with those good-for-nothing 'cullud pussons' out there?"

"Teach them a little responsibility, that is all."

"My sweet sister," said Elsie, rapturously kissing the pale face as she drew Margaret down into a rocking-chair, "you will kill yourself with trying to be the world's keeper."

"It is only a little thing, Elsie; the cup of cold water and no more."

CHAPTER VII.

It was June before the little Frenchwoman would hear to Margaret's making any effort to dispose of her produce in her own way. Regularly every morning Lizzette boarded the four-o'clock train for the city with her boxes of produce, which she pushed to the train in the hand-cart and wheeled from the train to her stall in the market. Until now the amount yielded by Margaret's garden had been small in bulk, but so well had it thrived under Lizzette's management and the comparatively good season, that the more bulky vegetables, such as spinach, peas, beans, etc., were coming on, and Lizzette found the yield of the two gardens more than she could well manage in her small way. Margaret, appalled somewhat, for all her courage, at having to face the multitude in a stall at the market, was for disposing of her produce to the commission merchants on South M—— Street.

"Non," said Lizzette emphatically. "Zere ees no money in zat. You make consignment and more likely zan not get back ze whole stuff wilted and good for nosing. I tried zat to my sorrow. In ze stall you sell all at some price. You no carry home ze stuff again."

"I know," said Margaret doubtfully, "but truly I

dread my ignorance and the contact with things wholly
unfamiliar."

"Ah, ze little brown Frenchwoman haf no such fear,
and she forget ze girlhood so long temps! Zare ees
Gilbert—ees he not old enough? I take him under my
wing, and he sall learn ze tricks of trade. N'est-ce
pas?"

"I will go with you to-morrow," said Margaret,
"for I must conquer my dread. Perhaps some time
Gilbert shall take my place."

Nothing in the line of work had ever seemed so distasteful to Margaret as wheeling the little hand-cart
through the streets of the city, and taking her place
within the stall next to Lizzette's. It was early when
they reached the market, and the buyers were not out
in full force; nevertheless Margaret fancied she saw
in every eye that lingered on her an impertinent curiosity. Self-consciousness was the least of her failings;
but there was an almost unacknowledged protest at
being compelled to stand up before the gaze of hun-
dreds and volubly offer her small wares for sale. Duty
certainly wore her most uninviting aspect that morning, and came nearer finding Margaret a coward than
ever before. She had never as yet shrunk from any
work, however menial; but there was a vast difference
between performing that work within the seclusion of
home, cheered and upheld by an atmosphere of love
and appreciation that made "the dignity of labor"
something more than the radiant utterance of some
visionary pedant, and standing in the full gaze of the
public, subjected to the whims, avarice, snobbishness,

and impertinence of the pushing, merciless multitude.
Oh, how she shrank from it all! How had she ever
thought it possible to have strength for such work?
Lizzette's quick eyes noticed the constraint of Margaret's manner, and she undertook, by a display of
more than ordinary volubility and gayety, to dispel
the gloom that wrapped her. She bustled about,
changing the position of that bunch of onions or
radishes, this head of lettuce, or endeavoring to display
more temptingly the measures of spinach, peas, beans,
etc. More than one would-be buyer halted, gazed at
the silent figure and white face, and passed on.

"Zis will nevair do," interposed Lizzette in a whisper. "You look truly seek; sit down here behind ze
cart, and I sell for bof of us. Vous avez ze paleness
I no like to see. Ze work ees too hard."

Margaret shook herself together with an effort.
No, she would not be beaten back at the first step;
it would be degrading. The mutiny in her breast,
whatever it was, whether a hitherto unknown undercurrent of false pride or a new and abnormal sensitiveness, *must* be conquered. With a smile that was
almost pitiful in its attempted bravery she said: "No,
Lizzette; it is now or never. You will soon see what
a brave market-woman I will make. I shall make
a sale to the next comer. Good-morning, madam!
How can I serve you?" she asked, as a woman who
wore diamonds and silk approached and sniffed con-
temptuously above the little display of greenery.

"Dear me! You don't seem to have anything fit
for a pig to eat," said the woman as with ungloved
6

hand flashing with diamonds she deliberately reached for a measure of spinach, and turned it bottom side up on the little counter.

"I presume not," said Margaret, quietly picking up the spinach and restoring it to its place. "We don't sell to pigs here."

"H'm! impertinent!" and with a haughty stare into Margaret's face, the diamonds and silk passed on. Lizzette was convulsed with laughter. Margaret stole a quick glance at her, and the white scorn of her face lit up with a smile.

"That was a tonic, Lizzette," she said. "I shall do better next time."

A second later a sweet-faced little matron stopped at the counter, asked for prices, made her selection, and looking earnestly at Margaret, said: "You are a newcomer here. I know all the old faces."

"It is my first effort."

"And you find it hard?"

"A little. I shall get used to it."

"Ah, yes, we get used to almost everything in this world. I shall remember you and look for you to-morrow. Good morning" And with a slight bow the little matron took up her purchases and went on her way.

Margaret's face softened as she glanced at Lizzette. "Eet ees not all bad," Lizzette found time to whisper.

"No," said Margaret, "a little smile lightens the whole world."

When the market hours were over, Margaret, to her surprise, found that she had sold out her little stock, and Lizzette was voluble in praise of her ability as a saleswoman. The generous-hearted little French-woman had nothing to say of the numberless ways in which she had contrived to bring Margaret's supplies within the notice of purchasers. Margaret went home with a lighter heart. After all, nothing was ever quite so hard when once the shoulder had been put to the wheel. Yet it was a white, tired face that greeted the three who at Idlewild were anxiously awaiting the result of the experiment.

"O Meg!" cried Elsie apprehensively. "You have gone beyond your strength, and I am to blame for coaxing you into this move. I am going to take your place."

"No, indeed," said Margaret decisively; "I'll not hear one word to it. This is my work until I have mastered it and am ready to give it up to Gilbert."

They knew persuasions were useless, and so she was left to work out the problem upon which she was just entering. It did not grow any easier as the weeks and months progressed. She never could quite put down the mute protest that arose within her against a conscious unsuitability for such work. It was always distasteful to her to mingle with the jostling crowd and urge upon fault-finding buyers the excellence of her wares; but she resolutely choked back revolt, and finding that she was gaining customers who grew to like the simple earnestness of her manner and to rely upon the exactness of her word and measure, and that there was at least a living profit in her calling, she learned to endure all its unpleasantness with no word of complaint. How bravely she bore it all no one guessed except Lizzette, who witnessed daily the struggle going on in the girl's breast.

"Ze instinct of ze lady rebelled, but ze heart of ze woman bear," she said sententiously.

The summer passed away quickly and uneventfully; the daily round of duties, of self-improvement, of little moments of relaxation over Elsie's organ or Antoine's violin, making the days bright with widening hope and prospects.

One late October evening, while Elsie and Antoine were filling the little house with music and Gilbert was buried in a book, Margaret seated herself before her father's desk and began a letter to Dr. Ely.

"In fulfilment of my promise, I inclose a summary of our summer's work. You will see that financially we are a trifle ahead. This is due to the wise forethought of our good friend Dr. Ely and the management of our wonderful little Frenchwoman. When I look at my own work, I realize that I have been but the obedient machine of wiser calculation than I could possibly have evinced, and I take no credit to myself for this happy state of our affairs. Much as I believe in and preach the independence of the individual, I realize more and more the absolute need of interdependent friendship. It is impossible to find healthy life in the isolation of self; and yet it is in the development of self that we reach the highest capability for perfect friendship. The wisdom of others has benefited me largely this summer. Through others' eyes I have seen with clearer vision many things which my own inexperience would have shown me but dimly. I feel that I have grown stronger and more steadfast by reason of this friendship that came like a waft of summer wind across my barren pathway; and that I may properly render unto Cæsar, I hereby make my acknowledgments for numberless good offices at your hands.

"As regards the garden, the hot-beds are made ready for the winter's sowing, and we have built a substantial hen-house and a miniature duck-pond at the foot of the raspberry patch. The yield of berries this summer was inconsiderable, owing to the vigorous pruning given to the bushes, but the growth has been fine. The trellises are all in good shape and we hope for a substantial return next summer.

"My experiment with Aunt Liza and Eph, about which I wrote you, has not been highly successful. Between the two they have managed to save about five dollars, and I've no doubt the community will be called upon as usual to keep the breath of life in their poor bodies until spring. For my part, since they are both able-bodied I shall *give* nothing. Whatever help I offer they must be made to pay for in some shape, since in that way only can they be taught independence and responsibility, and something like a solution be made of this problem of the poor whom we have always with us.

"As regards my market business, I do not think I am calculated for trade. The peculiar isolation of my life has unfitted me for contact with many-sided hu-

manity, and for that reason I tie myself to it with a
self-immolation of an Indian devotee. With not only
my own way to make in the world, but that of Elsie
and Gilbert, I can afford no mawkish shrinking from
unpleasant things. It will never be a pleasant business
for me, but as I find the newness wearing off, it grows
more bearable. I have established a regular line of
good customers who seem always well suited; have
quite a trade in butter, which I buy from the farmers'
wives hereabout, and a slight output of eggs and
chickens from our own hennery. Eph has promised
to keep me supplied for the winter with game, and
Lizzette and I will make our trips at six o'clock instead of four as the weather grows colder. So much
for material matters.

"In our Home Club we have done fairly well. We
have finished United States history, taken up the first
principles of political economy, made some studies in
Shakespeare and 'Ivanhoe' and 'Adventures of Philip,'
tried Browning and discarded him—our practical life
is too short to spend in solving enigmas that, however
charming they may be as poetical conceptions, have
nothing perceptible to teach us—and by way of dessert,
with Ruskin to fall back on, have taken up some slight
studies in æstheticism, the material result of which
has been innumerable 'love bags,' impossible 'head-
rests,' and indescribable nothings on Elsie's part. The
best part of our efforts, however, has been the practical value of our discussions following the presentation
of a 'blossom' or thought by each member. You
will recall my previous letter regarding this. Out of

this discussion has come wisdom, even beyond our hopes, and strength greater than our own. We scorn nothing here, not the simplest wayside weed, and we have learned much from each other and research. Antoine is making marvellous progress in his music. Already he is interpreting Bach and Handel, and even venturing into snatches of original composition. The lad's soul seems to have been lit at the altar of music; for on no ordinary presumption can one compute his wonderful development. Strength and a greater degree of comeliness seems to have come into his long thin arms and bent shoulders, while there is a constant glow in his dark eyes and an unusual gayety in his laugh. Lizzette is in a fervor of happiness and pride, and seems not to be able to do enough for us. Elsie has caught Antoine's faculty for whistling, and often makes a good second to the bird-like notes with which he accompanies his violin. It is a rare treat to listen to them as I am listening now—Elsie at the organ, Antoine with his violin nestled lovingly under his chin, and his deft bow bringing out with marvellous power its almost human tones, and both whistling! Elsie grows daily more charming and more expansive, and music seems to be with her, as with Antoine, the expression of much that is restless, wayward, and beautiful in her soul. Gilbert is docile and patient; but I notice a growing uneasiness and distaste for his work that must be met and overcome in some way. I have been thinking of putting him in the manual-training school in the city, but have not yet solved the problem of ways and means. I think you may perhaps be

pained to find that we do not attend church.   In the
first place, the purchase of the organ rendered necessary the most rigid economy in dress—in fact, Elsie
and I wear nothing but calico, and Gilbert's clothes
are growing decidedly seedy.   In the second place, we
went once to St. Paul's, in the city, and have had no
heart to go since.   My poor father long before his
death used to declaim against the growing tendency
to exclusiveness in the churches.   In the simplicity of
my country living, I thought him unnecessarily apprehensive.   The house of God was indeed to me so much
a sanctuary I thought worldliness was left at the outer
door; but I found my mistake upon entering the door
of St. Paul's.   The free seats, high-backed and un-
cushioned, were portioned off from the others with a
wide aisle.   In them were gathered a little handful of
people like ourselves, evidently the world's toilers and
God's poor.   The cushioned seats were filled with a
richly-dressed congregation.   The altar was superbly
decorated in white and gold, and the clergyman, as
white and high-bred-looking as his æsthetic surroundings, preached a sermon on the ' Beauty of the ideal.'
He found his text in the Bible, but he found nothing
else there.   The Bread of Life was not in it.   I glanced
around the congregation; those in the free seats sat
with blankly staring countenances, evidently victims
to a sense of duty.   The occupants of the cushioned
seats leaned luxuriously back and listened with a well-
bred air of interest; but as far as I could see not one
face glowed with an intensity of feeling or asked for
anything more than the rhetorical flourish.   We re-

mained through the communion service, but did not
partake of it. I think the divine symbols would have
choked me, my heart was so hot and bitter within me.
Clearly my father was right. The church of to-day is
not for the masses, nor of the masses, and yet I feel
sure that there is a great heart of humanity underlying
all this worldliness, and perhaps waiting patiently for
the time to ripen when the crust of wealth-worship,
caste, and place-hunting shall be burned through with
the white heat of its fires. God loves his chosen, and
they are of all the earth; some day he shall call them
together! We spend our Sundays at home. Elsie and
Antoine render beautifully those old arks of safety,
'Come! Ye Disconsolate' and 'Jesus, Lover of My
Soul.' We read, talk, study, and open our hearts to
the sweet graces of love and charity, and so we forget
that outside there is a world which scorns our poverty
and our calloused hands. Once in a while, drawn by
the music, old Aunt Liza and Eph—who by the way
begrudges the Sunday that takes him away from his
hunting—make an addition to our number. I don't
try to do any so-called missionary work with them, although Eph says suspiciously he 'specs dat's what
it all means, anyhow!' On the whole, life is very
pleasant with us. I am growing so accustomed to its
methodical rounds that I have no time for anything
like regret or vain aspirations.

"With the best wishes for the prosperity of the
school and the welfare of our good friend Dr. Ely,
I am   Sincerely your friend,

"MARGARET MURCHISON."

CHAPTER VIII.

THE ground was covered with snow, and with the thermometer registering ten degrees below zero everything creaked, tingled, and snapped in the frosty air. A keen, cutting wind whistled down from the North and made the comfortably-housed mortal shiver with dread at thought of being exposed to its rude blast. In the little house at Idlewild the three drew around the stove and discussed, gravely apprehensive, Margaret's dread trip to market in the morning.

"Don't go!" exclaimed Elsie. "It will be so bitter cold that precious few will venture out to buy."

"I wouldn't if it were not so near Christmas, and I shall have no money for remembrance if I do not sell off the little produce we have."

"Well, I'd rather forego a remembrance than have you frozen stiff in the act of presenting a cabbage-head to an indifferent public, while your very utterances crystallized on the frosty air and left you a touching monument to the ills of labor."

"Let me go, sister," exclaimed Gilbert. "I think it is time you let me bear a little hardship."

"Indeed it is," interposed Elsie. "You are spoiling the lad by forgetting that if he lives long enough he will be a man some time."

"Never fear! He will live long enough to see you

a sharp-tongued old maid," ejaculated Gilbert, who occasionally winced under Elsie's raillery.

"That doesn't frighten me a bit! I never saw a sharp tongued old maid who didn't have the right of way everywhere she went. Try again, Gilbert. Your picture is not half dismal enough."

"Hush, children!" interferred Margaret, laying a hand on the hand of each. "Suppose I accept your proposition and let Gilbert take my place to-morrow!"

"Yes, and the rest of the winter," said Gilbert earnestly. "It is too hard for you. I've noticed you were growing thin under it."

"And I too," added Elsie. "I should have said so before, but you have such a desperately calm heroism about you that it takes more than usual bravery to remonstrate with you."

"Desperately calm is an admirable expression, Elsie," said Margaret with a smile, "and now that you have exhibited so much bravery, I suppose there is nothing left for me but to succumb."

"Exactly. It is refreshing to find you so docile."

"I suspect it is because I am a coward physically. I have not much desire to stand in the front; in fact, I'd like to desert from the army of workers."

"Margaret, I'm afraid you are going to be sick," exclaimed Elsie, all the mischief dying out of her face.

"Nonsense, Rosebud. I never was sick in my life."

"Everybody finds his Waterloo some time, and now, Margaret Murchison, I'm going to exert my long-reserved authority and insist that you put up that book

—somehow I never see you of late without a book or a cabbage in your hand—and go to bed. You are completely tired out, I know, and there is no use in trying to make a martyr of yourself any longer."

With gentle insistence Elsie took the book from her sister's hand and dragged her off to bed, hovering over her with ostentatious airs of stern command that were as grateful to Margaret's tired senses as they were amusing in the blithe-hearted girl.

Some moments later, though it was still early in the evening, the little household was wrapped in profound slumber.

Fire! Fire! shouted a belated passer-by as he ran hurriedly toward the Idlewild cottage.

Fire! Fire! first took up one voice and another, and Fire! Fire! they cried almost under the windows of the little house. No response came from the inside. " Pound on the doors!" shouted a voice.

" Maybe they are not at home," responded another. " Pound away! wake them up! break in the door!"

Terrific blows were applied on the door, which yielded to the pressure and fell back splintered from top to bottom. Fire! Fire! yelled the foremost man of the party. Still no response from the inmates. By this time half a dozen men had gathered in the room, and were busily engaged in throwing out articles of furniture, hunting for water, and endeavoring to put out the fire, which, with the draft of the open door, was already encircling the room.

" Good God!" cried one of the men, opening a bed-room door and discovering Elsie and Margaret asleep.

"Here are two women! Wake up! Wake up! The house is on fire!"

Elsie sprang up dazed and bewildered.

"On fire?" she cried as if dimly understanding. "O Meg! O Meg! wake up! We'll burn!" and seizing Margaret by the shoulder she undertook to wake her. There was no response from Margaret, who lay like one dead.

"There ain't no time to waste," called the man. "Come, get up out of here," and he shook her vigorously. So heavy a stupor was upon her she could make no reply, and the man finally lifted her by main force and called to Elsie, "Come on, girl—there ain't no time to fool away."

Just then arose the cry, "We can't get a drop of water! Everything is frozen solid!"

"Let her go, boys! Throw out the things! No use trying to save her!"

At that moment Elsie appeared in the doorway. "My brother! My brother Gilbert! He's in there!" pointing to a door that seemed barred by the flames. "Let me wake him," and she was about to rush through the flames, clad only in her night-dress and with bare feet, when the little knot of men threw themselves in her way. One of them, axe in hand, dashed through the flames, and a moment later they heard the sound of shivering glass, while Gilbert awoke from a boy's sound slumber on the snow outside of his room. The man with the axe followed the boy's exit through the window, and appeared at the outer doorway a moment later. "Any one else in the house?" he asked.

"No," said Elsie growing cooler as she realized the safety of Margaret and Gilbert. "Save the books, the organ, and the desk if everything else goes."

"All right, but you better put for the neighbor's. We'll bring you some clothes and save the furniture too. Now, boys, pitch in!"

Elsie started out of the door at the word of command, and almost stumbled over Antoine on his knees in the snow. "O Elsie! O Elsie!" he cried. "I couldn't stay in. I was so frightened. Thank God, you're not burned!"

Elsie picked up the helpless lad in her arms and started as fast as the burden would permit her for the lad's home. At the corner of the house she met Gilbert in his night clothes, dazed and stupid. "Come, Gilbert!" she cried, "help me take Antoine home. I can hardly carry him."

"I want my clothes," he shivered; "let me get my clothes." He was just dodging into the door, when a hand seized him roughly by the shoulders and sent him flying into the snow again.

"Are you mad? The walls are just ready to fall. Get to the neighbor's! Here, take this blanket!" and the fireman tossed the shivering boy a blanket. Elsie was barely half-way up the path leading to Antoine's home, when she encountered Lizzette frantic with fear for Gilbert and Elsie. When she saw Elsie's burden she snatched the lad up with a startled exclamation.

"Mon Dieu, Antoine! Que fait il? Où va-t-il? I nevair know he leaves ze house, Elsie. Run, Elsie!

Margaret ees in a faint. I no wake her! Gilbert, mon pauvre garçon! Que dire? que faire?"

Hastily along the icy way the three ran, Lizzette having taken Antoine from Elsie's arms. They burst open the door of the little sitting-room, to find Margaret still and white on the lounge.

"Meg, darling," cried Elsie, sinking on her knees beside her. "Oh, look up! Speak to me! What is it? Oh, somebody tell me what is the matter! She breathes —see! she moves a little! Meg, Meg, speak to me!"

Her wild importunities only caused a little tremor to run through Margaret's frame. By this time Lizzette was at Elsie's side with a glass of brandy. "Here, drink zis, Margaret! Non? A teaspoon, Elsie! Now zen, open her teeth! Zay are not set! C'est tres-bon! She swallow? Oui! Her hands, zey are so cold! Ce n'est pas bien! Some hot cloths, Elsie. I go send for ze docteur!"

As Lizzette turned away there came a loud knocking at the door. Several men stood outside with clothing and furniture. "We have saved what we could. Where shall we store the things?"

"Oh, come in," cried Lizzette. "I know not. I only know ze young lady ees seek. Vill not some one be so kind to get ze docteur? She faint all ze time."

"Certainly," exclaimed one of their number. "I'll go at once."

"Ze furniture!" exclaimed Lizzette, suddenly recollecting herself. "In ze little room in ze back zare, vot you can find ze place for. Ze rest in ze hennery— anywhere. I tank you, gentlemen! Zese young people

so like my own eet break my heart," and sobbing bitterly Lizzette sank into a chair.

Elsie and Gilbert, wrapped in blankets, still cowered,
dumb with anguish, at Margaret's side. Antoine lay
back in his wheel chair as white as his pillows, but
with eyes that glowed like caverns of light in his white
face.

"It's hard, mum," said one of the men, as with quick
glances he took in the scene, "but we've saved most of
the stuff, and I guess the young lady will come to
after a while. Pretty nearly frightened to death, I
reckon."

"This is not a faint from fright," said the doctor
half an hour later. "It is the lethargy of typhoid
fever. Has she not seemed tired and languid for several days? Ah, I thought so! You could not wake
her? No; it will be some time yet before she realizes
her surroundings. A critical case; but not beyond
cure. Now, my good madam, can you put her to bed?"

"Oui—oui, at vonce."

Elsie and Gilbert, by this time aroused from the
vague horror and stupefaction which had overtaken
them, had managed to equip themselves in the various
odds and ends of clothing which the men had dropped
on the floor, and now sprang quickly to the aid of
Lizzette. In a few moments Margaret was safely bestowed in Lizzette's bed, and the doctor was pouring
directions in Elsie's ears.

"You are sure you are calm enough to remember
instructions?" asked the doctor, intently observing
her white face and darkly-circled eyes.

"'I am perfectly calm, now that I have hope for my sister. She shall not suffer for want of attention."

"Non, non," said Lizzette excitedly. "She ees ze angel of our lives. We sall nevair leave her von moment."

"It will be hard for you," said the doctor sympathetically, "but her case is urgent, and depends largely upon care. I will call again to-morrow. Good-night!"

"Now for some beds," said Lizzette, all her energy returning. "Antoine, mon garçon, venez avec moi! You sall sleep now, for ze great fear ees ovair. La fievre, eet sall be easy cure."

With tenderest ejaculations Lizzette picked up Antoine and carried him to bed. "Le bon Dieu!" exclaimed the lad fervently as he clasped his arms around his mother's neck.

"Oui," said Lizzette, kissing him. "He make all sings even."

For three weeks there was but one thought, one hope, one fear in Lizzette's little home. Margaret's fever was of that low, obstinate type which is all the more difficult of cure by reason of its seeming lack of violence. Day slipped into night and night into day again all unheeded by the quiet figure on the bed. She seemed neither to hear nor to see, and only responded to the care bestowed upon her as a new-born infant responds to the fulfilment of its needs. She lay like one sleeping peacefully, and seldom evinced restlessness unless this lethargy was broken by demands upon her attention. At the end of the twenty-first day there came a visible change. Her features grew drawn

7

and sunken; her hands became more restless, now idly picking at the bedclothes and anon clutching vaguely at the air. Her breath grew hourly and hourly more irregular; now sinking almost away, and again growing labored and painful.

"Now," said the doctor, "is the hour of trial. Keep her strength up and we shall save her. She has a magnificent physique to aid us."

Heavily dragged the hours as the four—Lizzette, Elsie, Gilbert, and the doctor—watched Margaret's painful struggle for life. There seemed to be so little to do to save her. It was like barbarism to sit there and watch the regular administering of the necessary stimulant, and realize that upon it, and the recuperative power in the frail body, depended hope and life. Elsie, worn as she was with watching, was nearly mad with the desire to do something worth while, to be active in rousing Margaret to recognition, and not to feel almost guilty in the passiveness with which she watched the approach of the dread crisis.

"I shall go wild with waiting, doctor. Is there nothing more I can do?" she moaned.

"Nothing, child," he answered sympathetically. "We are doing all that can be done."

"Waiting is such hard work."

"For youth, yes; for old age, its time of greatest cheer. When you are silver-haired, as I am, you will have learned to wait patiently."

"I never was patient; but God means to teach me, I see. It was Margaret who was always patient, always kind, always helpful. Dear God, we cannot live without her."

Down upon her knees beside the doctor's chair slipped broken-hearted Elsie, and grasping his hand she cried desolately: "Oh, may the good God strengthen you to save her, doctor! You don't know all she has been to us, to everybody with whom she came in contact. She has been one of God's good angels, sent by Him to make this selfish world more mindful of divine truth! He cannot mean to take her now with her work just begun. I know He will give you power to save her, and you will, you will, won't you?"

With all of a childlike innocence and pleading she raised her tear-stained face to his.

"My dear child," he replied, "all that I know I have so far applied to the case, and I am deeply interested in saving her. I have faith that I shall do it. Now, my little girl, it is not wise to give way to tears. You must keep up your strength to help me. The battle is only half-won when the crisis is passed."

At that instant there was a timid knock at the middle door, which speedily opened to show Eph's black face, as he whispered half-apologetically: "I don fotched some game, and reckon maybe I's gwine ter heah some good news. Mammy's out'n heah and we's come ober ter help take cah of you'uns fo' ter-night. Mammy says as how yer oughter hab some good strong coffee, an' she don tol' me ter ax yer should she make some ter hearten yer up a bit?"

"That's right, Eph," said the doctor, who knew Eph well. "Just tell Aunt Liza to go ahead; for that's the very thing we need."

"The world is full of kindness," said the doctor when Eph's black face had been withdrawn, "if one only knows how to strike the key-note."

The interruption had been in the nature of a tonic; for the wave of intensified feeling subsided before the simple offer of the good-natured African. Elsie bent over Margaret's bed with renewed faith and strength, and as the midnight hours grew slowly into early morning, she was as quick as the doctor to notice the least change in the symptoms.

"I think she is better, doctor," she whispered half-questioningly.

"You are right," was the answer. "She will live."

Swiftly as an electric message went the glad news from eye to eye, and "Thank God!" welled up from anxious hearts and lifted eyes overflowing with tears.

Margaret had been convalescent two weeks before she was permitted an answer to the wonder in her eyes. It was a disjointed answer at best. No one knew how the fire had originated, why it had been impossible to make connections with the water-mains, or why they had been so deplorably incapable of action. One fact alone stood out distinct and clear: Margaret's insensibility and the subsequent hard fight for life. Now that Margaret was recovering, the misfortune seemed to lighten. In fact, the old sunshine had come back to their faces, albeit the unpicturesque side of poverty stared them in the face. They had not as yet gone hungry, for Eph with the generosity and sympathy of his race had kept the table supplied with game; but Lizzette's slender resources were being daily lessened.

Of this, however, she gave no intimation, but cheerfully bore her increased expense and labor, thankful
above all else for the boon of Margaret's life, and the
opportunity to repay a debt which it had seemed to
her a life's devotion could never obliterate. Elsie was
quick to see how the slender means were being strained
to their utmost, but while Margaret was still so weak
and needing such careful nursing she could make no
effort to earn anything to help out the scanty purse.
She could only bide her time until Margaret was able
to wait upon herself, and then something must be done.
She and Gilbert must be bread-winners now. Gilbert,
in the mean time, had gone from door to door, shovel-
ling coal here, sweeping walks there, running occasional
errands, and doing odd jobs of tinkering, in the hopeful effort to eke out the scanty income. It was a miserable pittance at best that he earned, but it bought the
beef for Margaret's tea and occasional bits of fruit to
tempt the tardy appetite. If Margaret surmised the
severity of the struggle, she saw no evidence of it in
the serene faces about her. If the old gayety of Elsie's
laugh was a trifle subdued and Antoine's violin had a
more than usual plaintiveness, there had come a tenderer sympathy, a sweeter note of love, and a closer
bond of union that were even more grateful. By tacit
consent the old evenings had been resumed as Margaret's convalescence progressed, Elsie "serene presidentess pro tem.," as she styled herself, and Margaret
an honorary member, from whom nothing was permitted except smiles and occasional applause. It was
a great delight to Margaret to watch her Protean sis-

ter. How admirably the versatile little witch fitted into every niche! How beautiful she was in face and form, and more than beautiful in character! "God shield her!" was Margaret's inward prayer. "The world is full of danger for such as she, and I must hasten to get well, rebuild the home nest, and keep the home ties strong."

But Margaret's recovery was very slow. It seemed as if the red blood of renewed strength would never come, and it was with a bitter heart-pang that she listened to the doctor's statement that she would not be fitted to resume work of any kind before spring. The golden cord had been well-nigh snapped in the indomitable determination to conquer self and circumstances, and nature was taking her revenge. Gradually, sitting helpless and empty-handed in her chair, she began to notice the little evidences of desperate need which the others tried in vain to keep from her, and one morning, determined to try her strength, she crawled feebly into the kitchen to surprise them at breakfast with nothing on the table but potatoes and salt!

"We are waiting for the cook to bring in breakfast," exclaimed Elsie, noticing the pain in Margaret's eyes.

"O Margaret!" cried Lizzette, "zis ees too much. Here, sit down, and see what good appetite we haf. Ze pomme de terre, ze sel, bof of a superieur kind and so well served we eat and eat like ze epicure."

The humorous twinkle in Lizzette's eyes was lost on Margaret, for weak and disheartened she sank into a seat, bowed her head on the table, and sobbed like a

child. In a second Antoine was out of his chair and
his arms were around her neck.

"Don't," he whispered. "The potatoes are done to
a turn and you will spoil them."

The lad's keenness had touched the right chord.
To stand in the way of another's need or pleasure, even
in little things, was an ingrained abhorrence of Margaret's nature. Instantly she raised a half-smiling face.
"It is a good deal better than starving, after all," she
said.

"Vastly," responded Elsie. "Just watch Gilbert
stow 'em away! I'm not going to tell the result of
my tally this morning, for fear he'll take revenge on
me. We are growing to be experts on potatoes, and
can tell how they taste with our eyes shut."

The ripple of laughter that greeted this statement
chased the last tear from Margaret's eyes.

"Hereafter," she said resolutely, "there shall be no
beef, fruit, and creams for me. I intend to become an
expert too."

Lizzette threw up her hands in protest. "Non, non,
Margaret. Ze strength fail unless ze diet ees generous
for you. Ze waste tissue must be repaired first. Non,
non, cherie. Trust Lizzette to know ze best."

"Well, I submit on one condition," and Margaret
threw a quick glance at Antoine's pale face. "I must
share with Antoine. He needs rebuilding as much as
I do."

"C'est vrai," said Lizzette in a choked voice. "Il
est très souffrant; but aujourdhui I make some famous potage de lapin for all, and we dine like ze em-

pereur. Eph he bring ze lapin and say, 'Game mighty shy somehow, Missis Minaud, but I don't fergit Miss Margaret, nohow.'"

"Poor fellow! I am afraid he robs himself," said Margaret sympathetically.

"If he does, other people make it up to him," replied Elsie. "The community has had its usual call to feed him and his mother. I asked him one day when he was here with a brace of partridges if he shot enough game to support them. 'Lawzee, missy!' said he with a laugh that showed the whites of his eyes and the internal anatomy of a cavernous mouth, 'not by a jugful. Dis yere game law jest doin' a heep o' mischuf to po' men. I hez ter be mighty cahful.' So, Miss Murchison, on the principle that the receiver is as bad as the thief, I mistrust you've been cheating your beloved country of its just dues whenever you have smacked your lips over a bit of partridge breast!"

"Let us be thankful that rabbits are not interdicted, and that Eph's sense of kindness exceeds his respect for law."

"'How are the mighty fallen,'" quoted Elsie tragically. "I fully expected to see you rise in the might and majesty of insulted justice, and visit condign punishment upon poor Eph by refusing to be any longer a party to his crime."

"Hunger is said to know no law, and while I feel inclined to forgive Eph for past sins, I shall have to try to impress upon him a fuller sense of his obligations as a law-abiding citizen."

"A useless task, I fancy. Too many generations of

dependent blood run in his veins. His liveliest sense seems to be gratitude for some little acts of kindness on your part."

"I wonder what he did with the money he and his mother saved last summer," said Margaret reflectively.

Elsie laughed. "I asked him one day, and he hung his head as sheepishly as a boy who is caught stealing apples. Finally after much coaxing I got the information—'Deed, missy, specs you think I's nuffin but a po' fool niggah; but I's listened to you'uns playin' music till I's most dead, and I buyed a 'cawdion wid my part ob de cash and mammy she buyed a hat fur meetin'. I's larned to play on it too, Missy Elsie!' You see, Margaret, your idea of 'culchah' has taken deep root in unexpected soil."

"Is Aunt Liza's hat an outgrowth?"

"As an artistic idea I imagine it is; for more intensified reds and yellows never gleamed above a smiling black face. The poor old creature was so delighted with her 'speriment,' as she called it, in saving money for such an artistic triumph, that I hadn't the heart to do more than enjoy it with her."

"After all," said Margaret thoughtfully, "my 'speriment' was not a failure, even if it missed its objective point. I have aroused ambition in their apathetic breasts. See if it does not bear good fruit."

CHAPTER IX.

ONE afternoon as Elsie and Antoine were filling the little house with the notes of a Hungarian battle song, in which violin, organ, voice, and whistle played prominent parts, Margaret was startled by the sudden opening of the outer door, and the appearance on the threshold of a richly-dressed lady, who with a deprecating gesture which the carnival of sound alone permitted, undertook to explain her unannounced presence. Margaret stepped feebly across the room and hushed the players as the lady said laughingly:

"I rapped several times, but was unable to make myself heard, and venturing upon the freedom of long acquaintance, I opened the door. I think I must have made a mistake. I thought I was in the house of Lizzette Minaud."

"You are," said Margaret. "Be seated and we will call her."

The moment Lizzette saw her caller she cried in the freedom of her native tongue: "Madam Mason! Comment cela va-t-il, aujourdhui?"

"Assez bien. Et-vous?" was the answer in the same tongue.

Lizzette hesitated a moment and then said by way of explanation: "Zese friends of mine zay speak ze French wiz me."

"Ah!" and the lady glanced somewhat superciliously

at Margaret and Elsie. " It is immaterial to me which tongue we use. I have only a few moments to spare at best. I was not aware, Lizzette, that you were musical."

" Eh bien, eet ees only Miss Elsie and Antoine. I haf not ze time."

" I should suppose not," said the lady, still using the French tongue, in the evident belief that it might cover some slight impertinences of question and manner.

" Where did they learn that battle song they were playing as I came in ? "

" Zey learn zemselves," answered Lizzette. " Zey haf un grand penchant for music, and eet ees bread and meat to Antoine."

" Humph! Who are these girls ? "

The blood mounted to Lizzette's face, but restraining herself she said with a quiet dignity, that in the little market woman was evidently vastly amusing to Mrs. Mason, " Zey are my guests."

Mrs. Mason laughed. " Come, Lizzette——" she began, but her words were interrupted by a simultaneous movement on the part of Margaret and Elsie. Margaret arose from her chair, and Elsie as quickly offered her arm, and the two were on the point of leaving the room when they were arrested by a whisper from Antoine, " Take me too. I can't stay here."

Elsie put her hand to Antoine's chair, and in a profound silence the " funeral procession," as Elsie called it, marched out of the room.

" Come, come, Lizzette," exclaimed Mrs. Mason in English, when the door had closed. " I meant no

offence, of course.   You seem to have acquired an unusual dignity since I last saw you."

"For zose who deserve it, oui; for Lizzette Minaud,
non.   I know ze ladies when I see zem, if so be zey are
in calico or silk."

"Oh, of course, of course," replied Mrs. Mason somewhat impatiently.   "Tell me who they are, anyway,
and how they happen to be with you."

"Helen Mason," said Lizzette a little sternly, "if so
be I did not know you nearly ze whole of your life, I
nevair tell you von leetle word.   But since I think
vous avez ze heart under zat spoiled exterieur, I vill
tell you ze story."

Mrs. Mason laughed.

"The privilege of an old friend, Lizzette, is sometimes terribly abused; but I forgive you because of
my impatience to hear this wonderful story.   You've
really aroused my curiosity."

With all the eloquence of eye, voice, and gesture so
characteristic of the French, Lizzette gave the details
of Margaret's struggles and misfortunes.   The barren
story lost nothing under the glow of Lizzette's imagination and fertile tongue, and when she finished with a
glowing peroration on the virtues of the little family,
Mrs. Mason's eyes required several applications of a
dainty bit of embroidered gauze before they were restored to their pristine brightness.

"Very affecting indeed," she declared.   "It is singular how hard some people's lives have to be, but it
is fate, I suppose."   Mrs. Mason was evidently quite
resigned to fate.   "I declare," she exclaimed, "listen-

ing to the story of the trials of these people, I had nearly forgotten my own. I am in the deepest trouble, Lizzette, and of course I had to come to you for help just as I used to do."

"Tu as l'air triste," laughed Lizzette.

"Why, I am in despair. You remember that expensive Frenchman I took such pains to import for my kitchen a year ago, and who was such a splendid cook? Not quite equal to you, of course, Lizzette— nobody ever has been. Well, what did the beast do but get so drunk yesterday that he hasn't prepared a meal since and we are nearly starved!"

"Wiz all zose servants in ze house?" asked Lizzette incredulously.

"Oh, as for that, the maids have succeeded in sending up something, but then you know how exasperating it is to have meals so poorly served. Dear me! he was such a model on sauces!" And a sigh that was evidently drawn from the depths of her heart followed the plaintive ejaculation.

"Was? Ou est il?"

"Oh, Mr. Mason discharged him this morning. You know how rigid he is about drunkenness. I begged Mr. Mason on my knees to let me keep Joseph another month, anyway; for Herbert—your Herbert, you know, Lizzette—is coming home from Europe, and I've no end of dinners planned for him, and no cook in the house. What am I to do, Lizzette? Can't you come to me just for a month, Lizzette? I will pay you well if you will, and Antoine can stay here with these girls. Oh, do come, there's a dear, good Lizzette."

Mrs. Mason was gently patting Lizzette's brown hand with one of her own daintily gloved ones. Lizzette pondered a moment. "Vot you pay Joseph?"

"An enormous sum," answered Mrs. Mason, coloring. "He had such a reputation, you know, and one always has to pay for reputation!"

"Ah!"

The ejaculation was so dry that Mrs. Mason hastened to add: "But of course I shall not let money stand between us."

Lizzette ruminated a little: "Ees eet worth to you ze twenty dollars a week?"

"It is truly," she answered, feeling a sense of relief that it was not Joseph's usual weekly stipend of one hundred dollars.

"Eh bien!" said Lizzette, "I cannot go."

"Lizzette, you break my heart. Why not, pray?"

"Because everysing go to ze waste here; mais, I haf ze plan for you. I find you une cuisinière a cet prix."

"But ordinary cooks, you know, Lizzette, cannot earn more than five or six dollars a week."

"I know; mais, zis von ees so tres-bonne, I myself teach her. She lack ze experience, zat ees all. Elle à le genie sublime!"

"That may be; but such wages are too large to pay inexperience. I think you ought to get her cheaper."

"Ees eet not," asked Lizzette with a sly twinkle in her eyes, "zat le prix ees much sheaper zan you obtain Joseph?"

"Oh, of course; but Joseph was a noted chef."

"Haf you not ze grand need of a cook?"

"Certainly."

"Zen if I take l'avantage de votre need to obtain le bon prix for ze work zat ees very good *wizout* ze reputation, I only follow ze well known business principle: one zat Monsieur Mason take l'avantage of every day."

"Lizzette, you are too much for me. Where is your paragon?"

"Here. C'est Elsie."

"What, that young girl? You astonish me. She cannot be capable; besides, I thought you considered her a lady."

"Bah! Ze work ees not ze lady any more zan your robe de soie ees ze lady. Ven I say 'lady' I mean ze instinct, ze character, ze soul, ze nature. She cannot harm zat by working dans le cuisine. My word for it, you will nevair find Elsie Murchison ze trespasser of her place, if so be it ees in your kitchen or in your salon."

"Small likelihood of the latter! Go on, Lizzette— you are really eloquent."

"Mais, I feel ze indignation at ze misapprehension of your world ofer ze name of lady. In my leetle world ect means somesing besides ze airs and ze graces et l'argent."

"Your world and mine won't quarrel over it much, I fancy," said Mrs. Mason composedly. "It seems to me you've grown into a fierce little radical since you compounded such delectable dishes in mamma's kitchen; but as to the capability of that young thing, I doubt it much."

"I do not, for she learn so fast; and ven I haf vonce

taken her through ze maison and she know ze duties, you vill be surprised at ze ease she do zem. Besides, ze grand sing ees ze buying, and I vill do zat until she sall haf learned. Je vous le promets a treasure in El- sie, and you vill nevair be sorry zat Lizzette Minaud say so."

"I never have been sorry that I took any advice of yours. But how do you know your marvel will ac- cept?"

"Nous verrons! Elsie!" called Lizzette, stepping to the kitchen door. "Sit down," she added, as Elsie pre- sented herself. "Madam Mason haf ze offer to make to you," and thereupon Lizzette detailed the proposition that had just been under discussion.

Elsie's eyes grew big with wonder as she listened to Lizzette. "I am afraid I am not equal to it," she faltered.

"Lizzette vouches for you," said Mrs. Mason. "I have always found her advice good."

Elsie did not answer at once. A tide of thought was sweeping over her. The opportunity was like a tale from fairy land in the riches it seemed to offer; but how could she live under the domination of that supercilious woman she *knew* she should hate? But Margaret, Gilbert, Antoine—how much she could do for all of them! Courage! Now was the time to prove herself. The way had been opened; there could not be, must not be any shrinking back.

"Very well," she answered simply. "I am willing to make the trial."

"To-morrow, then," said Mrs. Mason, rising, "you

will begin under Lizzette's management. She knows my house as well as her own. At ten o'clock in the morning I shall be prepared to receive you. Good-evening, Lizzette and—Elsie."

With a scarcely perceptible nod Mrs. Mason hastened out to her carriage. When the door had closed Lizzette grasped Elsie by the shoulders and began an impromptu chaussée up and down the room.

"C'est trés-bon! C'est trés-bon!" she cried. "I prove ze sharper zat time; mais, le defaut ees in ze grand cause of humanity."

"I am frightened to death, Lizzette," said Elsie.

"Chut! Helen Mason ees only la femme ordinaire, and reech! Helas! l'argent zat petite femme frow to ze winds. Lizzette haf catch some for you, anyway."

Margaret opened the door just then and the three sat down to discuss the important move.

"Honestly, Lizzette, now, do you think I can manage their great dinners? Why, I haven't the least idea how to plan any work beyond my own little kitchen."

"Vraiment, c'est une bagatelle ven you haf got ze hang of sings. Nefer you fear. I take you under my wing for three, four days and zen we vill see! Ze chance was so tres-bon to help Margaret——"

"And all of us," interrupted Elsie softly.

"Oui; ze pomme de terre and ze sel go by ze board now, eh, Elsie?"

"O Lizzette, what a good friend you have been!" exclaimed Margaret.

"Bah! eet ees only selfishness. I want myself some good sings to eat. Now, Elsie, I gif you my recipes;

8

vous savez zat you read zem wiz care and learn zem by heart. Sans doubte, you exercise your skill to ze charm of madam."

"Tell us about her."

"Zare ees but leetle to tell. I vork in ze kitchen de sa mère zese many year. I make ze good friends of Helen and Herbeart—ah, Herbeart, mon cher ami, il est un galant homme, and I knows ze folly of Helen like ze book. She ees vain and haughty; mais, her heart ees not mèchante. You vill grow into ze good friends some time."

"I don't expect that," said Elsie. "All I ask is not to be tyrannized over. I am conservative enough to recognize the gulf society places between us, and I shall endeavor to keep to my side of the fence."

"Vous avez raison. Still, I make ze meestake eef Helen Mason do not herself some time break down ze barrier. Zare are some sings zat vill not be made to see de fausses idées de grandeur."

"It is not wise ever to hope for such a thing," said Margaret, fearful that Elsie might be carried away by Lizzette's volatile spirits. "We have our work to do in our own sphere, and we know that we can achieve all that is in us by working faithfully within our own lines. If we hope for recognition outside of these lines, it will but breed disappointment and discontent."

"Have no fear for me, my sweet sister," replied Elsie with sparkling eyes. "I shall never yearn for a world greater than that of our own little quintette, wherein Lizzette, Gilbert, and I furnish the brawn and *capital*—I feel like a bloated bondholder already—

and Antoine and Margaret represent the culture. But
to stop nonsense and come down to practical things.
Since I am to represent the capital of our community,
I must have the chief direction of affairs, otherwise
behold in me 'the iron hand,' etc. What are we to do
with our three-years' lease of our desolate home?"

"Eef ze agents vill not rebuild, Margaret and Gilbeart sall stay wiz me and so still work ze land."

"No," said Margaret decisively. "The hardest part
of this apparent good fortune that has befallen Elsie is
that it takes her from home. I cannot endure it long,
and if Elsie remains with Mrs. Mason I shall take
rooms in the city as near as I can find them, and Gilbert must bring her to us every evening. We must
not break the home ties."

"That will be glorious," exclaimed Elsie.

"Non," said Lizzette, tears springing to her eyes.
"Eet vill bring ze heart break to Antoine and Lizzette
Minaud."

"No, no," said Margaret and Elsie together, "you
shall come to us every day after market hours, and
Antoine can be with us two-thirds of the time."

"I know zat vill be ze best for Elsie; but ees ect
possible? Ze docteur, he say zat you vork not till ze
spring. You must obey ze command, if strength sall
come back to you."

"I know," replied Margaret. "How would it suit
you to take a sub-lease of the land, if satisfactory ar-
rangements can be made with the agents?"

"Eet vill be ze very sing."

"In that event the manual-training school for Gilbert is the next move, and I shall be compelled to ask Dr. Ely for a further advance on the books."

"And be sure to add that I can very soon repay it out of my independent income," laughed Elsie.

CHAPTER X.

THE mansion of Helen Mason was a treasure house of art in pictures, draperies, furniture, bric-à-brac, and all those distinguishing characteristics of wealth and culture. In one particular it was somewhat unique; everything was genuine, from the old masters to the spoons. The fair mistress of the house hated pretence, and although an ardent believer in the divine right of kings, she recognized none of them in a tinsel crown. The child of wealthy and aristocratic parents, in whom the old noblesse oblige had taken deep root, she had grown to look upon her station in life as the outgrowth of a certain fixed law which bestows upon men the positions for which they are best fitted. If there were suffering, struggling mortals on planes far below hers in social advantages, no doubt the sufferings arose principally from their efforts to fit themselves into niches for which they were not made. It seemed singular to her undisturbed mind that there should be such a seething discontent among the masses. Why couldn't people be satisfied to go the way they were called? Why were they trying all the time to subvert society and make one fairly afraid of her life with these horrible physical force movements and plots and counterplots of all kinds? It was so much better every way for people to learn contentment. She believed the doctrine was too little preached, and she meant to speak to her pastor, the white high-bred rector of St. Paul's, about it.   He must really exert his influence over these misguided people who were so clamorous for places for which they were not destined.   Believing as she did in the doctrine of every man to his place, she strove with a zeal of a prophet in her own little domain to make that place the best of its kind.   Her servants were accordingly well lodged, fed, and paid, albeit they were trained to their duties with the precision of a martinet.   Haughty, imperious in some things, while childishly dependent in others, she was at the same time a good mistress, and by no means unfriendly to her dependents.   She intended to accord them the rights of their class, as she exacted a reverent homage for the privileges of her own; but she was far from admitting that those rights could in any way transcend the limits of a certain material consideration. The finer qualities of the soul, such as innate delicacy of perception and the instinctive appreciation of true refinement, could not be theirs by reason of the stamp of poverty and the millstone of low association which precluded cultivation.   It was a theory of hers that only generations of wealth and leisure could produce the highest types, and she had consequently a great scorn for the nouveaux riches of modern society and their blundering attempts to imitate English customs and cockney "fads."   As a rule her servants were loyal and obedient, and she was wise enough to see that her little investment in humanity yielded usurious interest which she was by no means disposed to undervalue. She had been proud of having the best-equipped home, the most perfectly-trained servants, and the most noted chef in the city. It was, therefore, with no little trepidation that she awaited the coming of Lizzette and Elsie, and contemplated yielding the dominion of her kitchen to "that young thing." Mr. Mason had laughed at her when she recounted the result of her attempt to secure Lizzette, and had said, by way of administering comfort to her perturbed spirit: "That is just about as quixotic as women's schemes usually are. My word for it, she will not have been three days in the house before the present discomfort will be intensified, and we shall end by having to order our meals from the caterer."

It was now nearing the hour of ten, and she was impatient to settle details with Lizzette and feel the troublesome experiment partially off her hands. As she sat idly tapping one foot against the brass fender of the blue-tiled grate in her morning-room, she was a fair type of the cultured, self-poised, well-dressed woman of society. Her face was chiefly remarkable for a pair of keen gray eyes, with heavy black lashes and straight brows. The remaining features were nondescript, with a colorless skin and dark brown hair handsomely coiffured, for setting. A keen, cold, somewhat intellectual face had been Elsie's thought on first seeing her, and she felt sure that she should hate her. She felt the same conviction sweep over her now as she and Lizzette stood in the presence of the mistress of the magnificent home.

"Be seated," she said, motioning them to seats. "I presume Lizzette has informed you that I am a strict disciplinarian and require the most perfect obedience.   If that is rendered you will not find me a hard mistress."

"I should not have come if I had not expected to obey orders," replied Elsie.   "My only fear is that my inexperience may try your patience."

"As to that I shall hold Lizzette responsible; and now, while Lizzette will at once post you in regard to matters below stairs, I will give you our hours for meals, and shall expect you to report to me promptly every morning at ten o'clock to receive orders for the day.   Lizzette will at present do my buying; but you must of course go with her until you have familiarized yourself with prices and materials.   Here is to-day's menu, which by the way, as to the main dishes, I always prepare myself.   You may have noticed as you came through the house that the maids are in uniform.   I shall expect you to wear one, and you will find your allotment of white aprons, caps, and kerchiefs in this basket.   Here, Lizzette, you may as well invest yourself in one, too."

"Helas! zese new idees vill do for la jeune fille like Elsie.   Mais, ze brown face of Lizzette Minaud look not so well from under ze white cap.   Still I obey ze mistress !"

"Just as you always did," laughed Mrs. Mason, pressing an electric button, which almost immediately brought a maid to the door.

"Show Elsie, our new cook, to her room.   Stay with me, Lizzette.   I wish to speak with you."   Elsie picked up her satchel and basket and followed the maid, who eyed her curiously, but vouchsafed no word.   "Here," she said sententiously, opening a door of a roomy, comfortable bedroom on the third floor.

Elsie hastily entered and closed the door behind her. Then dropping satchel and basket, she threw herself on the floor beside them and cried out: "O Meg, Meg, Meg, how hard life is away from you and your serene courage! How lovely all our theories are until we have to put them into practice. I shall hate that woman, I know. Dear me! this won't do. I shall have a red nose. Now let's see how I look in the new prison garb," and volatile Elsie bounded to her feet, and speedily invested herself in the white muslin cap with its narrow frill and the accompanying kerchief and apron.

"Not so bad, after all," she said, as she eyed herself in the glass, and a roguish dimple nestled in her cheek as she viewed the picture. It was pretty enough to tempt the vanity of the Quaker maiden she resembled. The dainty frill above the black rings of hair, the fichu folded smoothly across her breast, and the long apron with its big pockets, seemed exactly fitted to the piquant face and slender form. "Well, there's some satisfaction in not looking like a fright," she said as she descended the stairs.

The morning-room door stood open and Mrs. Mason and Lizzette could scarcely repress a start of surprise as the dainty maiden stepped upon the threshold. "She look like ze picture of ze old time," exclaimed Lizzette. Mrs. Mason made no reply as she handed Elsie a memorandum-book and pencil, which with keys to pantry and store-room were to be suspended at her belt.

"Now you are equipped, I believe, and Lizzette will take you in charge. I wish you the best of success."

When the two had departed, Mrs. Mason stood where they had left her with downcast eyes gazing into the grate. "What a lovely face," she mused. "So full of fire and strength and—well, yes, I suppose I must admit it—refinement! She looked like a queen in masquerade as she stood in the doorway. But then nature indulges in freaks of that kind sometimes. Lizzette tells me they were always as poor as church mice. What an absurdity I am perpetrating in putting her in my kitchen; but my old brown Lizzette is always as good as her word, and we shall see what will come of it."

The force of servants in the Mason household consisted of James, the English-looking butler, of whom Elsie was secretly afraid, because his gaze of admiration was so open; William, the coachman; Martha and Mary, the two house-maids; and Jenie, the little kitchen-maid of twelve years. They all knew Lizzette, who, being a privileged character about the Mason mansion, was free to do pretty much as she liked, and when, in response to her call, they gathered in the below-stairs parlor, which also served them for dining-room, they received Elsie with unction.

"It hain't a bad place, miss," said James patronizingly. "I've been with the family five years, and I can't say as I've 'ad a 'ard time by no means."

"I should say not," laughed Martha. " James thinks as he owns the hull place."

"Ceptin' you," added Mary.

"I wouldn't own such poor property, no'ow," said James with offended dignity.

"That ain't me," exclaimed William with a sly chuckle. "I've just been a-dyin' to own both on you girls for months."

"Oh, you horrid Mormon," chorused the girls; "you'll be wanting the new cook too, next." The blood flamed into Elsie's cheeks and an ominous sparkle gleamed for a moment beneath the downcast lids; but, with a struggle that was only noticed by Lizzette, she raised her eyes to William's round, honest face.

"I think we shall all grow to be good friends; but you must be very patient with me until I have learned the ways here."

The sweet face, the timid, deprecating manner, the ladylike voice, awoke varying emotions in the breasts of Elsie's little audience. "You bet," exclaimed William hastily.

"Oh, of course," said James, and then stopped confusedly as he recollected how near he had been to saying "Madam!"

Martha and Mary looked at each other and sniffed. "Stuck up," they whispered as they passed out to their various duties; but little Jenie slipped her hand into Elsie's and said simply, "I like you."

"Courage, ma chere," whispered Lizzette; "now we haf nosing but ze dinner to sink of."

In recounting the day's experience afterward to Margaret, Elsie always alluded to Lizzette as her "colossal spinal column;" for in reality Lizzette was

the main director and executor of the day's work.
Elsie obediently followed directions; but her native
force and ingenuity seemed to have deserted her, which
made even Lizzette a trifle doubtful of the wisdom of
her experiment. But when everything was finally
made snug for the night, and Lizzette was leaving for
home, Elsie said bravely, though tears stood under
the curved lashes, "I shall do much better to-morrow.
Tell Margaret I've got the 'hang' of the ship's tackle,
and to-morrow she'll sail."

"Nevair fear," said Lizzette lightly, as she imprinted
a kiss on either rosy cheek, and steadily ignored the
trembling drops in the dark eyes. "Eet sall be ze
brave capitaine on ze deck, too."

The next morning, with the edge of strangeness
somewhat blunted, Elsie was able to send up the breakfast in excellent style, and Mrs. Mason was therefore
prepared to receive her with a manner a trifle less
severe than that of the day before.

"Your breakfast was well prepared," she said as
Elsie stood before her, note-book and pencil in hand,
to receive orders. "If the dinner is as satisfactory I
shall feel no further uneasiness."

"I shall endeavor to improve as I become accustomed to things, and I shall hope to satisfy you in
every way. I love to cook, and the kitchen is so admirably appointed that what has hitherto been a mere
passion I may be able to elevate into the great art
that Lizzette calls it."

"Lizzette is an enthusiast."

"It takes enthusiasm to succeed in anything, and it

is because I love my work that I expect to please you."

Mrs. Mason looked at Elsie curiously. How quietly, yet with what seemingly unconscious dignity, she uttered those few well-chosen words. If she had been mistress instead of servant they could not have been better expressed or more charmingly enunciated. There could be no question of efficiency with such intelligence; but oh, there was the fear, always oppressing one so with these "lady helps," that she would get above her business. So to Elsie's little burst of confidence she said coldly, "As long as you keep strictly to your line of duty I shall be satisfied."

"You have nothing to fear on that score, Mrs. Mason. I know my place as ' Elsie the cook.' Have you any further orders?"

"Nothing more to-day."

Mrs. Mason smiled triumphantly as she watched the blood deepen in Elsie's cheeks as she left the room. "The girl is as proud as Lucifer; but it is not a usual pride, I must confess."

At the close of the week Elsie found that her end of the domestic machinery was running quietly and smoothly. She had already made friends with the other servants, who, while recognizing the air of self-respecting womanhood that would neither give nor permit low jests or rude actions, could not fail to be drawn by the simplicity of her manner and her frank, straightforward way of looking at things. Insensibly the loud-voiced talk and rude horse-play formerly in vogue among them began to disappear. James' ostentatious display of knowledge gradually weakened before Elsie's clear eyes and plain questions; William left his stable-talk at the door, together with his coat and boots, and came to his meals in patent-leather pumps, velveteen roundabout, and hair saturated with patch-ouli. The house-maids had less gossip of the upper regions to retail, and Jenie's smutty frock was invariably replaced by a clean one at meal-time.

"Ze leetle witch," exclaimed Lizzette to Margaret. "She haf got zere necks under her heel so quick! And ze funny part ees zey know eet not at all."

"I doubt if Elsie does," replied Margaret. "For after all it is only the power of judiciously exhibited self-respect."

CHAPTER XI.

THERE was a subdued bustle in the Mason mansion which betokened an unusual event. Covers were removed from unused furniture, long-closed rooms were newly aired and decorated, windows were opened to the sunlight, and hot-houses were ransacked for potted plants and cut flowers. In the store-rooms of Elsie's department tables and shelves were piled high with viands of every sort, the combined result of Lizzette's and Elsie's skill; for Elsie had been afraid on so momentous an occasion to trust entirely to herself.

"And all this fuss is over one small man," whispered Elsie to Lizzette as they stood admiring the aggregation of eatables. "Has he been starving among the Hottentots all these years, or is he a great gourmand?"

"Nezair," laughed Lizzette. "Il est ze apple of ze eye of Helen Mason. Zay are alone togezzer in ze world, and ze one sweet sing in Helen Mason ees her love for Herbeart. Mais, he ees tres cher efen to me. So vot you call warm-hearted, wiz ze bonhomie zat make ze world bright. He travel in Europe zese several year, and like Helen il à l'argent in heaps I know not."

"What has he made of himself?"

"Eh bien. Vraiment, le galant homme!"

"A gentleman! A noble profession How does he do it?"

"Ze witch ees laughing!   I no explain to zose mocking eyes."

"Never mind, Lizzette.   There is something so charmingly indefinite about the term 'gentleman' that I was only trying to discover what particular form this rara avis took."

"He choose no profession zat I know. He no haf to work."

"Unlucky mortal!   How he will envy us, Lizzette! But tell me about him.   Does he resemble his sister?"

"Not ze leetle bit. · Il a les eyes like ze summer sky, zay are so blue.   Il est so tall like ze young tree. His hair ees ze sunshine of ze autumn, and his smile like ze warmth of ze summer sun."

"Scorching," exclaimed Elsie.   "How glad I am I shall not come under its gleams; for I would rather cook his dinner than be cooked by that smile!"

"Ze mauvaise Elsie!   She make ze fun of eferysing, efen my heart.   I haf loved him since many year he climb my knee, and I only speak ze figures de la poesie."

"My dear Lizzette," exclaimed Elsie contritely, "I do not make fun of your love, nor of your similes, which really are quite wonderful.   Indeed, I never knew you so eloquent before; but this worship of yours for the fair god is so new to me, I did not know that men were entitled to so much."

"Ze time vill come, ma petite Elsie, ze time vill come ven zat mocking heart sall take back zose idle words."

"How solemn you are, Lizzette.   You frighten me."

"Non, non, mais, zere ces no love like ze true love in ze heart of ze good woman."

"It may be," said Elsie lightly, "but like the old Scotchwoman's white linen, 'it taks a sair bit o' achin' ta get it,' and I've no desire to prove it."

"Eet vill prove itself in ze heart, and no ask desire."

'Dear me! how far we have wandered from our muttons. I suppose your paragon dines here to-night?"

"Oui, and to-morrow I sall go shake ze hand de mon Herbeart, and find him still ze same."

"Perhaps not."

"I know," said Lizzette positively. "My lad ees not made of ze sheap stuff zat wear out memory."

The next morning as Elsie, in response to Mrs. Mason's invitation, entered the morning-room, she became at once aware that its fair mistress was not its only occupant. Partially concealed behind a news-paper she saw a blonde head, out of which a pair of blue eyes gave her a quick glance, and she noticed with an odd sense of detail that their owner wore a dark blue smoking-jacket with facings of pale blue satin. There was also a running accompaniment of observation as to a slim white hand, the curling ends of a blonde mustache, and an air of indolent grace in the long lithe figure. Venturing but one glance, she stood with book and pencil in hand, quietly awaiting Mrs. Mason's orders. It had been one of the results of Elsie Murchison's secluded life and country rearing that no one had ever told her how beautiful she was, and if she could but read the pleasing tale in her

9

mirror she accepted it in as humble and thankful a
spirit as she accepted the sunshine and the flowers,
and there was always a refreshing unconsciousness
about her that reminded one of the innocence of a
child.   If she ever knew how charming a picture she
made as she stood before her mistress with downcast
eyes and flushed cheeks and the quaint cap and kerchief only intensifying her girlish simplicity, it was not
till long after.   The natural flush of youthful expectancy at coming in contact with the young and handsome man before her was crushed back under the self-
scorn with which she regarded any vague desire, as
she expressed it, to "look over the fence."   Not for
one moment would she allow herself to forget that
she was "Elsie the cook," and a little defiant curve settled around the dimpled mouth as she became aware
of the intent gaze of those blue eyes over the top of
the newspaper.   It was with haste amounting almost
to curtness that she received her orders and betook
herself out of the room.

There were two or three moments of silence after
Elsie's departure, and then Mrs. Mason's guest threw
down his paper with the question: "Where in the
name of all the graces, Helen, did you find such a
Hebe as that?"

There was a steely flash in Mrs. Mason's eyes as
she answered: "Have you been half the world over,
Herbert Lynn, only to come home and rave over the
beauty of my cook?"

"Cook?   I thought Lizzette was responsible for
that superb dinner last evening."

"So she was in part; but this girl, Elsie Murchison, is a protégé of hers whom I have engaged for a short time until I can do better."

"Well, if her cooking corresponds to her beauty she must be a treasure."

"That is what James and William both declare her to be;" replied Mrs. Mason calmly.

"Oh, of course, just their style of girl," and Mr. Lynn resumed the reading of his newspaper, as if the subject had no further interest for him.

"Singular," he mused, while his eyes roamed over an editorial résumé of the Parnell inquiry, "what surprises nature does love to work, putting the face of an houri over a mind that doubtless shames a Nancy Sykes. Helen's cook, indeed! but, by Jove! I never saw so lovely a face before."

After this, despite the black looks of his sister, Herbert took especial delight in haunting the morning-room at the usual hour of her conference with her cook. He was seldom rewarded by hearing the Hebe speak, and then only in monosyllables; but he noticed she had "that excellent thing in woman," a well-modulated voice, as well as a quiet and reserved manner.

"Herbert," exclaimed Mrs. Mason with an angry flash in her gray eyes, after he had been present at the third or fourth of these conferences, "I'll not have you watching that girl so, and I warn you that my house is not the place for any old-world gallantries."

The mild blue eyes met her own for an instant with an equally angry glance, which, however, speedily died

away by the time the nonchalant lips had framed an
answer. "I believe I've been doing nothing unbe-
coming a gentleman."

"Well, I only drop you a warning. I know what
the views of young men usually are after they have
spent a season in Paris."

"You are wise in your generation," he said with a
slight touch of scorn. "When did you learn of the
all-pervading blight of that modern Gomorrah?"

"Don't try to be lofty with me," pettishly exclaimed
his sister. "You know as well as I do that no good
can come of your admiring that girl."

"And what possible harm can come of it? I have
done nothing reprehensible, except to bestow a few
quick glances upon a fair and youthful face. If she is
not to be looked at, you must veil her like the prophet
of Khorassan. As for your insinuations—well, if men
go to the devil as regularly and deliberately as you
seem to think, it is often because they are driven there
by the cool assumptions of women like yourself. Now,
my dear sister, let me disabuse your mind once for all
of the fear that I have imbibed nothing but old-world
vices in my continental trip. I always did respect
virtuous womanhood and always shall. I shall not in
the least harm your Hebe of the pots and pans, but to
relieve your mind I'll read the papers hereafter in the
billiard-room."

"Well," said Mrs. Mason, after Herbert had somewhat ostentatiously departed, and she was left to
ruminate on not over-sweet fancies, "I fancy I've fore-
stalled any absurd ideas that might get into Elsie's

head, and although I am growing to like her better every day, just let me catch her making eyes at Herbert!"

"Elsie," said Mrs. Mason the next morning, "we are all going out for the day, and you may have your time to yourself. I've given the maids a half-holiday and there'll be nobody at home but James."

Elsie stood for a moment irresolute. A swift desire had all but leaped to her lips—but dare she make it known?

"What is it, Elsie?" asked her mistress, evidently more graciously disposed than usual.

"I would like to ask a great favor. If there is to be no one in the house may I try the piano?"

"I was not aware that you played the piano," said Mrs. Mason a trifle coldly. Elsie's face flushed.

"I do not. I never touched one in my life; but I have a longing to see what I can do. There isn't volume and scope enough in our little cottage organ, and I promised Antoine to ask permission to try the piano. He is so much interested in music and finds so much pleasure in learning that I love to help him even in little things."

"I see no objection in the present instance; but you of course understand that I regard the request as an unusual one for a servant to make?"

"I do," said Elsie hotly as she turned away, "and I will not——"

Back swept the red blood from Elsie's face, and a white, dull patience overspread it as she took up the broken thread of her speech.

"Mrs. Mason, I was going to say that I would not touch your piano for worlds ! You seem to be afraid all the time that I will forget the difference in our station and presume upon it. Have I done so? Have I been less than obedient, or indicated by word or look that I thought myself anything more than a servant ? But even servants have the common right of humanity, and I asked a favor, knowing it to be a favor, because of the crippled boy I love and the sick sister who taught me to love and do for all things helpless and dependent. If it were not for them no money would tempt me to stay where I am not trusted; but they are helpless and in need. I shall never ask any further favors of you, Mrs. Mason; but if you still wish to keep me I shall try, as I have tried, to be obedient and faithful to your interests."

Mrs. Mason sat for a moment without speaking, and then suddenly reached out her hand to Elsie. "Come back, child," she said, "and sit down. I want to talk with you."

Elsie came back from the door and stood before her mistress. "Sit down," reiterated Mrs. Mason.

"It is expected that servants will stand in the presence of their superiors," answered Elsie with the old mischievous sparkle in her eyes.

Mrs. Mason laughed. "I like your spirit, anyway. I really haven't any objection to your using the piano when we are away. I'm glad you are ambitious to cultivate yourself; but you mustn't make the mistake of regarding a little superficial finish as cultivation. Genuine cultivation strikes deep in the soil and takes hold of every fibre of the being.'

"Mrs. Mason," said Elsie, "you make a mistake if you think I have any longing for the mere name of lady. I believe I could be your cook all my days and yet make myself worthy of the character and appellation. It is not what one does so much as in the manner of doing it that lies the distinction, and I have as natural a longing for all things noble and beautiful as the flowers have for the sun, and just as good a right to reach for them."

"Certainly," assented Mrs. Mason; "but with such surroundings you haven't a very hopeful chance of obtaining them. Your life is not a very happy one."

"Yes, it is," replied Elsie stoutly, "because I make it so. I wouldn't change places with the richest woman in this city, if by so doing I had to lose the dear hopes and sympathies for every day living that make even our misfortunes bearable. O Mrs. Mason, before the fire and Margaret's sickness, nothing could have exceeded the daily delight of our lives, even with all their hard work and privation. Something to believe in, some hope for humanity, some trifle in word or deed for each other—why, it seemed like a foretaste of heaven. And now—well—" she went on, choking back the sobs, "it is a delight to me to know that my earnings have placed my brother Gilbert in the manual-training school, and are helping Margaret, Lizzette, and Antoine in numerous ways. I don't want anything in this world, but just to grow into light and life with the dear ones I love and who love me."

Mrs. Mason did an unprecedented thing for her.

She clasped one of Elsie's hands in her own, and said with a litle break in her voice: " My dear child, you must promise to forget my severity, and take me at my word when I tell you to use the piano as often as you find the coast clear, and also to help yourself to what books you like in the library. I shall never speak a harsh word to you again."

" Don't say that," exclaimed Elsie quickly. " I may need a good many."

" Well, the compact stands until you do need them."

Two hours later, having seen the carriage drive from the door, and supposing the house empty with the exception of James, who was dozing in his pantry off the dining-room, Elsie came softly down the stairs to the front drawing-room. She had taken off cap, kerchief, and apron, and wore only a dark cloth dress with a little knot of bright red silk at the throat. With childish curiosity she investigated everything in the handsome room, pausing longest before a Carrara marble statuette of Cupid and Psyche and talking aloud with all the abandon of a child.

" So that face of Psyche's was the best the sculptor could do to represent the soul. I should call it rather the absence of soul; but then I'm a Philistine, and lack culture; and as for Cupid, if the blind god is no fairer than he is painted — I should say carved—he wouldn't stand much chance of awaking immortality in me. I don't believe I've got a bit of poetry in me, anyhow; I'm so inclined to laugh at sentiment, or sentimentality—it all amounts to the same thing. In either event, I suppose it shows that ' Elsie the cook ' is made of coarser clay than those who find beauty in unmeaning faces. But I forget. 'Elsie the cook' has gone away, and Elsie the lady has come to stay."

A low ripple of laughter broke from her lips over the unintentional couplet. "A poet, after all! I guess, as they say below stairs, I'll throw up my job and get a quill and ink-stand."

At this juncture, a gentleman who had been stretched at full length upon a couch within a curtained alcove at the further end of the library, closed the book he had been reading, and shoving the curtain aside for an inch or two, gazed into the drawing-room through the half-open door. It chanced that the wide pier-glass was so situated that nearly the whole interior of the drawing-room was visible to the occupant of the alcove, and a half-smile gleamed beneath the curled blonde mustache as he listened to Elsie's amusing comments.

"Elsie the lady has come to stay," she repeated, "and now I'll see if I can play it as well as madam herself. I wonder if I look like one," and half-dancing up to the glass, Elsie stood for a moment looking critically at herself. "No, I won't do. My hair ought to be so," and she gathered it up on the top of her head, from which the riotous ends speedily escaped in a curling mass. "There! that's better; looks quite fashionable; gown is very plain, but then we'll suppose I go in for asceticism. No rings, but no pot black on my hands. Nails well manicured and tolerably aristocratic-looking. That is, there's quite a taper to the fingers, which I suppose puts the proper stamp on. Now that my lady has come to her own, let's see how she receives her guests. We'll try her cook first, so as to get the proper air of dignified severity. No, I'll not do it," she said thoughtfully, as she stood for a moment with downcast eyes. "She was kind to me after all, and I'll not repay it with mockery even to myself. It is quite evident that there is a great deal due to station in this world, and Elsie the cook must cultivate a little appreciation. Come, my Lord Snubbem, and teach me to be a Brahmin."

With a mock courtesy Elsie stood before a great sleepy hollow chair of blue velvet and went on with her soliloquy:

"You will no doubt understand, my lord, that this is my first appearance in society, and lacking the *savoir faire* of long acquaintance, I shall, I presume, shock you with some of my 'wild woolly western' ideas. Nevertheless, having seen that my brother, Mr. High-and-Mighty, just returned from 'the continent'—that is the way even Americans put it, as if there were but one continent—is paying his proper devoirs to Miss Bullion, and will probably fall in love with her, or rather with her money, which, entre nous, is all 'we' ask nowadays, I suppose I'll have to permit you, my Lord Snubbem, after a great deal of coaxing, to induce me to play for you. Of course you know all the time I'm dying to show off; at least that's the way they say it is in society, and so you offer me your arm and lead me to the piano, and I prepare to display my diamond rings—dear me, it's too bad I haven't any! —and my precious little knowledge of music. Let me see, how shall I begin? With a grand flourish, of course; now for that Hungarian battle song !" And almost forgetful of the character she was supposed to represent, Elsie struck the heavy chords of the overture, and became at once absorbed in the melody she was evoking. "Ah, that is grand," she sighed tremulously. "There is power, adaptability, volume in a piano that you can't find in a cottage organ if you smother your soul in it. Now good-by, Lord Snubbem. Elsie the cook and Antoine the cripple have come back and are going to forget all about you."

Presently, after a few drum-beats of the piano, arose the shrill, sweet notes of a trumpet-call. Again it came, louder, sweeter than ever, then the answering tones of the piano, until trumpet-call and drum-beat were blended in one brilliant clash of melody. Then the piano ceased and Elsie's whistle took up the plaintive solo of the violin, which is supposed to represent the pathetic heroism of the Hungarian mother in sending her loved ones to battle. Softly, yet clearly, and with such underlying feeling rang the bird notes through the room that the listener felt tears gathering beneath his eyelids. Scarcely had the sweet notes ended when louder and faster came the crash of battle, to be followed by the low dirge and moaning cries rendered by the resonant whistle. "Oh, dear," sighed Elsie, "if Antoine had only been here, it might have been worth while. What a grand thing the piano is! Poverty wouldn't be so bad if it did not exclude so much of the heaven of music and art, etc., etc., etc. Now, Elsie the cook, stop that vain longing ! Maybe you'll earn a piano yet with your immense riches.

Just one more try, and Elsie the cook must go into
the lower regions again; but it's been glorious to know
what such a life might mean. Come, old comforter,
and compose my soul," and she struck the accompaniment to the old, old song, " Jesus, Lover of my Soul."
The fresh young voice, gaining confidence as the feeling pervading the melody swept over her, seemed to
fill every nook and corner of the room and rise upward and outward until it was lost on the shining
pathway to the stars. It was dusk when Elsie closed
the piano, and with a sudden fervor she bent down
and kissed it. " The only friend I have in the house,"
she sighed aloud. A moment later she passed out
into the hall humming softly to herself:

> " Hide me! Oh, my Saviour, hide,
> Till the storm of life be passed!"

When the last notes had died away in the distance
Herbert Lynn sprang from his couch, and striking a
match, looked at his watch.

" Six o'clock!" he exclaimed. " Helen will be furious
because I've not kept my engagement; but I wouldn't
have missed that scene for all the dinners in Chris-
tendom. Heavens! what a nature there is in that little
girl!"

CHAPTER XII.

MARGARET sat reading a letter from Dr. Ely. The
faint blood of returning health was deepening in her
cheeks, and the glad light of her eyes intensified by
emotions which the letter evidently called forth. With
the freedom of the invisible biographer we will glance
over her shoulder as she reads:

"I have carried for months the picture of the cosey
sitting-room at Idlewild set like a gem in the silver
circle of memory. It is hard, very hard, now to feel
that it must be only a memory; that I shall never see
it again, and never be able to picture the little feasts
of reason which your letters have so charmingly described. Still, home is where the heart is, and I regard this misfortune as only a temporary interruption
of your plans. I know so well the motive springs of
action in your nature, that I feel sure as soon as your
strength comes back on perhaps a firmer basis, the old
progress will be re-established.

"I heartily indorse your move in placing Gilbert in
the manual-training school, and inclose a draft for
one hundred dollars to advance your efforts. You
need have no hesitancy in accepting it, as I find the
books are regarded by bibliophilists generally as pos-
sessing all the value I placed upon them.

"As regards Elsie's experiment in going as a cook, there is much to be said for and against. She will be subjected in such a position to much that will tax her high spirit; but if she is equal to it she will be the gainer in conscious strength and purpose. As a financial move, even at the average wages, it is undoubtedly the best thing that could be done; for even had the way been opened, there is no such money in teaching school or standing behind the counter. It is also a safer life for a girl of her beauty, because the seclusion of the kitchen has no such temptations as beset the workers in public shops and factories. The question of caste has evidently not entered into her calculations, because she looks upon life as it is developed from the standpoint of moral worth, and she is a charming example of the revival of primitive ideas. I shall watch the outcome of the experiment with a good deal of interest, not alone because I admire the fair experimenter, but because I also look upon the move as an incipient factor in social progress. The housekeeping and homekeeping questions lie at the roots of all philosophy; for man is by no means a sublimated mortal who can exist and theorize with no provision for his material needs. Still, if I could have had my way, I should have preferred that Elsie develop her character and fitness for the world's work under less trying circumstances. It does not seem fitting to me that women should bear the brunt of bread-winning; there is other and better work for them to do.

"As for my school and myself, I think we are both

growing in strength. I should indeed be faint-hearted
if I did not feel nerved for the battle when I remember the fearful odds against which you and Elsie have
set yourselves. I do not prophesy much in the way
of harvest for you, for I know the world better than
you do. Yet I know that with you a slender sheaf of
the gleanings will be as so much saved for the All
Father's granary, and I can only bid you God-speed
in all you do. I know those who come within the
radius of your presence are lifted, albeit unconsciously,
in aspiration, and I have no wonder at all at Eph's
devotion. I look upon it as a natural result of natural
conditions, and I predict that in your home in the city
you will find the question of how to find room for all
the demands upon your sympathies and interests a
much more serious one than it is now. I shall hope
to have in the future, as in the past, a full account of
the progress made by all of you, and trust that in trying to fulfil the purposes that actuate you, you will
not forget what is due your health.

" Sincerely your friend,

"CHARLES J. ELY."

Margaret read the letter very slowly, evidently finding much food for thought in the lines. That it was
happy thought the demure smiles that almost brought
dimples in her cheeks testified.

"It wouldn't be difficult to turn back now," she
mused, "but it would be cowardly. It will be easier
too to go ahead, knowing as I do that all my efforts
are watched by sympathetic eyes. The determina-

tion to stand by Elsie and Gilbert, until character shall
have been formed and purposes achieved, grows heroic
as I progress; for in it I already discern, thanks to
Dr. Ely's eyes, a lever for the good of others besides
ourselves. Duty has always seemed so simple and
necessary a thing to me, that I don't believe I have
properly appreciated Elsie's heroism. Poor little girl!
I wonder how she bears the brunt of the battle, and if
that tempestuous heart of hers is in daily rebellion.
Antoine!" she exclaimed aloud, "we are glad this is
Sunday and that Elsie is coming home to-day, aren't
we ?"

"So glad that I can't half read," said the boy, tossing
aside his book and looking up with a smile.

"It seems to me, Antoine, the violin has leaned more
to elegies and dirges than formerly. That won't do,
for I notice you are not looking as well as you were,
and I fancy you are missing Elsie too much. I'll tell
you what we're going to do. Next week I shall look
up rooms in the city, near Elsie, and we will have her
home every night, and you—now don't look so disconsolate—you shall remain with us and take lessons
at the conservatory. I've arranged it all with ma
mère, and I shall see almost, if not quite, as much of
you as I do now."

Antoine did not answer until he had choked back
one or two obtrusive sobs. "And ma mère ?" he asked.

"She will be back and forth every day, with two
homes instead of one."

"And am I really to have lessons ?"

"Really and truly," answered Margaret.

"I don't know how to be thankful enough," said the lad. "But who pays for them?"

"Never mind asking questions," said Margaret, smiling. "It is your business to accept propositions."

"I know—it is Elsie!" he exclaimed gleefully. "She said she should dispense charity like a millionaire."

Margaret laughed as she replied: "I don't think Elsie's princely income, as she calls it, will be equal to all the schemes she has in her bright head; but I know I am very glad of the prospect of having her with us once again. It's a dull house without her."

"And shall we have the old 'evenings' over again?"

"Indeed we shall, please God. We'll take up the thread where it snapped on that awful night of the fire, only a little wiser and tenderer perhaps in our judgments."

"How would it be possible for you to be any tenderer than you always have been?" asked Antoine.

"Because experience widens and deepens our natures, and

"'Hearts, like apples, are hard and sour,
Till crushed by pain's resistless power.'"

"God mellowed yours, then, in long-gone ages, for nobody ever found a hard spot in your heart."

"A royal flatterer!" exclaimed Margaret gayly. "I shall have to kiss you for that," and Margaret sank on her knees beside the wheel chair and printed a resounding smack upon the lad's pale cheek.

"I'm jealous!" cried a gay voice at the door, and the next instant Elsie was on the other side of the chair and Antoine's arms were around her neck.

10

"Home again! Home again!" he cried with a little break in his voice.

"For just about six hours, so tongues must fly at a mile a minute. I have heaps and heaps to tell," and breathless Elsie sank into a chair and said nothing.

"Why don't you tell it?" asked Antoine.

"It dwindles so when I stop to think of it. I guess it is all summed up in the statement that 'Elsie the cook' is very well satisfied with her place, and a good deal prouder of her two-weeks' wages than if somebody had earned the money for her. Just see!" and emptying the contents of her purse in Margaret's lap, she went on: "Now, I've come home for some music and to hear the rest of you talk. Where's the fiddle, Antoine? Let's wake the echoes and forget the frying-pan."

"O Elsie, life has come back with you," exclaimed Antoine fervently as he tuned his fiddle.

"To stay, I hope; for I don't want to be guilty of taking life when I go again."

An hour later everything had been forgotten in the rendering of the old hymns and psalms with which it had been their wont to delight themselves on Sunday afternoons. Margaret and Gilbert were joining in the chorus, and Lizzette was softly humming to herself in her work about the kitchen, when there came a gentle rap at the outer door. Lizzette opened it and with difficulty repressed an exclamation at sight of Herbert Lynn on the threshold. With a warning gesture he put his fingers to his lips and said in a low voice: "I did not want to interrupt the music or I should have rapped at the front door. Who is it plays and sings so charmingly?"

" Antoine and Elsie," said Lizzette proudly.

" Elsie? I did not know she was here. I had a little leisure and concluded I couldn't better employ it than in coming to see my old Lizzette."

" Vous avez ze welcome, just as in ze old days. Let me get ze leetle rocker, and you sall sit by me and talk," and Lizzette made a move to enter the little sitting-room. Herbert's hand was on her arm in an instant.

" No, no," he said in a whisper. " Let me sit here and listen. It will disturb them to know I am here."

Softly and sweetly from the other room came the strain, " 'Tis midnight, and on Olive's brow," and Herbert Lynn reverently dropped his head in his hands and listened. If there was to his critical ear a lack of technical skill, there was no lack of sympathy or feeling in every touch and tone. Neither was there lack of genius, although it was easily discernible that it was an untrained genius.

" What power Antoine gets out of the violin," he whispered to Lizzette, who nodded and smiled in proud acknowledgment of his appreciation.

" Il a——" she began, but the music had ceased and there was a rustle of turning leaves as Margaret took up the Bible.

" On second thought," she said, " I will ask for a subject. What shall it be, Elsie? You have been out in the world—what need has seemed greatest to you?"

" The strength to bear," answered Elsie soberly.

"It seemed easy to be patient and properly humble in this home of love and appreciation, but in this other world of place-hunting and time-serving the quick retort quite too often besieges my lips. You know, Margaret, it is only the old enemy, and as the horizon widens and I see what life might mean to me if fortune had been kinder, and I realize that I have a nature capable of profiting by the beautiful things of the world, I grow rebellious and dissatisfied. I try every now and then to imagine I am perfectly contented; but all the time I know I am deceiving myself. Help me, Margaret dear, with all your sublime patience and courage, to bear it, and not yearn after the vain things of the world."

There was a sound of tears in Margaret's voice as she answered: "Strength must come from within, Elsie. 'They that dwell in His house' know where the well of strength is, and 'the pools are filled with water.' As for the vain things of this world for which you sigh, the sin of it depends upon what those things are. I think I know your heart well enough to believe they are not selfish follies, but only healthy aspirations for broader fields of culture. I don't believe in repressing such aspirations. They are as natural to natures like yours as sunshine to flowers. Aside from my unchanging faith in the beneficence of God, I have always found the thought that the duty of to-day may be the pleasure of to-morrow my greatest source of comfort. Let us work faithfully, cheerfully to-day; the way may be a little rough, but after all we shall find many things to gladden it. A note from Antoine's

fiddle, a bit of Elsie's nonsense, have often made me
smile in the midst of the moodiest repinings. Our
work now, Elsie, is like the hard digging around the
roots of a rose-bush; by and by we shall look up and
see its crown of beauty and fragrance, and the roses
will be all the sweeter because our hands have sent the
thrill along their stems that roused them to life. I
haven't the least fear for my little girl when we re-
establish the old home life. Discontent will be left at
the door, and aspiration will find wings in Antoine's
fiddle and at the ends of her deft fingers."

"The first day I ever saw you," said Antoine to
Elsie, "you said your ambition lay all in learning to
cook like ma mère. What is the matter with it that
it does not satisfy you? Is the grand art of ma mère
no art after all?"

"Don't ask such heretical questions, Antoine! Just
ask ma mère if I don't put heaps of enthusiasm in my
work, and make perfect poems in pastry and sonnets
in salads, whose proof is in the eating! But one may
have a thousand ambitions in the course of a lifetime,
and to confess the honest truth—Margaret, hide your
face!—I've just now an absorbing ambition to have a
new gown in the very latest style, with velvet all over
it and some genuine lace at the throat, and all those
refined ladylike things that make you feel so—so satisfied with yourself! See, I bow my head and meekly
await the avalanche of reproaches from this virtuous
and austere household!"

"Well," said Gilbert from his corner, "I haven't any
for you; for the threadbare appearance of my knees

has filled me with a similar ambition. The fellows at the training school are mostly sons of well-to-do men, and they eye me in a way that doesn't make me feel so—so satisfied with myself."

In an instant Elsie jumped from her chair, and patronizingly patting Gilbert's head exclaimed: "My dear brother, how glad I am to know I'm not the only black sheep of the family! Meg, you see what comes of letting the lambs out in the world's pastures!"

Just then Elsie, glancing out into the kitchen, caught sight of the amused faces of Lizzette and Herbert Lynn, and consternation, fright, and astonishment so overcame her that she could only stand still and scream.

This at once brought Lizzette and Herbert to the door. "Margaret," exclaimed Lizzette, "zis ees my old friend, mon garçon Herbeart Lynn, who coming to see his old Lizzette haf ze desire also to know her friends. He haf zair welcome, I believe?"

Lizzette looked appealingly from the white scorn of Elsie's face to the surprise of Margaret's; but before either had time to speak Herbert said eagerly and with flushing cheek as he glanced at Elsie: "I can explain my presence here as an involuntary listener in this way. Lizzette, as you probably know, has been more than half-mother to me. Taking advantage of a day when I felt sure of finding her at home, I came out for a little visit. As I neared the door I heard such charming music I hesitated to interrupt it, and so I crept like a culprit to the back door and listened—very reprehensibly, I know—to a discussion which was so full of strength and interest to me I had not the courage to interrupt it. Lizzette, can you not help me to be forgiven?"

"Helas," said Lizzette. "I am ze grand culprit. I take ze pride in vat you list."

"Lizzette's friends are of course welcome to us, since we are trespassers upon her kindness," said Margaret brightly. "And as we have no state secrets, I think we can forgive an unintentional listening. This is my sister, Elsie Murchison, whom perhaps you know serves your sister, Mrs. Mason, as cook."

Margaret's countenance hardened a trifle as she looked at the young man's handsome face and again at Elsie's, coldly repellant, and she laid a stress upon the last word that brought an involuntary smile to Elsie's lips. The nod which she bestowed upon Herbert was, however, so ostentatiously distant that the pleasant augury of the smile was speedily dispelled.

"An' zis ees my good lad Gilbeart Murchison, et zis mon garçon Antoine," said Lizzette hastily, in an endeavor to smooth over the awkwardness of the situation.

Herbert turned quickly to the boys, and taking the proffered seat eagerly clasped Antoine's hand in his own. "You've changed a good deal, my boy, since I saw you, and you are growing to be quite a musician. Your genius must be cultivated."

"It is going to be," answered Antoine, "thanks to my Elsie."

Herbert glanced up as Antoine spoke, in time to see Elsie slip into the kitchen.

"Eet ees ze dinner hour," said Lizzette, looking after her. "I sall leave you, Herbeart, in ze good care of Miss Margaret and ze boys."

"I shall be well cared for, no doubt. I always have been in your house."

"You have but recently returned from Europe, I understand," said Margaret as Lizzette left the room. "Were you there long?"

"Some three years," replied Herbert.

"Long enough, then, to become somewhat imbued with old-world ideas and customs."

"To the extent of finding democratic America the most delightful place on earth to live."

The air of constraint, so foreign to Herbert's usual suavity of address, dropped off under the stimulant of Margaret's calm eyes and interested face, and he presently found himself talking and laughing with her and the boys with the freedom of long acquaintance. In the mean time Lizzette had been bustling about the kitchen on hospitable thoughts intent, and wondering vaguely where Elsie had gone. In honor of her home-coming she had sacrificed a couple of plump chickens which she had stuffed with truffles grown in the darkness of her cellar. On the case of wooden shelves which, with the romanticism of her race, she loved to dignify with the name of "beaufet," stood a glass bowl of snow cream flanked by a basket piled high with yellow sponge-cakes.

"Zere ees ze pineapple jelly, ze salade de cresson, ze cold sliced ham, ze duchesse potatoes, et ze cream chocolate—ah, well, Lizzette's table ees not so empty after all."

She was bending over the oven door, watching the browning of the chickens and letting a flood of savory steam into the kitchen, when she felt a warm kiss on her cheek. Glancing up in surprise she saw Elsie, cloaked and bonneted, before her. "Fie, fie, Elsie," exclaimed Lizzette. "Zis vill not do. You no leave before ze dinner."

"I must," said Elsie, putting her hands on Lizzette's shoulders and looking into her face with her eyes full of tears. "Don't you see how the case stands? This 'petit curieux'—there, don't be angry, I can't call him anything else—has followed me here, and if Mrs. Mason hears of it I shall lose my place. Don't you see I could not sit at the table with him and defend myself against her attacks?"

"Oh-h!" It was a very long and expressive "oh" on Lizzette's part, and her eyes grew round with wonder and amusement as she glanced at Elsie's perturbed face. "I nevair vas so big dunce in my life. Haf Herbeart efer speak to you?"

"No," said Elsie, crimsoning, "only—only looked at me!"

Lizzette burst into a laugh so resounding that it penetrated the room beyond; but Elsie's distressed face was too much for her tender sympathies. "Ma petite fille," she exclaimed, "how stupid ees your old Lizzette. Eh bien, I vill explain. Herbeart know not you live here; he tell me so, and I nevair know Herbeart Lynn to lie. So you see eet ees not ma petite Elsie zat bring him——"

"Lizzette! Lizzette!" cried Elsie, beside herself with

mortification. "I did not mean it that way! I'm not so vain as you think; but to tell the truth he has always eyed me so, when I went to confer with Mrs. Mason, that I have noticed she was uneasy and cross when he was in the room. That is all in the world there is in it, except that as 'Elsie the cook' I decline to sit at table with his high mightiness. Honestly, I do not want ever to speak to him."

"Herbeart haf ze good heart zat harm nobody."

"That may be true; but the gulf between us is considered too wide by his circle ever to be bridged over by the commonplaces of even the simplest association. You know I am right, Lizzette, and no false vanity prompts what I say. I do want to keep my place, and Mrs. Mason would be furious if she knew I broke bread at the same table with her brother."

"Ah, zat Helen! Oui, Elsie, vous avez raison. Zis ees too bad. Mais you sall not go hungry; here in ze pantry I set you some dinner."

"No, Lizzette, I can't eat," said Elsie disconsolately. "I'll just go down to Aunt Liza's and stay till the six-o'clock train. Tell Meg how the case stands. I know she'll approve my view of it."

"Helas," said Lizzette sorrowfully. "Ze dinner vill be spoiled for Margaret and ze rest of us; but maybe zat vill be ze best way out of trouble."

It was growing dusk when Elsie took her seat in the car on her way back to the city. She was tired, faint, and over-wrought. A disturbing influence had set again at work all those little discontents which Margaret's calm reasoning had well-nigh dispelled, and she fairly gasped with horror when she saw Herbert Lynn enter the car and deliberately take the vacant seat beside her.

"Miss Elsie," he coolly asked, "will you be kind enough to tell me why I am an object of such aversion to you?"

"I—I—don't know what you mean," she stammered helplessly.

"Aversion, Miss Elsie, is said by Webster to mean dislike, disapproval, detestation, repugnance, antipathy, abhorrence, loathing, etc., and so on. I trust you understand me now," and he looked down on the flushing face with a marked little smile of triumph.

"The definitions are all a blank to me, and relate to nothing with which I am familiar."

"Let me enlighten you, then. Do you think I am not aware that I drove you from the house this afternoon, and Lizzette's delicious dinner? I am truly sorry that my mere unexpected presence in that little house should have been productive of so much mischief. I assure you I am not half as bad as I look, and I feel as penitent as a small boy who is caught stealing apples, and just about as guilty."

Elsie sat with her face turned toward the window and made no reply. Not to be balked, Herbert went on:

"I never enjoyed—or would have enjoyed but for the unlucky fact of your displeasure—anything so much as acquaintance with your sister and the atmosphere of Lizzette's little home. It is something new to me, and I am not so case-hardened as to be wholly insensible to it." Still Elsie vouchsafed no word as he paused in evident expectation.

"Well, if I am to have all this conversation to myself, I shall take the liberty of saying just what I think. I think a certain Miss Elsie Murchison is decidedly unreasonable, and is determined that the culprit's sentence shall be a severer one than he deserves. She will not even permit him to plead his cause. Nevertheless, as he is satisfied of its justice he proposes to go on. The brother of Mrs. Helen Mason, an acknowledged leader of the haut ton, is neither a knave nor a fool; at least he is not prepared to so view himself just yet, and because his well-beloved sister has certain views in accordance with the creed of her set, it does not follow that he must blindly indorse all those views. He may have sufficient independence to recognize worth when he sees it, regardless of its environment."

Still no response from stubborn Elsie. The hot blood mounted to Herbert's brow. Bending forward so that he might get a good view of her face, he exclaimed impetuously:

"Miss Murchison, if this is really a matter of personal dislike I have nothing further to say. Until I am satisfied that it is, however, I feel that I have a right to understand the meaning of your persistent silence."

Thus brought to bay Elsie raised her eyes, and Herbert saw that they were full of unshed tears.

"Mr. Lynn," she began tremulously, "it seems almost cruel in you to press me for an answer; but since you force it you shall have the plain truth. There is no personal feeling at all in the matter. I neither like nor dislike you, and simply ask to be let alone. I am your sister's cook, between whom and Mr. Lynn there cannot be even common acquaintance."

"My sister's cook!" repeated Herbert. "It is as I suspected, a mere matter of pride on your part."

"No," said Elsie desperately. "It is a matter of bread and butter. As your sister's cook I am earning good wages, that are of incalculable value to those I love and for whom I work. If I lose my place, it means deprivation and distress. Can you not see my reason and be generous?"

"Generous, most certainly; but not for any reason you advance. I am not under my sister's dominion."

"But I am; and if I in any way incur her displeasure, I shall suffer for it."

"Not through me," said Herbert stoutly. "I shall take good care of that."

"You can only do it by refusing to notice me any further; a favor which I particularly request."

"I do not know that I ever before flatly refused a lady's request; but this time I am compelled to do so by circumstances beyond my control."

The mischief in Herbert's eyes was too much for Elsie's volatile nature, and she greeted his audacious statement with a ripple of laughter which she bitterly regretted a second later.

"There!" he exclaimed. "I am glad the statuesque repose of the De Veres has been broken. I think we shall understand each other soon."

"We do now," said Elsie hastily. "I cannot speak any plainer."

"Well, I can; but here we are, and while we walk
the rest of the way home I'll endeavor to be explicit.
Please take my arm."

There was no help for it. Eight or ten blocks inter-
vened between them and the Mason mansion; it was
dark and physical fear prevented Elsie's refusal of the
proffered escort.

"Now," said Herbert as she meekly placed her
hand on his arm, "things are just to my satisfaction. As regards your place, it shall be yours in-
definitely so far as I am concerned. I promise not
to annoy you in any way—that is, whenever I think
that way is consistent with my way. I admire your
sister very much, and she has already accepted my
offer of comradeship, which, by the way, shows her good
sense. As for her rebellious little sister, I shall be just
as much her good friend as if she were forty times a
queen in her own right, which she undoubtedly is. She
cannot prevent my admiration of her independence
and heroism if she snubs me twenty times a day, as,
judging from the past, I presume she will. That, however, will be the least of my distress, so I succeed in
making her believe I am not a wolf in sheep's clothing.
I assure you, upon the honor of a gentleman, that I
shall be guilty of no more reprehensible act than to
claim the kindly consideration of one friend for another."

Elsie found it difficult to frame a reply. Animosity
was fast breaking down before the simple, candid words,
and in its place had come a not wholly definable sense
of companionship that was strangely sweet.

" But the social gulf——" she began feebly.

"A fig for it! Are you not of that heretical sect which believes only in an aristocracy of moral worth and cultivated brains? Are you going to deny me the privilege of proving my claim to distinction among you? 'Your sister has already outlined your little evenings to me, and I am going——"

"To do what?" asked Elsie quickly.

"Look in upon you occasionally, that is all. You fancied I was going to apply for a membership. I am afraid if I should, one of its brightest members would stay away. But we are almost home, and you haven't told me yet that you have forgiven my unintentional transgression of the conventionalities this afternoon; nor have you promised to believe in my integrity and good-will."

"I promise on one condition," said Elsie, stopping suddenly. "There is only half a block further; let me go alone. It would be so unfortunate for me if—if any one saw us together."

"Certainly, if you wish it. I suppose there is no law to prevent my walking a few steps behind you."

"I don't think there is any law anywhere for you. Good-night," and with Herbert's laugh ringing in her ears Elsie hastened down the area steps and swung open the kitchen door.

CHAPTER XIII.

"ELSIE," said Mrs. Mason the following morning, "I am going to give a reception in my brother's honor to-morrow evening, and I shall put the dining-room and kitchen in the hands of the caterer. If you like you may assist Mary and Martha in the toilet-rooms during the evening."

"Very well," answered Elsie soberly; but there was a light in her eyes which made Mrs. Mason say interrogatively, "You are pleased at the change?"

"Indeed I am! I shall see a little of the pageantry of life, and I love to look at beautiful things, fair ladies, and brave men. The whole thing will be a living picture, and while I hand a pin to this one, or a fan to that, I shall be stealing something that will be neither coats nor diamonds."

"Something less tangible, but more valuable, perhaps."

"I am not so sure of its value as I am of its pleasure."

"Pleasure in what way?"

"In the way that a rose is just as beautiful to my eyes as to those of a princess; in the way that this reception will be just as much for me as if I wore satins instead of a house-maid's cap and apron."

Elsie had been for the nonce aroused from her usual reserve, and as she caught the coldly critical glance which Mrs. Mason bestowed upon her, she exclaimed eagerly: "I beg your pardon, Mrs. Mason. I did not mean to inflict my small enthusiasms upon you."

"I was only thinking," replied Mrs. Mason, "that the world seems to open a vista of enjoyment for you which many apparently more fortunate would give half their years to possess. What is the secret of your happiness?"

"'Secret?' I have none, unless it is that I am still a child, in heart at least, and accept life as unquestioningly."

"But by and by the heart of the child will have grown old, and you will be like the rest of us, tired, disappointed, doubting."

There was a note of sadness in Mrs. Mason's voice that appealed at once to Elsie's tender sympathies. Involuntarily she reached out a hand as if to lay it upon the white jewelled one of her mistress; but with a sudden start of recollection she drew back and said simply: "There is so much in this world to hope for, so much that may be had even by the poorest, that disappointment and doubt need affect one only as externals. I hope I may never grow wise if wisdom brings only bitterness of spirit."

Mrs. Mason made no reply; she was watching the fine mobile face before her, with its blending of pride and guilelessness. "The girl gains on one so," she mused, "that I could almost make her friend instead of servant, if it were not for——"

At this juncture Elsie, uneasy under the prolonged scrutiny of the gray eyes, asked hesitatingly: "Do

11

you wish anything further, Mrs. Mason? May I go now?"

"You might have gone some time since," was the calm reply, given with all the iciness of manner she knew so well how to apply to the impulsive girl.

Elsie's face flushed painfully as she left the room. Mrs. Mason smiled grimly as she saw it. "I treat that girl horribly sometimes; but it is the only way I can preserve the proprieties."

The next evening, when everything had been put to rights in the kitchen, Elsie and Jenie, the little maid of the scullery, climbed the back stairs with many a ripple of laughter. They were deeply engaged in the all-important subject of dress, and were as keen in their enjoyment of the good points of attire as many a society belle who would grace the Mason parlors.

"Oh, but you are just lovely," exclaimed enraptured Jenie as Elsie invested herself in a cheap lawn of rose pink, and fastened a coquettish lace cap above her curls in place of the frilled muslin of every day. The dress was as straight and plain as that of a Puritan maid; but the soft lace of a Martha Washington fichu and a jaunty lace-trimmed apron with pink bows on the pockets, created a costume that only needed the dark eyes and tinted cheeks of the wearer to complete it.

"I lack one thing," said Elsie, critically surveying herself in the glass. "I wish I had one of those Bonsilene roses that the florist has massed in the parlors. I'm going to ask Mrs. Mason for one."

"I wouldn't," said Jenie. "I'd just take one. It would never be missed."

"Jenie," laughed Elsie as she placed a hand under the little maid's chin, "I should miss it, and that would be the worst miss of all. I like to keep my fingers clean, you know."

"Well, it ain't like takin' clothes and such like."

"Not exactly; but all the same it *is* taking what doesn't belong to me."

"It's such a little thing I wouldn't have minded it."

"It is the 'littles' that make us, Jenie. Lookout for the little foxes and the lions will keep away. Now, let me see how you look. As sweet and clean as a whistle. Let me straighten your cap. Dear me, there's a button off your shoe. I must sew that on right away. It doesn't look ladylike, you know, to go with the buttons off."

Jenie laughed. "Me a lady!" she exclaimed as if the idea were preposterous.

"To be sure," said Elsie seriously. "You can be just as much a lady in your work as Mrs. Mason in hers."

"Humph! She'd laugh at me."

"That wouldn't affect the fact, and nobody will laugh at you for respecting yourself. Only you must lookout that you don't think so much of yourself that you neglect your duty. People would have a right to laugh at you then. Now I'm going for the rose;" and having seen that Jenie's belongings were in order, she opened the door and started for the lower hall, humming a gay chansonette and emphasizing its tune with a step as graceful as if art, not nature, had prompted it. Herbert Lynn's door stood open, and unseen by Elsie, he watched the lively patter of a pair of bronze slippers along the hall with a light that was somewhat deeper than amusement in his eyes.

"Good-evening!" he exclaimed as Elsie neared his door. "These buttons on my glove are a trifle refractory. May I beg you to fasten them?"

The song on her lips met instant suppression as she glanced up with heightened color into the blue eyes that were smiling down at her. It seemed to Elsie that it was rare good fortune which sent James at that moment across the hall.

"James," she called, "Mr. Lynn would like to have you button his glove," and without pausing a second Elsie walked soberly along the hall to Mrs. Mason's room. Herbert bit his lips in vexation, and re-entering his room, he slammed the door in no very amiable frame of mind.

"The witch!" he exclaimed, throwing himself into a chair and scowling like a thunder-cloud. "How cavalierly she does treat me! Jove! isn't she lovely in that cheap finery! She ought to 'walk in silk attire and siller hae to spare' instead of being doomed to the round of Helen's pots and pans. How unequally the good things of life seem to be distributed, and how singular it is to find such pride of character in a girl occupying her position in life. Well, I'd give 'Jupiter and his power to thunder' to break that stubborn pride of hers, and I'll do it or die in the attempt."

A look of resolute will settled over the bright, almost boyish, face and gave it an added strength and beauty, which struck Elsie wonderingly as a moment later she encountered him in the hall with her hands full of roses. He bestowed upon her only the slightest nod as he passed rapidly down the stairs, and Elsie climbed to her room and pinned the roses at throat and belt with a feeling that something had taken the glamor from the evening's enjoyment.

"I don't care," said she defiantly. "I knew my hands would tremble if I tried to fasten those buttons; besides, I don't thank him for noticing me in the least. I'm only 'Elsie the cook' and he knows it, for all of his pleadings to the contrary. I just want him to let me alone, and there's all there is of it."

This stalwart enunciation of wishes was not wholly borne out by the misty eyes that greeted her from the glass, and it required several little pattings of her handkerchief to clear them so that she dare trust herself in the waiting-room below. The guests were already arriving as Elsie entered the dressing-rooms, and her services were at once called into requisition in undoing trains, buttoning gloves and slippers, making up faces and arms, and arranging dishevelled coiffures. More than one quick glance was bestowed by the guests upon the pretty maid in pink who so deftly ministered to their various needs, and one tall, statuesque girl of superb grace and unusual elegance of costume attempted to slip a dollar into Elsie's hands as she was about to leave the room.

"I beg your pardon," said Elsie, flushing. "I—I cannot accept the money. Mrs. Mason pays me for my work."

The lady laughed as she tapped Elsie's cheek with her fan. "You must be a new acquisition of Helen's.

I do not remember to have seen you before, and as for the money, my dear child, I always bestow it upon those who serve and please me."

"It doesn't seem right for me to take it," replied Elsie; "and I hope you won't think me ungrateful if I refuse."

"Why, if you will be so quixotic I will not urge it upon you, of course; but you are the first of your class I ever remember to refuse a gift. I must congratulate Helen on her rare good fortune. Your action is quite unusual, I assure you."

At the first opportunity Elsie turned to Martha and Mary, who had smiled audibly behind their handkerchiefs at witnessing the little scene. "Did I do anything wrong?" she asked pitifully.

"Don't know as it's very wrong," answered Martha, "but it's awful silly, and you'll find out that the tips the rich folks give you'll buy lots o' nice things."

"If that's all I don't care," said Elsie. "I don't want to be rude."

"Why didn't you want it?" asked Mary curiously.

"Because I am paid by Mrs. Mason for my work, and because somehow it touched my pride to be offered money for nothing."

Martha and Mary laughed. "That's a queer pride of your'n, Elsie. I never seen none like it before," exclaimed Martha.

"It is a pride I hope that harms no one; not even myself."

"I don't know about that! You'll always get left if you stand too much on your dignity."

"Not if I am faithful in my work, and that I mean to be."

The evening was after all a great delight to Elsie, who never allowed any misgiving to long cloud her skies. The beautiful costumes, the light laughter, the gay banter, the strains of music that floated up-stairs from the mandolin orchestra stationed in the library behind banks of ferns and roses, all seemed a dream from the fairyland of the imagination. She hovered over the balusters in the hall, and watched the moving panorama below with all the intoxication of youth in bright and beautiful things. Later in the evening she crept down-stairs with the other maids, and hiding herself behind a screen of palms in the hall, could see in the drawing-room beyond the bevy of belles and beaux in the exercise of all the graces of refined intercourse. She could see that Herbert Lynn was everywhere welcomed by bright eyes and cordial words, and a little pang of regret shot through her heart at the injustice of fate. But it was only for a moment, and then, with an effort of will so strong that it sent the blood out of her face, she trampled the rising regret to death.

"I will not, I will not," she said between set teeth, as she walked wearily along the hall to her room when the last guest had departed.

"You've dropped your roses," said Herbert's voice behind her just as she reached the foot of the stairs.

"No matter," she said, half-turning. "A withered rose is valueless."

"Not to me," he replied emphatically, as he gathered them up and deliberately placed them inside his vest.

A look of innocent wonder swept over Elsie's face, that was not altogether successful in its effort to appear natural. "A wilted rose, I suppose, will answer for a rose-jar! There are oceans in the parlors, and I can bring you a panful if you wish."

Herbert took a quick step that brought him to Elsie's side. "Elsie Murchison," he exclaimed half-savagely, "do you know I never was baffled in my life?"

"First times have come to a good many of the world's conquerors. Mr. Lynn would be a most notable exception if he continued an unbroken line of victories."

"You may mock me as you choose. I have been candid to the verge of bluntness with you, and you know very well I am desirous of obtaining your friendship."

"And you know very well," answered Elsie, all the brightness dying out of her face and leaving it gray and cold, "that there is no friendship possible between us. I resolutely refuse to consider the slightest chance of such a thing."

Stung to the quick, Herbert turned on his heel, saying vehemently, "Very well. So emphatic a statement as that must be heeded; but I am very much mistaken if you do not some day regret it."

Elsie had never known such a weariness of body as she carried up the long flight of stairs to her room, and it was with a feeling of having been hunted and driven to bay that she threw herself across the bed and burst into tears. All the pent-up feeling of years seemed to burst its bonds as sob after sob shook the slight frame and floods of tears rolled their tempestuous way over her cheeks. At last the force of the storm was spent and she sat up in bed, weak but relieved.

"I couldn't have been fiercer if I'd been Vesuvius in action," she said ruefully as she tried to collect her scattered senses. "But I've done one virtuous act, anyway! 'Regret it!' Ah, if he only knew the silly little heart I carry here, and how heavy it is and always will be! Meg, dear, duty didn't find your little Elsie on the coward's side, after all, and yet how I should have enjoyed saying 'Thank you, sir,' after the regulation order. He'll forget all about me in a day or two, and it is a good deal better than if I had tried the miserable farce of friendship only to have it surely end in trouble. Now I'm the only one to suffer, and henceforth I shall look upon myself as quite a heroine. I don't think there's much fun in being one, though," and with this doleful reflection Elsie, like a sensible girl, turned off the gas and went to bed. If her sleep had not the peace of the care-free, it was yet sufficiently healthy to bring back the color to her cheeks and the lustre to her eyes, and no one dreamed of the tempest of pain that had swept over her the night before.

CHAPTER XIV.

THE week following Elsie's memorable visit to Idle-wild found Margaret and Gilbert domiciled in rooms some ten blocks removed from the Mason mansion; that being the nearest approach of cheap rents to the aristocratic thoroughfare. The rooms were situated in an apartment-house, as such are nowadays called under the approved nomenclature of progressive ideas; but the building was some decades behind its imposing name. It was indeed a type of the old shabbily-built, inconvenient, and miasma-breeding tenement-house. It was a long, narrow, five-storied structure, poorly lighted and equally as poorly ventilated; but it was in fact the only house with a reasonable rent which could be found near enough to Elsie to warrant a nightly visit from her. Margaret chose, out of several vacant rooms, four in the fifth story, because in these she had both light and air, and she felt she could better endure the inconvenience of the four long flights of stairs than the absence of two such essentials to health and comfort. The condition of the halls, which the majority of the tenants seemed to consider a lodging-place for refuse of various kinds, was a terrible eye-sore to her housewifely instincts, and she had not been many days in her new quarters before she put her wits to work to effect a change in their untidy aspect.

So far as her own flight of stairs and its contiguous hallways were concerned, the solution was simply a compound of soap, water, and muscle; but when it came to the consideration of those below her, something like generalship was needed to induce the desired cleanliness. To perform an undue share of the public work did not by any means enter into her scheme of the general good. The responsibility of the individual was the one hobby, if such it could be called, which Margaret permitted herself. To arouse the latent instinct of self-dependence and development was an almost unconscious exhalation of the sturdy faith which had always made circumstances only a means unto an end, and that end the uplifting of the better elements of character. To be her brother's keeper in so far as that keeping could induce a heartfelt aspiration or a simple kindness, had been but an outgrowth of the unselfishness of her aims. Few people looked with as lenient an eye upon the shortcomings of humanity, or were actuated by as sincere a desire to lend a hand to retrieve a false step, as Margaret Murchison. Yet it was with a good deal of delicacy that she reviewed the means whereby she might bring an air of greater thrift and cleanliness into the desolate halls below. Like all refined and sensitive people, she felt a hesitancy about bringing even an inferential reflection of uncleanliness upon those whose co-operation she desired.

"It will be impossible to do it," she sighed, "until I have made their acquaintance, and won their confidence. They will be distrustful and think in their vernacular that I am putting on airs if I broach the subject before."

If the condition of the halls dismayed Margaret, the condition of the living-rooms of the inmates of the building was much more disheartening. Not that poverty in its severest aspect was present, for in nearly all cases the rooms were occupied by the families of porters, office clerks, and under salesmen, and although a decent amount of food and clothing was to be had by the closest economy, there was such a lack of homeness that it turned Margaret heart-sick. The women were, for the most part, good-natured, well-intentioned souls, but tried beyond endurance in the almost hopeless task of making both ends meet on the scanty dole of the one wage-earner. Children were everywhere; for whatever other blessings may be denied the toiler, the children always come to lighten his heart and empty his pocket. Ambition was well-nigh dead in their bosoms; for the daily grind of hard work, the lowering cloud of capitalistic oppression, and the constantly-increasing tide of mongrel, half-starved immigrants, who stood ever ready to snatch the crust from their lips, had left very little opportunity for the better classes of American workingmen to look forward with any degree of hope.

There was a wholesomeness about Margaret that made both men and women trust her, and with the natural volubility of their class, the women had poured the whole story of their daily struggles into her willing ears before she had been ten days in the house. There were twelve families in the building, a number of rooms being unoccupied; and barren as had been Margaret's own life in the little parsonage at Barnley, and later at Idlewild, she felt that it had been a broad way of peace and plenty beside the narrow line of these toilers. With her, above meagre outlines and practical details had been the wide field of growth, the plenitude of hope, and the infinite realm of thought. With these people, cabined and confined year in and year out within smoke-begrimed walls, life had become a sordid round of ministering to material needs, with no blue skies to call their eyes upward or song of birds to awaken benumbed hearts.

"I would not have thought poverty could wear so pitiless an aspect," she mused. "Something must be done to bring back the revivifying influence of hope to these people. But what can I do, burdened with a like poverty, against the greed and extortion of these capitalists? Just think of men with families compelled to live and pay rent on six, seven, and nine dollars a week, working twelve and fourteen hours a day, and Sundays too, if the 'boss' so wills, without a penny's extra pay! Oh, it makes my blood boil when I see such injustice! Is there no relief for all this? Are there no thunderbolts of heaven to strike these slave-drivers who compel their men to this life, by telling them the market is overstocked with unorganized workers, and that a body of lean and hungry wolves stands ever ready to snatch their scanty crusts? Small wonder that ambition dies, and that there are only mutterings of discontent and savage envy and malignant plottings against the mighty magnates who instigate and abet this monstrous cruelty. What can I do for these overworked and disheartened mothers, these joyless children and sullen fathers? How can I help them to smile, to look for sunshine instead of clouds? Out of the abundance with which I am blessed I must devise some way."

Margaret's abundance was certainly not that of money, for she had been forced into taking "slop-work" from the factories, at forty-five cents per dozen for men's hickory shirts and fifty cents per dozen pairs for men's overalls. The winter's indebtedness was draining the greater share of Elsie's abundant wages, and Gilbert's expenses at the training school were already eating into the carefully-guarded one hundred dollars that had been sent by Dr. Ely. It was evident that what help Margaret gave could only be that of interest and suggestion. But how to make suggestion inoffensive, and how to stimulate ambition without arousing antagonism, were questions which puzzled her not a little.

One Saturday morning, returning from the factory with her arms laden with work, she stopped at the doors of the various rooms on her way up-stairs and asked that all the children who were large enough to climb the stairs be sent to her rooms in half an hour.

How joyfully they swarmed the halls long before the appointed time, and what a time Margaret had counting them! Forty-eight above five years and the eldest not above nine. "How many go to school?" she asked as she ranged them along the wall.

Fourteen little hands were raised; of these eight were boys.

"Now, boys," she exclaimed, "I'm going to begin with you. What do you like best, or would like best, if you could have your wish?"

The answers varied from peg-tops to balloons and locomotives.

"How many hours do you have out of school?"

"School's out at four.

"Till half-after six, then—two good hours. Now, how many are willing to work to earn money?" Every hand went up. "Well, after four o'clock to-night I want you to come up again to see my brother Gilbert. He has fitted up a work-bench in one of the rooms, and those of you who are willing to work, and work hard, for two straight hours a day, can earn some money by and by. It will not be so much fun, perhaps, as racing through the halls, sliding down the stairs, or playing out in the street; but it will buy the peg-tops and locomotives one of these days, and there isn't much in this world we can have without paying for it in one way or another. Are you all agreed?"

"You bet!" came the unanimous response. Margaret smiled as she turned to the girls.

"How many know how to sew?" Not a single hand was raised. "How many are willing to learn?" Every hand in the room went up. "Boys and all," exclaimed Margaret. "Now let's make a test. Who has a button off his shoe?"

"Jimmy! Johnnie! Nell! Sue! Mary! Jane! Jack!" sang out the noisy chorus.

"Down on the floor, every one of you. Now, I'll furnish needles, thread, and buttons, and I want every one who has a button off to sew it on, and sew it strongly, too. Now, the one who sews a button on the best and quickest shall have that card," and Margaret pointed to a brilliant chromo-lithograph of angels with impossible wings and beatific smiles.

"Oh, my!" chorused the girls.

"Jiminy crickets!" ejaculated the boys, with now and then a more forcible expletive thrown in. It took some time for the clumsy little fingers to get to work; but Margaret, noting down time and names, kept close tally, and at last pronounced every button in its place, and proclaimed the name of the winner of the prize.

"Now," said Margaret, "this is not all. If every little child here will agree to keep the buttons on his shoes, I'll give every one, at the end of a month, a still handsomer card, and by that time perhaps the boys will have learned how to make frames for them."

"All right!" "Betcher sweet life!" "You're a trump!" "Bully for you!" were the expressive answers with which this proposition was met.

"I want to get up a little club among ourselves and call it the 'Busy Fingers Club,'" Margaret went on, "and I want to see how much real good work this little club can do. I expect to be mistress of the club, and the first thing I shall ask will be to see how neat and clean you can keep yourselves. Now, take this hand-glass and begin at the head, and tell me how many are sure that their faces are as clean as soap and water can make them."

It was a shamefaced little group as the glass was passed from hand to hand, and hitherto unnoticed and unthought-of streaks and specks came into view. The girls eyed each other askance and surreptitiously applied their aprons to several more obtrusive marks, but the boys made no attempt at self-improvement and shouted their approval when one of the older ones exclaimed: "Boys and dirt go together. 'Tain't no use to try to keep clean."

"Trying does a great deal in this world, and I suspect it is equal to making a boy declare war upon dirt. We'll hope it is, anyway."

Thereupon Margaret proceeded to state the plan and laws governing the Busy Fingers Club, whereby every member was to become an important factor in the great work of self-government and improvement. When all the details had been submitted, the children gathered around her enthusiastically. "It's just the jolliest thing," they cried. "We'll work like tigers so long's you're our captain."

And they did. Under Gilbert's tutelage the boys developed skill and industry in wood-carving and amateur cabinet work, while the girls from big to little grew deft in the use of the needle, and lifted many a burden from the shoulders of tired mothers in timely patching and darning. Elsie became deeply interested in Margaret's efforts, and begged silks and velvets from Mrs. Mason for the girls' fancy work, which was one day supplemented by a huge bundle containing everything in the line of material for such work. The bundle was sent anonymously, and great was the wonder of the girls and Margaret as to its source. If Elsie guessed she was discreetly silent about it, athough she was possessed of no small curiosity to know how the scheme had become so well advertised. Her wonder would have been greater, if her curiosity had been less, could she have seen the companion of Lizzette in her daily walks between market and station, and some times to the very door of Margaret's hive of industry. Since the evening she had so resolutely refused to consider the possibility of association between them, Elsie had not encountered Herbert Lynn. Once or twice she had caught a glimpse of him in library or dining-room as she passed up-stairs to her daily inter-view with Mrs. Mason, but he had always seemed en-tirely unconscious of her proximity. Evidently the whim which had seized him had passed, and Elsie as-sured herself, with somewhat remarkable frequency, that she was glad the young man's reason had returned, and that having been "baffled" at last, she hoped he would not be so boastful in the future.

One morning, some three weeks after Margaret's re-moval to the city, Lizzette left Antoine at Margaret's door with a hurried exclamation ·

"I haf not ze moment to spare. I haf ze business engagement zis morning. I no return perhaps zese several hour. Delay not ze dinner for me," and with a kiss upon Antoine's cheek, she hastened down the stairs. Half-way up the block she gave a signal to a gentleman driving leisurely along on the opposite side of the street. A second later he drew rein at the curb-stone, and alighting, assisted Lizzette to the seat be-side him.

"O Herbeart!" she exclaimed, "I know not how to tank you. You haf given me ze hope once more. Mon Dieu! Eef eet be true ze light of my life vill shine again."

"It is only a hope as yet," he answered, "for I was not sufficiently posted about his case to enter into particulars. However, this morning's interview will probably determine it."

"And ze docteur assure you he tink Antoine can be made to walk?"

"There is a chance for him, he thinks, but it will be months of pain and tedium for the poor boy."

"And after zat zen his music vill make him ze grand maestro, and I need not to toil till my hands—see!" and she drew off a shabby cotton glove, "be so like ze iron. Antoine ze grand maestro, and Lizzette ze—ze—lady," and she gave an arch glance, half-smile and half-tear, up at Herbert's sympathetic face. "Ah, eet ees ze dream of fairy land!"

Herbert smiled down at the wrinkled brown face with the affectionate sympathy of the old boyish days, and Lizzette grasped his hand and patted it softly. "Eet ees all so dear zat I haf mon garçon Herbeart to do zis for me in my old age. I could take ze loan—Antoine sall repay—from no one so easy as my Herbeart. Eet ees no offence zat I say eet seems like von of ze family?"

"Offence! No," laughed Herbert. "I don't hedge myself around with any absurd notions of caste, although E— By the way, what a peculiar little body your friend Elsie Murchison is!"

Lizzette's eyes twinkled, but she was resolutely obtuse. "Je ne vous comprend pas! Please explain."

"Oh, well, she is so—so—proud."

Lizzette laughed. "Elsie! ze cook de votre sœur
Madam Mason!"

"Yes, cook, cook, cook!" exclaimed Herbert vehemently. "She's thrown that in my face a half-dozen
times, and now you do the same. What's the matter
with all of you?"

"Ze matter ees wiz you, Herbeart. Vot do you
care to know ma petite Elsie?"

"Because she is the most charming person I ever
met. You needn't look so incredulous. There's an
originality and a sweet womanliness about her that is
exceedingly rare in these days. I suppose I may as
well tell you the whole story of what first attracted
me, although I shall enjoin secrecy upon you," and
thereupon Herbert proceeded to relate the scene in
the parlor which he had witnessed several weeks before.
Lizzette's enjoyment of the recital was keenly por-
trayed in her sparkling eyes and expressive features.

"Oh, zat Elsie!" she exclaimed. "She ees such a
witch!"

"A most unapproachable one, too," answered Herbert. "I had a strong desire to make her acquaintance
after the unconscious revelation I witnessed, for I felt
that it would not hurt a certain conscious complacency
of mine to brush it against the rugged sense and keen
satire of such a nature, and you know, Lizzette, that
I don't care a fig for the creeds of society. I can recognize a gentleman in the man who drives my coach,

if he exhibits the qualities of one. But your Miss Elsie is decidedly averse to any advances in that direction. In fact, she has snubbed me so emphatically that I can't help thinking she has a personal dislike for me."

"Ah, Herbeart, you reason like ze boy. I know Elsie haf ze desire to please your sister, and Helen! ze hurricane ees no comparison to her anger eef her only brother should disgrace——"

"Take back that word, Lizzette!" exclaimed Herbert hotly. "Disgrace and Herbert Lynn never went together, and never will, please God. It is no disgrace to love—what is beautiful and right."

Lizzette caught at his words quickly. "Tell me, Herbeart, ees eet only ze passing fancy, or ze strong man's love?"

The blood flamed into Herbert's face as he answered passionately: "Would to heaven it *was* only a passing fancy; but I am afraid the ugly truth is that I'm in love, as it is called, for the first time in my life."

"C'est triste! C'est triste!" murmured Lizzette. "Helen vill be zo angry, and eet ees so—so—out of ze right vay."

"Nonsense!" exclaimed Herbert. "The right way doesn't depend upon any old-world ideas of aristocracy. Were I ten times a King Cophetua, I should sue my little maid right royally, if there were only a little less scorn in her eyes. I tell you, Lizzette, there is so much unhappiness bred in this world by false ideas as to what is due to position, and there are so many mercenary and loveless marriages, that I am sick of the whole empty pageant. I cannot see that I am to blame because I happened to be the only son of a millionaire, nor do I feel bound to render myself miserable for life to please the whims of those who enjoin certain obligations upon the possessor of a little inflated position. As regards Elsie, I'd give a good deal to be able to lift her out of that drudgery, even if— yes, I'm so far gone as that—I never saw her again. Can't you help me to help her, Lizzette?"

"Eet ees all ze grave meestake, Herbeart. Elsie ees so—so vot you call independent zat she no take von sou in charity. I can see no vay except you forget her and leave her to her own place. Eet ees often so mooch meestake to marry beneath von too."

"That isn't the question, at least not now. Such gifts as Elsie's ought to be put to better use than the making of sauces and salads in Helen's kitchen——"

"I take eet you vould not mind eef ze talent vas changed to Herbeart's kitchen," interrupted Lizzette. "Zat ees just like ze man; he want eferysing to himself."

"You wouldn't have found me quite so selfish if you had waited a moment. I only desire a chance for the best development of Elsie's gifts. Now I needn't appear in this matter, and a few thousand dollars, I'm sure, couldn't be more worthily bestowed."

"Non, non," said Lizzette with a sober shake of her head. "Elsie guess in no time, and ze cake be all dough. Not von sou vill she take if she earn it not. I haf tried her and I know. Zare ees only zis to hope for, if so be you not forget her: leave her to her

place—eet would be von bitter blow to her to lose it—
and trust to ze change in time and circumstance. Eef
some time I sall find zat ze tangle may be made straight
and no hearts break, I vill tell my Herbeart."

"A dubious promise, considering the view you take
of the situation; but there is one thing you can do.
Antoine tells me Elsie is to pay for his music lessons;
let me pay for them, while you put the sum, small as
it is, in the dime savings bank to her account. That
will not be charity."

" Merely a loan zat Antoine sall repay!"

" Oh, certainly! What strict constructionists you
and your little circle are!"

" Eet ees ze old-time construction of self-dependence
and respect zat I haf learned of Margaret and Elsie.
Ze self-pride ees wiz zem ze grande idée."

" Good doctrine, I'll admit; but there are times when
it is excessively inconvenient."

" Such times as mon Herbeart like to play ze philanthropist, eh? Neffer mind, I feel ze day come ven
ze vay vill open for ze help you like to gif to humanity."

" But I am decidedly indifferent to humanity in general. My philanthropy is specific."

"And goes no more beyond ze rosy cheeks and
bright eyes of a pretty girl!· Fie! fie! Herbeart, zose
bright eyes transfix you wiz zere scorn if she know
zat. So often I sees zem dimmed wiz tears ovair ze
pain, ze loss, ze trial of ze vide strange vorld. So
often she vish for money zat she might build up ze
strength of independence for ze suffering. Ah, you

tink you know ma petite Elsie. Je vous dis, zat she haf ze heart of ze angel in her breast. L'homme zat vin ze love of ma petite sall take heaven to his home."

"Amen," said Herbert reverently.

"But eet will not be ze selfish heaven; eet sall be so vide as ze earth, so long as ze life!"

"Lizzette!" exclaimed Herbert with a start. "All this shames me, for I realize the selfishness of my aims. But let me once win Elsie, and by all that is sacred I promise to be as wax in her hands."

Lizzette regarded Herbert's flushed face with grave eyes. "I tink you meestake her still. To vin ze spurs and vear zem make ze knight in her eyes, I fancy."

"Ah, well, I see you are bound to convince me that the way is difficult; but I do not despair yet. To tell the truth, it is a new and somewhat depressing knowledge to learn of how little value Herbert Lynn is in this world. He always fancied himself quite a personage until he chanced on your quixotic circle."

Lizzette's eyes twinkled. "Eet ees good sometimes to see ourselves in ze truthful mirror of unflattering eyes. Still I do not tink mon Herbeart ees all so bad. I haf some fond hope for him yet."

"It is fortunate that you have; for with the unpleasant truths I've been hearing lately, there is great danger in my finding this world a hollow mockery and betaking myself to a monastery. But here we are! Now for a consultation with Dr. M——. We shall know the truth about Antoine's case soon, and then, if favorable, we can tell the lad what the future has in store for him."

Glancing up, Lizzette saw before her the façade of a large hospital, into which they were speedily ushered. It did not take long to establish the fact that so far as could be determined without actual examination there was hope for Antoine, and it was safe enough to arouse the lad's anticipations; a thing which Lizzette had hesitated about doing without strong presumption of success. A personal examination the following day gave still greater color to hope, and with glowing anticipations for the future, it was settled that within two weeks Antoine should take up his abode for six months at the hospital.

That night Elsie and Antoine held high carnival, and between them there was a wild commingling of laughter, tears, kisses, and music. Every now and then Elsie would turn from the organ to print a kiss on the lad's pale cheek, and Antoine would throw down fiddle and bow to clasp his arms around her neck and whisper:

"Only think, Elsie, if it hadn't been for Herbert all this would never have happened. Isn't he good!"

CHAPTER XV.

IT was the night before Antoine's departure for the hospital, and already April breaths were balmy with Southland odors. Through the open windows of Margaret's room there floated down to passers-by the vanishing strains of a deftly-handled violin. Antoine and Elsie were giving a farewell concert to Margaret's Busy Fingers Club, and the strains of music had drawn first one inmate of the house and then another up the long flights of stairs until the rooms were full. It was a treat to which the children had long been looking forward, and their elders found a short surcease of care in the delight and abandon of the two untrained musicians. Elsie and Antoine were in their gayest mood, and violin and organ seemed to laugh with them. Like the birds they had tried to imitate a year ago, music seemed to be innate in their breasts, and they flung off gay quicksteps, ariettas, and rondos until hands, feet, and heads of the little audience kept almost unconscious time, and smiles flitted from face to face in self-forgetfulness.

The music came in fitful gusts through the open windows, and passers-by paused to listen, seemingly loth to lose a note of the gladness trembling on the air. Across the street in the shadow of a portico a man had stood for some time in a listening attitude, and as the music seemed to grow madder and merrier, a certain restlessness became apparent in shifting feet, and an uneasy tapping of fingers on the wooden column against which he leaned.

"Antoine is gay to-night," he thought. "Hope has been awakened in his breast, and if it were not that I might seem to be seeking his thanks I should climb the stairs and make myself known to them. I wonder if my Lady Scornful would be as unbending to-night as she is within my sister's walls! I'm strongly tempted to try her—yet I'm afraid it would be an unwise thing to do; for as Lizzette counsels, it is best to await developments. What an extraordinary position this is for me, anyway! I've tried my best to reason it out on one of Helen's hypotheses, but it all comes point-blank against the fact that life isn't worth living without that little bunch of spitefulness. And, after all, she moves in an orbit that is distinctly outside of mine and with which, to tell the truth, I have very little sympathy. She and her sister are charming types of self-cultured women, and worthy of any man's or society's recognition; but their quixotic notions regarding a regenerated humanity seem the veriest nonsense to me. Every man for himself—et sauve qui peut is, as the world makes it, a fairly good doctrine. What is the use of being burdened with the sins and sorrows of the world? I don't consider myself responsible for them or that they would be materially lessened if I threw away my money in clothing the sans culottes. Such people are as ragged as ever the

next day after your philanthropy, and you are certainly none the better for it. Indeed, the leaven of
generosity, like that of love, ought to have a narrow
circle; it grows too pale if you widen it. And yet
those two slender girls would build up a social para-
dise in which the ignoble qualities of humanity have
no part. Greed, avarice, jealousy, insincerity, are en-
·tirely eliminated from their scheme of life. Surely in
their position they must have encountered all these
evils, and still they ignore them! They look upon
others as themselves in replica, at least in motive. A
natural conclusion, no doubt, but one the facts do not
bear out. One may safely prophesy regarding the outcome of these Utopian ideas. There never can be,
never will be, anything but the survival of the fittest.
I suppose if Elsie heard me she would say that the
fittest ought to include the majority at least, and that
it is in the hands of the fittest to help the unfit to become fit. But that is what Christianity has been trying to do all these years, and still the cry is, 'save us
or we perish.' These slender girls, hearing this cry,
have offered their empty hands to the multitude. And
the result ? Well, from what Lizzette tells me of that
little club of Margaret's, the outlook is by no means
disheartening; but how will it be as the circle widens ?
How much of heart and hope—for it is all they have—
will they be able to bring into the work ? I rather imagine that unknown quantity is beyond my arithmetic
at present. How long am I going to be content to
let this pathetic little drama go on ? Elsie seems to
have locked the door against me in that pitiful plea of

hers not to jeopardize her standing with my sister, and I am more completely shut out of her sympathies than if I were the beggar at her door. Even Lizzette shakes that sage head of hers and says it is not right. Right! what's wrong about it? If I had a perverted taste and Elsie was coarse and ignorant, and the chances were all against the ultimate happiness of such a union, perhaps I might be induced to see my error. But when did reason ever lend her balances to a man in love? I always supposed I was sane enough until a certain Miss Elsie Murchison took to snubbing me; yet here I am, a love-sick boy, mooning outside of her window, and like Benedick, 'a college of wit-crackers cannot flout me out of my humor.' Dear Lady Disdain, good-night! I'm going home to read my Shakespeare once more and learn of my prototype how to rail at and forget you––if I can!"

It was late in the afternoon of the next day, and Margaret sat alone in her room thinking wistfully of Antoine and the long six months of his stay at the hospital. The lad had gone cheerfully to the loneliness and pain before him, never doubting that the glad promise of walking like other men and awaking to the joy of vigorous life would be fulfilled. Indeed, his faith was so absolute that it took away much of the pang of separation, and Margaret and Elsie had choked back unbidden tears and promised him a weekly visit of long talks and merry times. Books, violin, and a mandolin, the gift of Herbert, had been sent with his other belongings, and a daily order for flowers had been left by Herbert at the florist's. All that loving hands could do to smooth the painful path had been done, and now there was nothing left but to hope and wait. But how they all missed him! The pale quiet face, the great dark eyes, the loving smile, and the sweet strains of his violin had so entwined themselves around their hearts that not to find them daily ministers to their need seemed a sore deprivation. "Elsie's smile will be more infrequent now that Antoine is no longer with us," sighed Margaret. "I am afraid our loved evenings will be doleful enough without our laddie. Still there must be the same adherence to duty wherever the lines fall, and perhaps our progress will be all the more substantial when we realize that hard work is our only master."

There was a sudden scurrying of feet up the stairs and several children burst breathlessly into the room. "O Miss Margaret!" they cried, "just come and see what some men have done to the new tenant—the one that only moved in a week ago! They've just come and took every bit of furniture, and the woman is sick, and they took the bed from under her and left her only a straw tick and a quilt, and she's crying awful, and the two little babies are squalling, and—oh! it's dreadful!"

Margaret quickly followed the children down two flights of stairs, to find the scene even more pitiable than the children had described. Upon a thin straw mattress in the corner lay a woman with her face hidden in her arms, while heart-rending sobs shook her frame from head to feet, and two little children, as yet only prattling babes, crouched beside her crying:

"Mamma, mamma, look up. Talk to baby. Don't cry! Mamma! Mamma!"

Margaret knelt beside the agonized form and softly stroked back the hair from the face that remained persistently hidden, and then, taking both of the wondering babies in her lap, said softly to the group of children at the door: "Now run away, dears, and shut the door."

The children obeyed instantly, and Margaret remained softly stroking the woman's hair and hugging the now quiet babies to her bosom. Under the soothing influence of Margaret's touch and presence the violent sobbing soon ceased, and a tear-stained face, lit up by a pair of hollow eyes, glanced up at Margaret. One glance caused a sudden transformation in the convulsed and agonized face, and a thin hand crept out toward Margaret as the woman said brokenly, but in the unmistakable voice and language of refinement: "You are good not to pass by on the other side. What made you come here?"

"Love," said Margaret simply.

"Love?" repeated the woman interrogatively. "Love died long ago, and the devils of greed and pride danced at his funeral."

"Not in all hearts, I trust. Love lives to help and strengthen sufferers like you. Can you tell me any way to help you?"

"Yes—kill me!" The hollow eyes gleamed with sullen despair.

"And the babies?" asked Margaret as she stroked back the rings of flaxen hair above the fair little brows.

"Oh, God forgive me! I am so wretched, so desperate."

"I know it, and I do not blame you; but let us see if there is not some way toward the sunshine. Tell me all about it."

"It is only a little to tell. The marriage of a petted, only daughter, with a head full of romantic notions, to a man whose only fortune was head and hands; but who held, at the time of my marriage, a salaried position as manager of a prosperous business firm. A panic, a failure, and consequent loss of employment, followed by unsuccessful attempts at re-establishment in the old line, the yielding of health at the shrine of motherhood, the gradual settling into bare and bitter poverty, the disposal of every article of value, and that last resort of the impecunious, the buying of needed furniture on the instalment plan, followed by the forcible taking back of the furniture just before the last payment could be made."

"And your husband?"

"He went out again this morning in the old, well-nigh hopeless search for work."

"Your parents?"

"They live in a distant city and know nothing of this. I married against their wishes. There were just five dollars more due on the furniture, but the chattel-mortgage shark exacted immediate payment, and of course I could not meet it. He was kind enough to leave me this," and the thin hands pulled at the tattered quilt.

"Oh, it is pitiful! Shameful!" exclaimed Margaret. "You must not be left to lie here. Can you walk?"

"I haven't walked a step in three months. Edward, my husband, has lifted me in his arms and managed to care for me and the babies. Oh, it is terrible, the way we have been compelled to live." And sobs again shook the slight frame.

"Never mind," said Margaret soothingly. "It will be better soon. My rooms are two flights above, so it will be impossible to take you there, but you shall have a comfortable bedroom and kind friends to look after you. I shall be compelled to leave you for a few moments, until I can ask some of these friends to make room for you."

"Oh, don't trouble anybody! I can't bear to be thrown upon charity. It hurts my pride so."

"We won't call it charity; we'll call it love. The love that prompted the Samaritan and a greater than he to moisten parched lips with cooling waters and taught mankind the constant need they have of each other."

"And do you believe in Him?"

"With an everlasting faith," answered Margaret.

"I did once until the inhumanity of the world made me doubt."

"Doubt no longer," said Margaret, smiling, "for He has raised up succor for you." With these reassuring words Margaret sought the rooms of several good women of the house, to hold counsel with them and determine the best course to pursue. Margaret's story evoked such a storm of indignation and invective against the mortgage shark that, if it could have gathered sufficient volume, would have swept the whole guild from the face of the earth. And yet, one and all counselled Margaret not to meddle with the matter.

"You can't do nothin' with 'em. They've got the power and they know it," was the unanimous conclusion of the little circle.

"But the injustice of it," exclaimed Margaret. "I can't stand tamely by and see a helpless being robbed."

"No more could we if there was any chance, but you'll find, the longer you live, that the poor don't have no justice in this world. The laws is all made for the rich."

"Then it is the fault of the poor man if he has no justice, for he is a recognized factor in the vote that sends men to make those laws, and if he knows his rights he can have them maintained."

"Well, I don't know how it is, but my man has to vote as the boss tells him or lose his place."

"Shame! Shame!" said Margaret indignantly, "and this is America's boasted freedom of life and thought! But we are forgetting that poor woman. Who among you will take her in until something can be done?"

"I," exclaimed Mrs. Smith, a motherly woman whose rooms were on the same floor. "We're a good deal crowded now, but she shan't lay there and suffer so long as I have a crust."

"Let us hope it will be only a temporary inconvenience. I am going to find some way to unravel this web of injustice and regain possession of those goods."

"You'll have your trouble for your pains," said Mrs. Smith dubiously as they walked along the hall.

"It may be, but there will be some satisfaction in trying. Here we are!" Margaret exclaimed as they entered the sick woman's room "Now we'll make a chair of our hands and between us carry you to Mrs. Smith's room, whose heart is as large as her back is broad."

"You're making it pretty big," laughed Mrs. Smith as she presented her ample form to the sick woman's view. A faint smile at the pleasantry played over the wan face, as she allowed them to lift her to the improvised seat and carry her to a bed.

"Now," said Margaret, when their charge was safely bestowed between clean sheets, and the babies were softly cooing on either side of her, "I want all the information you can give me, and all the papers you have relative to this furniture. I am going to make an effort to get it back."

"You will find an old portfolio in the tick I was lying on. All the receipts for money paid and the contract are in it."

As Margaret returned with the portfolio, a sheet of paper fell from it and fluttered to the floor. She picked it up and was about to restore it, when the sick woman said: "Read it. It will verify the statement I made a few moments ago."

Margaret glanced along the page and saw that it was poetry written in a free-flowing hand. Seating herself beside the bed she read:

"O Soul, I am tired of you, tired !
  You do nothing but think and feel,
    And often you weep,
    In some sensitive deep,
  O'er wounds that you cannot heal.

" O Soul, I am tired of you, tired !
  You have threaded the paths of life,
    And found the sweet,
    Too incomplete
  To answer the pain and strife.

" O Soul, I am tired of you, tired !
  You give me no peace or rest ;
    The blinding steep,
    Or lonely deep
  I walk at your stern behest.

" O Soul, I am tired of you, tired !
  You have only your faith and prayer ;
    For every ill,
    Their utterance still
  Comes back on the empty air.

" O Soul, I am tired of you, tired !
  How often with faith and you,
    I have tried to soar
    Where doubt is no more,
  And humanity's sometimes true.

" O Soul, I am tired of you, tired ;
  Why ask for an endless day?
    I am tired of the light,
    And long for the night,
  To rest forever and aye !

" O Soul, I am tired of you, tired !
  Go ask of Time, and find
    Some quiet spot,
    Where feeling is not,
  And oblivion conquers mind !"

As Margaret finished reading she bent over and kissed the white face. " Is this yours ? " she asked.

"Yes, and dozens of others. They have been my safeguard against insanity. Only when I could go outside of myself, could I find anything to make the barren life endurable."

"Have you offered any for publication?"

"No; I have neither stamps nor courage."

"May I keep this?" asked Margaret, referring to the one she had just read.

"Certainly, if you like it."

"I do, very much; and now let me see the contract and receipts."

Margaret found that the original bill and contract called for one hundred and fifty dollars, but that the expense of making mortgage and the interest had been compounded until, although one hundred and seventy-five dollars had been paid, it still called for a balance of five dollars, which remaining unpaid, permitted fore-closure and forcible seizure of the furniture.

"A Shylock's bond!" exclaimed Margaret indig-nantly. "It is so manifestly unjust that I feel sure there is a law somewhere to cover it."

"We knew at the time the goods were bought that it was an unjust contract, but we had no money to pay down, and what could we do? It is just the way the world takes advantage of necessity. The trite maxim that 'sentiment and business have nothing in common' you'll hear on the lips of every man in trade."

"We shall hear how justice agrees with business, then," said Margaret, rising. "I should like to put the bitter dose of equitable payment for these crimes against common humanity, between the teeth of these

sharks. At any rate, if there is no justice for such des-
picable creatures it is time it was known."

"Humanity has a grand defender in you," said the
sick woman, looking admiringly at Margaret's flushed
cheeks and flashing eyes.

"Not so," she replied, shaking her head. ".I know
my weakness and ignorance too well. I only recognize
the truth that the primitive idea of equal rights seems
to have been utterly lost in this avaricious world. But
so long as I have voice I shall speak for it. The good
such speaking may do remains to be seen."

Margaret went up to her rooms and opened her
purse to see how much money she had at her command. Of the money Dr. Ely had sent, but five dollars
remained. "If worst comes, and I cannot regain the
furniture, this will at least buy them something to eat,
and I can loan them Gilbert's bed while he takes the
lounge, until the way is opened for something better.
Now to find a lawyer in whose hands to put the case."

Once on the street, Margaret realized that in all the
great city she knew no one to whom she might apply
for advice. She wandered down toward the business
part of the city, intently scanning signs and inwardly
praying that she might be directed to some one who,
with the profession of lawyer, combined the outlawed
sentiment of humanity. "J. Brown, Attorney," glit-
tered in gilt letters before her, and up the two tall
flights of stairs she followed the beckoning sign. A
gentle rap, answered by a gruff "Come in!" and the
room of J. Brown, Attorney, opened to her view.

"Is Mr. Brown in?"

"I am he. What can I do for you, madam?"

"I desire advice on a matter of business."

"Ah, be seated, please. You may state your case."

Margaret lost no time in doing so, relating the pitiful story with such succinct detail that the lawyer beamed at her with evident admiration.

"Very well stated, madam—very well, indeed. Are these people in any way related to you?"

"They are entire strangers."

"And you have taken up their case from pure charity?"

"From pure humanity, rather; as, indeed, I would that another should do for me."

"Very admirable of you, indeed; but you are doubtless aware that it takes money even to champion the cause of humanity."

"I am," said Margaret briefly, though with sinking heart.

"Then you will readily see that I can give you no advice on this matter without cash in hand."

"How much does it require?"

"In consideration of circumstances, I'll make it merely nominal. Say five dollars!"

Margaret arose to her feet somewhat unsteadily. "I have but five dollars in my purse, sir," she explained, "and I shall need it to buy food for the sick woman. I shall be compelled to look further."

"As you like," and J. Brown, Attorney, stiffly turned his back on Margaret and returned only a slight acknowledgment of her faint "Good-afternoon." Somewhat depressed by this encounter, Margaret wandered

on and entered no less than six offices, to be met with
very nearly the same treatment in every case, and the
identical result in all. "The cause of humanity cannot be championed without money!"

These words seemed burned in on Margaret's brain
as she left the last of these offices and stood irresolute
and disheartened upon the sidewalk. How could she
take the story of failure back to that suffering woman?
How could she bear to tell her that the promised succor was only a chimera of her own quixotic brain?
"I'll not do it," she said resolutely. "I'll go tell that
little sister of mine, and though I know her purse is
always low, perhaps her fertile brain may suggest
what my own stupefied one fails to apprehend."

Margaret was coming up the area steps of the Mason
mansion with her purse reinforced by two dollars, the
entire contents of Elsie's pocketbook, when she encountered Herbert Lynn just descending from his
buggy.

"Miss Murchison, I'm delighted to meet you once
again," he exclaimed as with smiling face he advanced
to greet her. There were tears on Margaret's cheeks
and trembling on the heavily-fringed lids of the blue
eyes. "Pardon me," he cried solicitously. "You are
in trouble." Margaret hastily brushed the tears away
as she answered:

"Only a little overwrought. I've been passing
through some trying scenes to-day."

"You were going home? Let me take you there.
Fortunately my buggy is just at hand."

"Thank you! I'm not going home at present. I

have some purchases to make, and I do not like to detain you."

"I have ample leisure, and it will be a new sensation to be of some use. I beg you to command my services."

Margaret glanced up curiously at the eager, almost boyish, face. "Perhaps if I were to tell you my errand you would not be so ready to offer your services. It is not pleasant to one who cares for his own peace of mind."

Herbert laughed. "I shall insist now where before I begged. Perhaps my own peace of mind will be all the dearer by contrast."

"If you insist I accept gratefully; for the truth is, my self-reliance is a good deal shaken."

When they were seated in the buggy and driving leisurely along the boulevard, Margaret said: "I am glad I have met you, for I have a story to tell and advice to ask." Without further prelude she detailed the events of the day. Herbert listened attentively until the whole story had been told, and then, with a new look of earnestness on his face, he exclaimed emphatically:

"Miss Murchison, if there are brains enough in C——, this dastardly outrage shall be probed to the bottom. It is enough to make a man's blood boil to think of the injuries inflicted on suffering women and children by such overpowering greed. But," he added, glancing at his watch, "it is five o'clock and already past office hours. Nothing can be done until to-morrow. If you will trust me with these papers, I will make an early effort to-morrow to regain the furniture. In the mean time, allow me to supply a bed and immediate necessaries for the sufferers."

"That will not be needed," interposed Margaret. "I have a bed of Gilbert's which I can loan them——"

"And turn the poor fellow on to the floor!" interrupted Herbert. "That is philanthropy gone mad, Miss Murchison. I shall insist upon supplying the bed."

"I am perfectly sane, Mr. Lynn," laughed Margaret, "and contemplate nothing worse than asking Gilbert to occupy a lounge."

"We'll forestall that by the purchase of a bed. Now that you've taken me into partnership, you must not deny me my rights."

"Not if you look upon it in that light," said Margaret seriously. "Still I should regret it, if it seemed a charity that was forced upon you."

"You would rather inconvenience yourself than ask a favor of one whom you knew to be perfectly able to grant it?"

"I should, if I thought the favor would be bestowed as a mere matter of form, without the promptings of a generous spirit."

"'The gift without the giver is vain,'" quoted Herbert musingly. "You can trust the spirit this time, Miss Murchison," he added, with a half smile. "It has lighted its torch at your altar."

"Thank you," replied Margaret gratefully, "but only for the time being, I am sure. The embers are glowing on the home shrine."

"Belief from such a source is most highly treasured," commented Herbert smilingly. "Now that you have complimented me so generously, perhaps you will tell me what I must do to deserve it."

"Buy the bedstead," said Margaret dryly.

"To hear is to obey," and putting whip to his horse, Herbert soon drew up before a down-town furniture store, where bedstead and clothing were purchased and dispatched on their way. A huge basket of provisions was next procured and stowed away in the buggy, while Margaret carried a smaller one of fruit.

"Let me carry these to your room," said Herbert as they drew up before Margaret's home. "You are to be sole almoner, for I beg you not to let my name appear in the transaction."

"I shall be compelled to," said Margaret, "if only as the mythical great and good man of all such works of charity. I could not truthfully bear the burden of so much generosity."

"Paint me as glowingly as you please, if only you give me no local habitation or name."

"Your wish shall be respected. Will my presence be necessary to-morrow?"

"No, I can save you all further trouble. And now good-night, and thank you for having given me a few genuinely happy hours."

CHAPTER XVI.

"WELL, we've won!" exclaimed Herbert the next day as, having mounted the stairs two at a time, he thrust his head into Margaret's open door. "The men are putting the furniture into the room, and I've a little sop in the way of damages," and he drew from his pocketbook a bank-note for ten dollars and laid it in Margaret's lap.

She looked at it dubiously. "Oh, it is honest," he laughed; "there's no taint of charity about it. Such high-handed crimes against justice must be made to suffer the penalty. It has set me to thinking, too, that it is time something was done toward establishing justice for these helpless poor. Why, the case would never have been won if I had not employed some of the best talent in the city."

"And that, of course, is costly."

"Of course; often more than the little sum in question. By the way, have you seen the head of this distressed family down-stairs?"

"I saw him for a few moments last night. He seems to be a gentleman in bearing and acquirements, but he wears a depressed, hopeless expression and a listless, half-hearted manner, that I can see are a constant thorn in the side of his more energetic, if enfeebled, wife."

"Well, no wonder, if half the story she tells is true. This seems to me a case of genuine humanity; one that appeals directly to a man's soul if he has one. That man ought to be given work."

"True, but he says he has sought for it far and wide."

"I don't think he need seek any further. I have a friend who is a wholesale grocer down on S—— W—— Street, and in relating the story to him, he offered the position of porter at eight dollars a week. Not a munificent salary, certainly, but a good deal better than nothing."

"Oh, I am so glad!" exclaimed Margaret. "And how happy that poor wife will be. I've grown very much interested in her, for the reason that such an ambitious spirit seems to dwell within the enfeebled body. How terrible it is when body and spirit are so at odds!"

"Terrible indeed! I really hope the good news of a place for her husband will act as a tonic. I leave the matter entirely in your hands and empower you to deliver the message."

"I will go now, if you will excuse me. I am in a hurry to tell the good news."

"Oh, certainly! Never mind me."

Margaret returned with a dismayed and crestfallen countenance. "He refuses it!" she exclaimed breathlessly as she sank into a chair. Herbert gave a long low whistle, and elevated his eyebrows in a cynical grimace that was not at all becoming.

"I am ashamed to tell you his reason," Margaret went on. "It seems so trivial under the circumstances.

He says he is fitted for higher work, and, in short, cannot accept such ungenteel employment."

"Well, that settles the Hon. Edward Carson, Esq.," said Herbert briskly. "I shall waste no more sympathy on him."

"But the poor wife," said Margaret, the tears standing in her eyes. "It was pitiful to see the look she gave him and hear her voice as she urged his acceptance of the place. 'Anything is better than starving,' she cried. 'And perhaps you can work up to a better place; I am sure you can when your employers learn your fidelity and trustworthiness;' but her entreaties were useless. He was stubborn with that white determination of an iron will. Neither the poor woman's tears nor prayers had any visible effect upon him."

"What does the fellow intend to do?"

"Oh, he has some little peddling devices, out of which, I believe, he expects to realize the fortune of a Vanderbilt in a short time. In fact, he informed me that he considered himself fully equal to managing his own affairs."

"He has proved it. Well, Miss Margaret, this only strengthens my belief in the folly of attempting to help such incapables."

"But think how the innocent suffer with the guilty! Think of the sick wife and the helpless babies! Because the man is stubborn and ill-natured, must those who are dependent on him be left to starve?"

"It seems a hard doctrine, born of that old pagan idea of brute force; but I sometimes question if it would not be the shortest way of ridding the world of

its great army of incapables.   Don't look so horrified,
at least until I have finished.   Take this unfortunate woman, delicately reared, educated, refined, sensitive; charity is, no doubt, nearly as offensive to her
as starvation.   Such people are proud of their independence of character, and what can she hope for in a
future that sees only the hand of charity between her
and the grave?   The helping hand in an extremity
like this is different from a bounty that must be a
continued obligation."

"Looking at the question from her standpoint, perhaps you are right; but in looking at it from ours, I
think you are wrong."

"There's the rub!   These ethical questions demand
some other solution than expediency."

"Christianity alone can solve them, as indeed it is
the only true solution of all the great questions of the
world.   The simple truth that we are our brother's
keeper acknowledged by mankind would be an easy
method of settling this omnipresent and embittering
war between labor and capital."

"A method the world has been slow to accept."

"In one sense, perhaps, but as we view the long
night of darkness and degradation before the coming
of Christ, we can only marvel at the progress that has
been made in less than two thousand years.   Some
day in God's great harmonies we shall hear the rhyth-
mic heart-beats of an altruistic faith, binding the
whole world together in a common brotherhood."

"And you are doing your best to strike a note in
that great harmony?"

"With Mr. Lynn's help," laughed Margaret. "He is going to advise me how to assist that suffering and unfortunate woman down-stairs."

"Impossible! He can only be the humble tool in your wiser hands. However, I've been wise enough to think she ought to be put under the care of a physician. That can be safely managed through you, as indeed can all delicate commissions."

"Thanks," said Margaret. "I always try to put myself in the sufferer's place, as I have known what it was to need help, and be grateful for it."

"When my hour of tribulation comes, may I have just such a ministering angel!" exclaimed Herbert warmly.

"Tribulation and the prosperous Mr. Lynn are a singular and almost unlooked-for conjunction."

"A man may have a great deal and yet want more. In fact, if he owns the earth he usually wants the moon, or something equally impossible."

"Is that one of your longings?"

"No; mine is more sublunary, if you will permit a pun so atrocious. The truth is there's another Galatea in whose marble veins I should like to see the warm blood of feeling run. My presence always seems to congeal the red current that glows for others."

"You speak in enigmas."

"Just now, perhaps; but by-and-by you will understand. By the way, there is one intense longing you can gratify. May I drop in some time to one of those charming 'evenings' Lizzette and Antoine have described to me? I have a sincere desire to consider myself a beneficiary."

"I am afraid I should say 'no,' if I did not begin to realize a little the earnestness of your nature. We are sensitive to our shortcomings."

"An equal sensitiveness inspires me with the desire to find a motive as admirable as that which actuates your little coterie. Besides—I suppose I may as well be honest, since you will be sure to find me out—I play the violin a little myself, and would be most happy occasionally to supply Antoine's vacant niche, provided your sister could be prevailed upon to accompany me."

A new light dawned upon Margaret as she watched the boyish blush that mounted to Herbert's brow. "And so you have already found out what an uncertain quantity my little sister is?"

"As regards your humble servant, she has been a profound certainty. A block of ice could not have been a colder reality," answered Herbert with a rueful smile.

Margaret's face grew suddenly thoughtful, but after a moment's hesitation she said bravely:

"I believe there are times when only the truth should be spoken regardless of conventionality. For my own part, Mr. Lynn, I like you exceedingly, and should gladly welcome you to our little circle; but my little sister is young, beautiful as you know, imaginative, sensitive, and—well, is it not best under the circumstances, which you so well understand, that she should continue a cold reality to you?"

"No!" exclaimed Herbert emphatically, as he sprang to his feet and placed a hand on the back of

14

Margaret's chair. "I am no cowardly trifler, and I have an honest admiration for Elsie that has a right to crave its legitimate outlet. I ask only a fair field."

Glancing up at the earnest, flushed face, Margaret smiled as she rose and laid her hand on his. "You shall have it," she said. "Bring your violin and be your own propitiation. I never interfere in matters of this kind."

Herbert raised Margaret's hand to his lips, and murmuring something wholly unintelligible, he snatched his hat and left the room. Margaret sat long buried in thought after he had left her. Elsie's doubts and misgivings in no way troubled her. Love in her eyes was too sacred and too rare to hamper it with the chains of caste or clothe it in false conventionality. But until now the thought of love and Elsie had not come to her except in the vague sometime that comes to all women. Elsie was so young, so inexperienced, yet, strange as it seemed, so wise. She had looked apprehensively upon the volatile nature, fearful that its buoyant wings would be sadly singed in the candle of life. Yet by Herbert's own confession the little maid had been as wise in her demeanor as if whole generations of elder sisters had stood sponsor for every utterance. "I am glad," she sighed tremulously, with that sweet enjoyment of love which all women have. "I could not be better pleased if the selection had been my own; but I mistrust that little sister of mine will lead him a wild dance before she surrenders, if she ever does. There are graver thoughts in that young

head than I ever dreamed of.   But all I can say is,
God speed an honest love!"

An hour later Margaret was on the street, intent
upon a purpose which had been gaining strength ever
since the invalid, Mrs. Carson, had given her the poem
she had read at her bedside.   There seemed to Margaret to be too much merit in the poem to forego the
effort to find for it, not only publication, but pay.
Margaret had become strongly possessed of the primitive idea that the laborer is worthy of his hire, and
that merit had the right to demand recognition.   Her
contact with life had so far been so simple and direct
that the complexities governing man's progress had
only just begun to confront her.   It was, therefore,
with the bravery born of ignorance that she entered
several editorial sanctums connected with the various
leading papers and periodicals of the great city and
offered the poem for inspection.   The contemptuous
glances, and decided snubs she received, disturbed her
equanimity rather than her purpose; although if the
matter had been a purely personal one, literary ambition would have met instant death in these en-
counters.   But Margaret's strength was always greater
for others than for herself, and not until she had exhausted all avenues did she intend to turn back.   Finally in the eleventh venture she encountered an editor
who, listening to her story and becoming interested,
volunteered the information that the poem had merit
and was worthy of remuneration.   A check for five
dollars gladdened Margaret's heart, and her smiles and
expressions of gratitude must have made a bit of sun-

shine in the soul of a just man. Margaret hurried home, her face glowing with happiness, and hastening into the invalid's room, produced the check with infinite satisfaction. There was no answer, but a pair of thin arms reached up and clasped Margaret's neck, while sobs and tears contended for the mastery. Margaret waited until the storm had subsided and then said gently: "You will have a chance now to turn your talent to account."

"What an angel you are! Sent by the God whom I doubted! How can I ever repay it all?"

"By reawakening a slumbering faith, getting well, and working cheerfully," and with a kiss upon the invalid's agitated lips, Margaret went up to her rooms.

CHAPTER XVII.

ONE evening, a week after Antoine's departure for
the hospital, Elsie sat at the organ, idly picking out
the melody of several of his favorite airs and dreamily
wishing the lad could be with them once again.   Margaret was busied over her books, and Lizzette, who
was with them for the night, was knitting the stocking
that always grew but never seemed finished, and Gilbert was putting some decorative touches upon a
small medicine cabinet.   Suddenly Herbert Lynn appeared in the open doorway, his arms filled with books
and a violin case in one hand.

Elsie arose from her seat as the others greeted him,
and stood with her slight figure as erect and indignant
as her mutinous spirit could make it.   Herbert turned
toward her.   "I am here by permission of high authority," he laughed, glancing at Margaret.   "I have
no apology to make this time."

"My sister's guests are always welcome," said Elsie
icily, as she sank upon the piano stool and industri-
ously undertook to rearrange several sheets of disordered music.

Herbert made no reply, but stood composedly watching the trembling· fingers and the swiftly-mounting
blushes on the fair face.

"You are nervous," he said at last.   "Let me do
that for you.   I am delightfully calm."

Sometning in the exasperatingly cool tones made Elsie glance up, and then as quickly glance down again.

"It is useless to keep on the defensive any longer," Herbert resumed as he coolly took the sheets of music from her. "I've come to beg a truce."

"And have you forgotten all I said?"

"Not altogether; but I am of a forgiving disposition."

"You forgive very easily, it seems to me," said Elsie haughtily.

"Sometimes, and one of these times is when a spiteful little girl says things she doesn't mean."

Elsie tried hard to keep a sober face, but Herbert's good-nature was irresistible, and the corners of her mouth relaxed in a smile as she looked up and asked: "What occult wisdom taught you she didn't mean them?"

"The science of physiognomy, if there is such a science. A face that is all sunshine for others cannot surely mean to keep all its thunder-clouds for an inoffensive young man like me."

"Some people attract lightning," exclaimed Elsie mischievously.

"By reason of superior magnetism, it is to be presumed. Thanks!"

At this juncture Lizzette came up with the violin case in her hand. "Herbeart, zis ees ze reminder de mon petit Antoine. Let me hear ze fiddle speak again."

"Willingly, if Miss Elsie will accompany me."

Elsie looked up, mutinous still; but meeting Herbert's eyes, defiance gave its last gasp as she said under her breath: "You are an arch conspirator. I suppose there is nothing left for me but submissiveness."

Herbert's blonde head bent low over the pile of music he was ostensibly examining as he whispered: "You shall see how generously I can conspire. Trust me to be magnanimous."

Elsie's nimble tongue was silent, and a sudden wave of intoxication seemed to sway her back and forth in a rarefied atmosphere where breathing was impossible. When at last she dared to glance again at Herbert, he was tuning his violin with such a look of beatific contentment on his face that pent-up feeling, on the perilous edge of a tear, seized the other alternative and burst into laughter. With instinctive quickness she dashed into a noisy jig on the organ, and by the time she dared to glance apprehensively around, Herbert had selected the piece of music and was striking its key-note on the violin. Elsie played very badly that night, and Herbert was several times obliged to point out little mistakes and make corrections with all the gravity of a professional music master. But the tumult in her veins rose higher and higher, and with a sudden crash on the keys the music came to a stop. Glancing down at the perturbed face, Herbert turned to the others:

"My violin is evidently not Antoine's and Miss Elsie looks tired. Have you examined the new books, Miss Murchison? There is one on sociology, by Sir Lyon Playfair, I thought might interest you. And there is Henderson's 'History of Music,' the 'Journal of Marie Bashkirtseff,' 'The Three Germanies,' and two or three newly-issued volumes of poetry by Meredith, Lover, and others. I thought before I dipped into them I should like your opinion."

While Margaret, Lizzette, Gilbert, and Herbert were discussing the new books, Elsie slipped away, too perturbed to do anything but throw herself on the bed and cry. Just why she cried it would have been difficult for her to tell. But she did not try to tell; she only knew, like all volcanic natures, that safety and reason lay in a copious burst of tears. Half an hour later she presented herself in the sitting-room, her old, calm, smiling self.

"Now that the ice is broken I shall hope I may come often," said Herbert as he bade them good-night. And saucy Elsie had no retort ready.

The summer wore into early autumn with busy days and brightening prospects for our little circle. Antoine was making slow but evidently sure progress at the hospital, and was hopeful and happy at the Sunday receptions of the friends who clustered around him. Lizzette beamed with joy and gratitude and seemed to have thrown discretion to the winds in the praises of Herbert which she constantly chanted in Elsie's ears. The treaty of peace to which Elsie had so unwillingly committed herself had, after all, been a very simple affair. Herbert had been generous, as he promised, and beyond occasional evenings together over violin and organ, at which Elsie was learning to acquit herself with greater credit than on their first venture, they did not often meet. Contrary to her usual custom, Helen Mason had not closed her city home for the summer. Herbert, much to her chagrin, refused to seek the seashore, and with wise forethought, as she fancied, she filled her house with gay company. Among the guests was a certain Miss Alice Houghton, who, an orphan and the sole possessor of great wealth, lived, together with a duenna aunt, at one of the great family hotels in the city. She was a tall, fine-looking, well-bred girl of twenty-three or twenty-four. Her distinguishing characteristic was an air of pronounced weariness, that reminded one vividly of Young's "Languid Lady." It was a difficult matter to interest her in anything, yet her attention once caught, her face would light up with unusual intelligence and animation. Herbert at first regarded her simply as an exponent of the system of purposeless education which is bestowed upon the average society girl; but after several weeks of acquaintance he became convinced that a secret grief was preying upon her. He was consequently not greatly surprised when he found her one morning in late summer in the drawing-room, with a ghastly look of horror on her face as she clutched a newspaper and read the head-lines concerning a sensational suicide of a fast young man about town in one of the gambling hells of the city.

"My husband!" she gasped, pointing to the head-lines and then lapsed into insensibility.

Elsie was on her way to her morning conference with her mistress when she encountered Herbert, pale and distracted, with the limp burden in his arms, calling wildly for Helen. There was no time for explanations as Helen Mason ran quickly down the stairs, and Elsie returned to her work with a clouded face and defiant air that did not escape Herbert's notice. The story of Alice Houghton's life was soon told to the two sympathetic friends. A marriage, secret at first from mere caprice, but afterward guarded because of shame, to a handsome but dissipated and entirely character- less man of fashion, who, having spent his own and a considerable portion of his wife's fortune at the gam- bling table, had deliberately shot himself rather than face the consequences of his evil deeds. The story never became known beyond the three or four sym- pathizers within the Mason household, and the death of a relative furnished ample excuse for the deep mourning and grief-stricken air with which the young widow again faced the world. Herbert was very kind and attentive to her in the early days of her grief, and in consequence his sister drew some exceedingly flat- tering pictures as to his future.

With Margaret the summer had been productive of much good. The little leaven of her kindly nature and generous deeds had permeated the whole tene- ment-house and extended even beyond it in sundry additions to her Busy Fingers Club. She was idolized by the children of the neighborhood, who hailed her as the patron saint of all their little schemes and am- bitions. Under her fostering care and that of the physician which Herbert had ordered, the invalid, Mrs. Carson, was slowly gaining her health and some slight encouragement in her literary ventures. There was a cloud, however, hovering in Margaret's sky. Gilbert, who had already reached a man's stature, had

acquired as well a man's independence, and had taken
to absenting himself from home evenings, much to the
annoyance of both sisters. It had been his custom
during the spring and summer to go for Elsie and
bring her home for the night, and there had been a
substantial progress made in their studies in consequence. Of late, however, Elsie had found herself
dependent for escort upon the good-natured William,
who had shown himself only too happy to be of use
to her, and had grown alarmingly confidential as a
result. This state of William's mind being duly im-
parted to Margaret, she had resolved to forestall
trouble by insisting upon Gilbert's usual attendance
on his sister. But the lad was sullen and unresponsive
when she broached the subject, and when night came
he put on his hat and went away without a word.
Margaret brooded for some time over Gilbert's changed
demeanor, and with a feeling of impending trouble
which it is so often impossible to resist, she dressed
herself for the street and went out, resolved to discover the places he frequented most. Fortune favored
her, for at Mrs. Carson's door she learned that Gilbert
and Mr. Carson had held a discussion about a meeting
of some kind which they were to attend that evening
at Harmonie Hall. The nature of the meeting the
invalid did not know, but she imagined it was semi-
political in character, as she had found that her husband had become interested of late in municipal poli-
tics. There had been strange mutterings in the air
for some time among the inmates of the tenement-
house, and Margaret's heart instantly took 'he alarm.

What had Gilbert, a minor, to do with municipal poli-
tics and this spirit of discontent that she could but
notice among the laborers with whom she lived? The
great strife between labor and capital had never come
actively home to Margaret. Indeed, so simple had
seemed its solution to her upon the broad basis of brotherly love and active Christianity, that she had worked
on quietly, hopefully, in the firm faith that she was only
one of millions of like factors in once more establishing the kingdom of Christ. Like one who watches
the battle from the hill-top, she believed the contend-
ing forces were only seeking their way up to the clear
sunshine. It was, therefore, with something like consternation that she found herself among the disorderly
crowd in the hall. Here and there little groups of
men and women were noisily discussing various topics
and paying only occasional attention to the speaker,
a swarthy, wild-eyed woman, who was shouting in a
shrill, rasping voice the most astounding ideas that
had ever greeted Margaret's ears. Drawn by curiosity
as well as interest, she quietly worked her way up to
a position near the platform and sank into a seat to
listen.

"Talk about freedom," yelled the speaker, waving
her long thin arms like a revolving windmill. "I tell
you we are slaves—handcuffed, manacled, abject
slaves." This assertion brought a round of applause.
"Talk about the great American eagle—it is only a
superannuated old crow that lets its blind followers go
where the witches dance on the point of a needle."
This witticism provoked a loud guffaw of approval

from the crowd. "I tell you, men, what we want is to preach the gospel of discontent. We want every one of you, all thinking people, to be anarchists. We don't believe in statutory law; we don't want any law but natural law."

"Hear! Hear!" came in shrill calls from various parts of the room.

"But you say," resumed the speaker, "that anarchy is disreputable. That is just what we want it to be. We want to find the gospel of discontent in the gutters. We don't want to be reputable, and I thank God that I am absolutely disreputable. We leave respectability for the Christian capitalist, the slave-driver, the monopolist. Why, a man cannot be a Christian anarchist, because anarchy is only of the earth. The only class of people who can regulate this dismal condition of society, at which so many are just now trying their hands, are the anarchists. Think of it: the telegraphs in this country are owned by one man, the railroads by sixty families, and into the hands of the few is fast being gathered the country's wealth. Impracticable dreamers propose to remedy this evil by making the state or nation responsible, but the anarchist says no, he doesn't want any interference, for he has had too much of it. The state resorts to armed force. If we want liberty, there is no other way to get it but to do as the state does and resort to armed force."

The speaker sat down amid a great wave of applause, and Margaret shrank back in her seat with her cheeks burning and eyes flashing with indignation. A man with long black hair and ragged beard next occupied

the platform, and held forth on the cruelty of the
bloated capitalists and a monopolistic press.

"Why, all attempts at pacification," he cried, "are
dead failures. Monopolists are more arrogant, trades
unions more bitter than ever. 'Give us more wages,'
we cry; 'We'll give you less,' they say. 'We don't
want to work so many hours a day,' we respond; 'You
shall have more,' they answer. 'We won't work under
such conditions,' we declare; 'Then starve,' they hiss.
Do you know there are over three millions of workingmen who are crying all this? And the capitalists
ask: 'What are you going to do about it?' We'll
show them what we'll do about it. Let them beware!
Let them remember the dark days of the French Revolution, and note how many patrician heads went under
the axe because the rabble like us—the sans culottes
like us, if you please—went crying for bread, and when
they couldn't have bread they cried for blood and had
it. Why, men, this is the greatest war of history. It
is a war not of countries, but of the globe, and the two
great forces, the very rich and the very poor, those
bonded slaves of an arrogant aristocracy, are closing
in upon each other. As yet it is a bloodless strife;
but let them beware, I say, let them beware! This
trouble will never cry itself to sleep. There are too
many mighty passions surging through the bosoms of
outraged and insulted beings. There are too many
hungry wives and freezing children. From the Bastile
to the portals of this hall stalks a long line of men-
acing ghosts, who with pointing fingers demand that
the cause for which they died shall yet be made tri-

umphant. Blind is he who cannot see that the edicts
of society are crushing to the wall the helpless toilers,
the unfortunate women and innocent children of this
world. Blind is he who looks upon the cruelties in-
dorsed by capital without rising in righteous indignation to echo the cry that rings along the line, ' Down
with the aristocracy! ' It is a lie that all men have an
equal chance in this world; I tell you the competition
is unequal and capital forces the issue. Success! success! is the Moloch of the world's worship, and into
its ravenous maw you and I and every one of the
toilers feed daily the writhing bodies of wives and children. It is feasting on the putrid carcasses that are
crushed under its triumphal car. And all the while
there is wealth enough in this world for every man to
have and to spare. I tell you, fellow-mortals, the
torch and the shotgun, the bomb and the bludgeon,
are as much for the toiler as the blue-coated minions
of the law."

The man took his seat on the rear of the platform
amid the wildest cheers, and Margaret watched the
eagle-like face and the trembling, attenuated form with
more than usual interest. There had been many
grains of truth in his wild harangue, and they had
inspired her conservative breast with an enthusiastic desire to behold the wide gulf, between the two
great opposing forces of the world, narrowed down to
the line of arbitration and adjustment, to which all
such questions must finally come. But she shuddered
with horror at the sanguinary battle which the speaker's
inflammatory words had conjured. A second French

revolution, intolerably bitterer, bloodier, more wide-
spread than its prototype! God forbid! There was
just then a call from the chairman for volunteer speak-
ers, and Margaret's eyes became stony in their wonder
and terror, as she saw Gilbert rise from his seat and
advance to the front of the platform. Tall, lithe, like
a young sapling, with a wealth of dark hair pushed
back from a high, straight brow, piercing dark eyes, a
square, firmly-set mouth and chin, and fine thin nos-
trils expanding with the fire of enthusiasm, he stood
before them all. For the first time in her life Margaret realized the singular beauty and magnetism of
the boy's presence. To her he had been always only
Gilbert, to be watched over and taken care of with
a mother's unfailing forethought. Now she saw, with
a bitter wrenching of her heart-strings, that the
chrysalis had burst and her lad had gone away forever. Before her stood the man Gilbert, on whose
utterances she hung in breathless apprehension. There
was something almost wonderful in the boy's self-pos.
session as he stood and gazed the noisy crowd into
curious silence.

"Friends and brother toilers," he began in a rich,
sonorous voice that filled the hall. "You have called
for volunteer talks, and although I am not yet fully
come to man's estate, the impulse to speak is too
strong to be resisted. It is time that something was
done to lift this burden under which we are groaning,
and yet it is the old, old question that for thousands of
years before Christ oppressed the bondsmen of the
earth. How long, O Lord, how long, before this

world shall see the fruition of the mighty labors of the millions who have gone down to death for the good of their brothers? How long before vengeance shall overtake the insatiable greed of capital, which has no more care for the toiler in its grasp than the tiger in the jungle for the man he has smitten with his paw? What is it to capital that labor goes unshod, to the well-fed gourmand that the slave who serves him is starving for the crust he despises? What does the capitalist care for the wails of woe that go up from thousands of infantile throats, for the shiverings of the naked wretches at his door, so that piled higher and higher in his safes he sees the gold these wretched toilers have wrested from the mighty bowels of the earth? Who cares for the wretched twenty-four thousand souls that live in one precinct in this great and wealth-rolling city, within a compass of two small blocks? Who cares for the nobodies that live in hovels where the water from the street pours in on the floors, and where sixty or seventy people live in eight or ten rooms and exhibit the morality of the dogs they repre-sent? What millionaire philanthropist goes down into his pocket to pay his men living wages, so that the poverty which shames old-country degradation need not be re-enacted here? Where is the churchman who, giving largely to conspicuous charities, would be will-ing to turn that charity into specific help in business to the man or men who do his bidding? It is only a few years back that the 'boss' worked at the same bench with his men. Now this is all changed. Now he has his elegant office, his carriage, his fine attire; but the

15

workmen show no such advance in prosperity. They
work for even less wages, wear the same cheap clothing, and toil just as many hours as when they and the
'boss' were co-workers. What has wrought this change?
What has made these conditions possible? I will tell
you. It is governmental aid. It is because the government has fostered the schemes of the rich man and
made him a ward of the nation. But it is unjust, and
a relic of the old feudality that the government should
recognize one son to the exclusion of the others equally
well-born, and equally deserving. On this principle,
therefore, we demand that we be made wards of the
nation. We demand a distributive justice, by pacific
means if possible, and if not, then by a retributive justice, by force of arms——"

"Gilbert! Gilbert!"

A hand laid on the lad's shoulder caused him to
turn in wonder and confusion to meet Margaret's
pleading face and terror-stricken eyes.

"You are wrong, Gilbert," she cried earnestly.
"Wrong! wrong! You must not incite to violence.
Just see what turbulent elements are before you!"

There had come an instant hush with her appearance on the platform; men and women had risen to
their feet and were peering curiously at the two.
Flushed, trembling, intoxicated wi h enthusiasm, Gilbert cried: "But the terrible wrongs of the poor! You
know what they are—you who toil for a daily pittance!
They must be avenged!"

"But not in the way you indicate. Not by blood-
shed or violence. See! we are attracting attention!
Will you let me speak for you?"

For a moment resentment gleamed in Gilbert's eyes, and then, as he glanced at Margaret's uplifted earnest face, he answered: "Yes, correct me if I am wrong. God speed you!"

Gilbert sank back into a chair, his eyes intently fixed upon his sister's face as she advanced to the front of the platform and stood looking out upon the sea of wondering faces.

"Friends," she began in a low voice, "I have a story to tell you. The lad who has just addressed you is my brother. For seven years I have been mother, counsellor, friend to him. I promised his dying father to watch over him with unremitting vigilance until his feet should be firmly set in the paths of upright man-hood. That father was a man who believed in and practiced the doctrine of the universal brotherhood of man. He recognized not that all men are created equal mentally and physically, for that is a manifest absurdity, but that there is a principle underneath all conditions of society calling for the respect, venera-tion, and love of man as man. We must respect hu-manity in all its phases, and there is no right, divine or earthly, that permits us to cripple it, enslave it, or destroy it. This idea was one of his ardent beliefs; but it would have cut his gentle heart to the quick to know that his son would ever be misled into uttering words that could in any way incite to violence or wrong-doing. I have listened to-night to words that made my heart bleed; not only for the evils afflicting labor, not only for the misguided ideas of the so-called upper classes, but for the deeper wrongs you are in-flicting on yourselves."

A stir among the audience and a few hisses for a moment disturbed Margaret's equanimity, but gathering heart again she went on in a voice of deep and commanding earnestness: "Nay! hear me out. I premise here that I am not against you; indeed, I am one of you. I toil for my daily bread, and I receive but a pittance for my work. I take slop-work from the factories, and make men's shirts for forty-five cents per dozen, and men's overalls for fifty cents per dozen pairs. So you see I know what labor has to contend with."

Shouts of "You're a good one!" "Go on!" encouraged the increasing tide of thought that surged to her lips. She stood before them pale, earnest, like a prophet, and forgetting time, self, place, she swept the now listening throng with the full force of the unselfish convictions which had made her mistress of herself and untoward circumstance.

"Once more I say to you, O my brothers and sisters, you are wrong, and I repeat it with the facts of history as a bulwark of defence. Let us go back a little to the dim days of which we catch but faint shadows, two thousand years and more before the Christian era, when there were but two classes of men, feudal lords and bondsmen. Let us trace up through the freedom given the slaves under Moses, fourteen hundred years before Christ, and through all the struggles of the toiler up to the present day, the results of violent uprisings of brute force. History gives but two evidences where such uprisings on the part of labor's slaves were not terribly disastrous to the insurgents. Thousands of years have passed away, men have fought with the desperation of tigers for their rights, and still these rights are in a measure denied, and the millennium of labor is not yet in sight. You may strike the torch to the factory, aim the shot-gun at your fellow-workman because he refuses to listen to your dictation, put your bombs on railroad tracks before the midnight express, leave the ship without sailors or the printing press without workers, because any or all of these are not conducted with a true regard for mutual welfare, and you will only find yourselves still deeper in the mire of dissatisfaction and wrong. You cripple your own resources and injure your own prospects when you preach the doctrine of physical force. Leave the development of that doctrine to the brute whose only resource it is, and lift yourselves up to the higher plane where exists the reason of man. But you are no doubt asking where that reason must begin. Back of all sophistries, back of all calculation, on that primitive plane of the newly awakened—the conscience! This, in the age of intricate reasoning and perplexing sophistries, may seem to you but the utterance of a simple-minded woman; but history proves, through experience, that the great and seemingly complex problems of the day never can be and never will be solved on any other basis. It was not indeed until the gentle Nazarene walked the earth that its toilers began to grope upward toward the light of reason and conscience. He it was who first took the taint from the grimy hand of the worker; He it is who ought to-day to be the sole advocate and

mediator in all your wrongs and suffering. I am not
talking to you of the religion that the occupants of
velvet pulpits preach to the occupants of velvet pews,
nor of the Christianity, so called, that is reserved for
the rich man who builds churches where he and his
class may worship in unsullied seclusion; but of that
fundamental principle which led the Carpenter of Nazareth to render absolute justice to all men and which
prompted the good Samaritan to do a generous deed
to his fallen neighbor. Yes, you say all this would do
very well if men could be made over on a higher basis;
but they are greedy, avaricious, and prompted more
by self-interest than brotherly love. True; but there
is always the acorn before there is the oak. Social reforms must begin with the individual. In order to
have an upright community it must be largely composed of upright individuals, and if every man reformed
himself the proposition of a reformed society would
be of very simple solution. It is wonderful indeed
how the little leaven leavens the whole lump. Wonderful how the gulf between classes is already being
widened by these injudicious threats of violence. Let
us beware, then, of incendiary words! We are all of
us, Dives and Lazarus alike, striving for the same goal;
we would all be rich, prosperous, happy if we could.
We are indignant because Dives gets in our way and
hinders our advancement, when he ought, by all the
laws of good-fellowship, to give us fair play and equal
chances. But when we as Lazarus, by a fortunate
conjunction of circumstances, come at last to Dives'
importance, how is it that we take the same mean

advantage of some less capable or lucky mortal? Ah, my friends, until we learn that all these great problems lie partially at least within ourselves, and, like Atlas, are willing to bear the world on our shoulders, we shall never gain the object we are seeking. In the conscience of every individual lies the hope of the world's progress. Let us seek, therefore, to cultivate that light within our own breasts, so that, feeble ray though it may be, it shall illumine the pathway of some weaker brother and help him toward the diviner light of the gentle Nazarene. I protest against the indiscriminate and wordy assaults upon rich men. Not alone in the poor man's breast are all the virtues. Much of the poverty of the world is the fault of the individual. Natural thrift and industry have their reward even in the present untoward industrial conditions. You cannot smoke away, and drink up your income, and justly blame the bloated capitalist who employs you if your children are shoeless and the table stands empty. But you can use your reason, you can be thrifty, careful, and educate yourselves on the side of conscience and humanity. I look upon this talk of reform which is in the air as excellent for the great cause of universal brotherhood. This is the tendency of the times; the cardinal truth underlying the welfare of the world. Capital is identical in interest with us, and must recognize sooner or later the trite truth that we are only the fulfilment and complement of each other. Let us beware, then, my friends, how we antagonize those whose help we need. Let us make capital feel, by reason of our foresight, our fidelity, our judgment, our generosity, that it cannot afford to ignore our rights and must open wide the doors to human progress or fall a victim to its own inertia. With you I believe in organization; organization upheld by, and upholding, the rights of the people, irrespective of class; organization prompted by the still small voice of conscience, which abridges no man's freedom while seeking its own. In this way only can your wrongs and mine be righted. But before we mend the steps of those who oppress us, let us as individuals sweep the inner chambers of the heart, and garnish them anew for the long-waited guest of universal justice."

CHAPTER XVIII

THE night of Margaret's meeting with the anarchists was an eventful one for the three members of the Murchison family. Elsie, tired of waiting for Gilbert's appearance, and strenuous in her desire to spend her nights at home, had been again compelled to ask William's escort, a fact which raised the spirits of the mercurial young Irishman to a point of emphatic self-gratulation. He felt sure, to use his own phraseology, that " Elsie was getting soft on him," and while preparing himself for the walk he resolved to put into definite shape his growing fondness for her. It so happened that when he and Elsie left the area door, Herbert Lynn, violin case in hand, walked down the front steps of the Mason mansion and leisurely followed them up the street. As William possessed the native wit of his race, together with an abundant fund of good-humor, Elsie's laugh was frequent at the droll remarks and anecdotes he poured into her ear. This only increased the self-elation with which he viewed his prospects, but lacking the finesse of language wherewith to proclaim his passion, he allowed the precious moments to slip by, until, having reached the dimly-lighted entrance to Elsie's home, he felt that decisive action alone could serve his purpose.

"Good-night, and thank you," said Elsie as they stepped within the narrow hall.

"Not so fast," he cried, clutching at Elsie's dress and detaining her. "I must be better paid."

"To be sure," answered Elsie, reaching into the depths of a woman's long pocket and bringing her purse to view. "How careless I am."

"No, you don't! Put that pocket-book up. Sure an' this is what I mean," and grasping Elsie round the waist he strove to imprint a kiss upon her lips.

"Let me go! Let me go!" cried frightened and struggling Elsie.

"Sure an' I'll not, then! I'll jest have a kiss and maybe more from the swate girl of my heart," and his strong arms were just about to bring the flushed and frightened face within range of his lips, when a firm hand clutched his coat collar and sent him spinning into the street. Glancing up he met the indignant eyes of Herbert Lynn.

"It isn't a very safe thing, young man, for you to insult ladies in this manner, and you may congratulate yourself on getting off with scant justice. The best thing you can do is to go home and reform some of your free-and-easy habits."

William shuffled off maddened and revengeful. "Ah, but I'll fix him and the girl too. Sure and the high hand isn't always for the mighty millionaire. And it's him, is it, that's stealing my girl's heart away? Well, then, an' I'll 'umble 'em, sure. I'm after thinking the mistress with her fine airs will not be as swate as the summer when she finds her brother is comin' it asy over the purty cook."

Elsie, released from William's grasp, darted up the

stairs, but half-way up the first flight she sank down in fright and exhaustion. Springing up two steps at a time, Herbert followed and bent over her. " Elsie! Elsie!" he cried, " what is it? Are you faint? Here, let me steady you," and with the same audacity which he had indignantly rebuked in William, he slipped an arm round Elsie's waist and endeavored to lift her up.

" I don't need any help," she said, struggling to her feet and making frantic efforts to free herself from the detaining arm. " I can go alone a good deal better Please take your arm away."

" No, thank you; it is quite too comfortable," replied Herbert composedly.

"And succeeds in making me very uncomfortable. I entreat you to release me." Elsie glanced up into a pair of blue eyes, in whose depths lay a light so warm and tender, that she staggered dizzily against the wall when Herbert's encircling arm was removed.

" There, I knew you couldn't go alone. Now I insist upon being permitted to help you up the stairs. I therefore offer you, in the most decorous manner possible, the despised and rejected arm."

Herbert stood before her with crooked elbow and attitude so ludicrously stiff, that in the laugh which rose to her lips the constraint of the situation passed away, and she not only accepted the arm, but made no remonstrance when, before the third flight had been reached, the despised member, by some legerdermain best known to lovers perhaps, had been restored to its original offensive position. It still lay supine and satisfied around the slender waist when the two reached Margaret's door and found it locked.

"Here's a go!" exclaimed Herbert slangily.

"No," said Elsie, attempting to remove his arm, "it seems to be a stay!"

Herbert caught at the word instantly, even while his laugh echoed along the corridor. "A stay!" he echoed, tightening his grasp. "Elsie, darling——"

No one will know quite just how it happened, but drawn by an overmastering impulse, he drew the dark head to his breast and pressed a fervent kiss upon, I grieve to state, a pair of unresisting lips.

"For shame!" cried Elsie when she found breath. "A second William. Young man, go and reform some of your free-and-easy habits! You're infinitely more cruel than he, because you know better. I am ashamed, indignant, heart-broken," and Elsie burst into tears.

"My darling," cried Herbert for the second time, as he prepared to do penance by repeating the crime of which he was accused, "you may be just as indignant as you choose so that indignation does not take you away from me. Here, take your kiss back again! I am perfectly willing to return the jewel I stole," and grasping the flushed face in both hands, he held it in a vise-like grip while he bestowed upon the ripe lips the principal with usurious interest. There was no time for protest or further explanation. There was some one coming up the stairs, and it was a hurried assumption of composure that greeted Margaret and Gilbert as they reached their door.

"We have been waiting for you," cried Herbert,

adding audaciously, "It seemed to Miss Elsie, I've no doubt, as if you never would come."

"Margaret, dear," exclaimed Elsie, "how pale you are! What has happened?"

"Come in and I will tell you," wearily answered Margaret as she unlocked the door.

"As it is late," said Herbert hesitatingly, "with your permission I will leave my violin here and come for our music to-morrow evening. Good-night."

Elsie could not raise her eyes to his, such a tumult of wounded feeling, love, shame, and regret surged through her breast, and Herbert was obliged to depart without the glance he coveted. Elsie listened to his merry whistle as he ran down the stairs, and cowered, shame-faced and despairing, in the shadow of the window curtain. How weak she had been! She had struggled so hard not to notice him, not to think of him, and all the time the victim of a relentless fate, had at last yielded to his kiss and let him see she had given her love unasked! What a state of moral degradation she had reached! How Margaret would despise her if she knew it! How everybody with any fine moral sense would be contaminated with her presence if it was known how really bad she was!

Sleep did not visit the perturbed brain that night. In dry-eyed misery she lay through the long hours of darkness by Margaret's side, and when at the first break of dawn she returned to her work, she carried a pale, conscience-stricken face. The other servants eyed her curiously, giving her already crushed spirit unmistakable evidence that William had heralded the evening's adventure. It was with lagging footsteps and a colorless face that she dragged through her morning's duties, and finally mounted the stairs to her usual conference with her mistress.

Mrs. Mason was alone when Elsie entered the morning-room, but she did not look up. She was apparently busied over a small account-book, in which, with the gold pencil attached to it, she now and then jotted down figures or memoranda. The coals in the grate glowed warmly; the mocking-bird in his gilded cage chirped cheerily; the flowers and potted plants in the windows seemed to smile a welcome to the disheartened girl, but the fair mistress had no greeting for her. Elsie waited some moments, and then, seeing that Mrs. Mason was purposely silent, she asked, but with a note of despondency in her voice that was only too apparent, "What orders, Mrs. Mason, have you for me this morning?"

"Only one," replied the lady, for the first time turning a darkened face upon Elsie. "Take this envelope, containing your week's wages, and leave my house at once. I have no further need of your services."

The room grew so dark to Elsie that she reeled and clutched at the door-post. Mrs. Mason watched her, secretly glad to see the shaft strike home.

"Will you tell me why you dismiss me?" asked Elsie faintly.

"Why? How innocent you are! You know very well why I will not keep such a dissembler in my house. Attempting to deceive me with your assumption of flawless honor, and then using all your arts and graces to ensnare the fancy of my brother, who——"

"Stop!" cried Elsie, all her strength returning under the sting of Mrs. Mason's words, and with indignation firing voice and attitude. "You make unjust accusations. I never have deceived you in any particular. I never sought to ensnare the fancy of your brother. Instead, I have begged him to let me alone. I told him I did not want his acquaintance, and I repeat it to you, his proud and aristocratic sister. I have my own life to live irrespective of your creeds and caste, and I have endeavored to keep both of you at arm's-length."

"You are as brazen as the generality of your class. It is useless to attempt any justification. The fact remains that you have accepted the attentions of a man infinitely above you in station, good-breeding, blood——"

"I deny it! Neither in blood nor breeding are you any better than the girl you despise. In station—you but emphasize the arrogance of your nature and standing when you attempt to heap unmerited abuse upon one whom you know to be defenceless; a thing which 'Elsie the cook' would scorn to do."

"You insolent thing! Leave the room at once, and if you ever dare to speak to my brother again, I'll publish you from one end of the city to the other, and then we'll see whether 'Elsie the cook' will continue to flaunt her good breeding in the face of her betters."

The hot blood surged to Elsie's face until the purple veins threatened to burst. "Have no fear!" she cried. "I despise——"

At that moment the door opened and Herbert entered the room. He glanced at the flushed faces and turned to his sister for explanation. Elsie, trembling in every limb, rushed through the open door, heedless of Herbert's earnest entreaty to remain. How she gained the street and flew up the long flights of stairs and buried her head in Margaret's lap, she never realized until long after. What a tumult of anger, shame, and wounded love raged in the girl's breast. How black her sky seemed, and how pitiful the story was when, by snatches of incoherent words and bursts of passionate tears, Margaret finally became possessed of it. She could only bend over the writhing form and press kisses upon the disordered hair, while endeavoring to soothe by touch and voice the violent storm of sobs and tears. Calmness had not yet come back to them and reason could only dimly see its way through the darkness, when there came an imperative rap at the door, followed almost instantly by Herbert's appearance.

"Elsie," he cried, tossing his hat into a chair and coming up to her as she lay with her head buried in Margaret's lap, "I have come to make reparation for all that you have suffered this morning. I have learned the whole disgraceful story, and I have come to offer the hand with the heart that has been yours for months. Look up, Elsie, and answer me. Margaret knows that I have loved you long."

"Oh, go away and leave me," moaned Elsie. "I cannot bear any more."

"Come!" exclaimed Herbert, bending over her and

attempting to lift her from Margaret's lap. "I am impatient. I want a decisive answer."

"You shall have it," said Elsie, pulling herself away from him and raising a tear-stained and mutinous face to his. "It is a most unqualified No."

Herbert staggered back a few steps and gazed with evident surprise at Elsie's resolute face. "You cannot surely mean it," he cried. "I thought you loved me, or would love me."

"Over-confidence is sometimes disastrous, even to young men who fancy the world is 'mine oyster.'"

"Dear child, you are hurt, unstrung by the distressing events of the morning. I wish I could make you see how pained I am that you should have been made to suffer so. I wish you would let me make reparation."

"I do not need any," said Elsie proudly. "I find myself able to survive even your sister's insults."

"Do not refer to them. Helen has a great many false ideas, but you ought not to punish me for them. I have never willingly harmed you."

"Yes, you have!" Elsie broke out impetuously. "Did not I beg of you to let me alone, to keep to your own devices and let 'Elsie the cook' go her own way?"

A pained look overspread Herbert's face as he answered: "If I have wronged you, Elsie, I offer you as honorable a reparation as any man can offer a woman."

"And do you think because, to please your own fancies, you have despoiled me of a chance to earn my bread, I can accept so great a condescension? I had rather starve than be made the recipient of any man's tardy sense of honor."

Stung, but not baffled, Herbert answered: "I loved you almost from the first time I saw you. I sought to win your regard with a scrupulous sense of honor, and if this offer of my hand is tardy, it is only because you have so persistently kept me at bay. Elsie, I beg you to forget my sister's taunts and let me prove how devotedly I can make amends for the suffering I have caused you. Margaret, help me to prove how true my statements are."

Herbert turned, only to find that Margaret had slipped away. "Elsie, darling," he added, going up to her and attempting to take her in his arms, "I cannot believe, after last night, that you do not, at least cannot, love me. I was the happiest man last night that ever sat in the glow of the fire-light and drew pictures of the future. If we had not been interrupted I should have told you then all that I tell you now. Elsie! Elsie! trust me to make you happy."

But Elsie drew herself away from the outstretched arms and sheltered herself behind an intervening rocker. "I cannot," she said resolutely, although the pleading tones no less than the supplicating eyes had well-nigh broken her composure. "Even could I so compose my heart as to contemplate the possibility which you picture, there is an insurmountable obstacle in the way."

"And that is?'

"Your sister! Never will I enter a family, were it ten times mightier than the one you represent, where I could be the object of such undeserved scorn as was heaped upon me this morning."

"My poor child! I will put the globe between us."

"And let me be the means of separating an only brother and sister? No! Go back to your sister, and marry some one who represents her idea of respectability—Miss Houghton, for instance—and be sure that family approval and society will bless you forever after."

"Thank you for the suggestion," said Herbert dryly. "I am, however, neither marrying my sister nor her ideas."

"No, I don't think you're marrying anybody at present."

"And am not likely to, you doubtless mean to suggest? Elsie, what makes you punish me so?"

"I am only paying you what I owe you."

"That is honest; now give me back the heart you've stolen."

"I have no heart to give."

"Elsie Murchison!" exclaimed Herbert with a new sternness, "I have one question more to ask you, and I demand a straightforward answer. Tell me by all the truth in your nature—do you love me?"

Driven to bay, Elsie stood alternately flushing and paling, and with her frame in such a quiver of excitement that the hand which rested on the rocker shook perceptibly. "I decline to answer," she finally faltered. "You have no right to question a foregone conclusion. I have told you I will not marry you."

"Is that decision final?" asked Herbert as he picked up his hat. "Can no pleading, no proof of devotion change it?"

White to the very lips, Elsie answered: "It is final and absolute."

"Then God pity us both!" cried Herbert as, with a face as white as Elsie's own, he left the room.

Elsie threw herself on the floor and writhed in the agony of mental torture.

"Love him? Love him?" asked the tumultuous heart. Did she not rather idolize him. And now she had signed her own death-warrant. "God keep him wherever he went—how could she live without him?" A tempest of tears answered this question as she saw days stretch into months and months into years without one glimpse of the sunny blue eyes, one sound of the melodious voice, or touch of the kindly hands that had been so glad to anticipate any need or desire of hers. "How can I live, how can I live without him?" she sobbed aloud, writhing in absolute physical pain. "Oh, I shall die! I shall die! It will be too dreadful to live now!"

A second later a pair of strong arms gathered her within their embrace, and Herbert's lips were raining kisses upon brow, cheek, and lips. "I knew it, Elsie," he whispered. "I couldn't give it up so easily. You do love me, I know you do. You dare not deny it."

With sudden impetuosity a pair of lithe arms crept around his neck, and hiding her face in his bosom Elsie sobbed: "I don't want to deny it now, for it has almost killed me. But truly I'll never marry you."

Herbert laughed. "Tell me the reason."

"Well, it wouldn't be right, and not even my love for you will make me do what is not fair and just."

"That's right, my little girl," answered Herbert between kisses. "We'll try to remove the wrong. Now that I know I'm held fast in the stronghold of your heart, I can conquer the world."

"Can you?" asked Elsie, the old mischief coming quickly back. "Can you make your sister, Mrs. Mason, get down on her knees and beg me to marry you to save you from a decline?"

"I'll try," said Herbert with a grimace, "although I beg to be delivered from the decline."

CHAPTER XIX.

LIKE Byron, Margaret awoke one day and found herself famous. The daily press, in keeping close watch of the anarchist movement, had reported nearly verbatim the speeches of both Gilbert and Margaret. Editorials had been written upon Margaret's utterances, and one enterprising daily had printed a supposed portrait of her and given a brief account of her work in the tenement-house, wherein she had been glorified beyond her just deserts and made to wear the mantle of the professional reformer. Margaret was by no means pleased with this unexpected notoriety, and particularly displeasing to her sensitive nature was the attitude in which she had been made to stand with reference to those whom she had sought to aid in the quietness and sympathy of her home life. As a friend, she was sure of their appreciation and co-operation; as a reformer, she felt fearful of their mistrust and the gradual withdrawal of the sympathies she had grown to depend upon for her own guidance and happiness. It was, therefore, with no little vexation of spirit that she found herself waited upon one day by a committee of ladies who urged her going upon the platform as the advance agent of a board of foreign missions.

"It is impossible," cried Margaret when the object

of the visit had been explained. " I am not fitted for such work. Indeed, it was a mere accident which caused my appearance in public, and I hope never to repeat it."

The ladies looked at each other aghast. Here was good timber obviously going to waste. Something must be done to secure it. " But," they argued, " you must have the interests of our work at heart, as your utterances gave evidence and as your work in your own home circle proves. Why not be willing to broaden it and bring the suffering ones of earth, whom you evidently pity, a little relief ? "

" Because," said Margaret, smiling, " I believe, in the truest sense, in the old saying that ' Charity begins at home.' I have a home to make, first of all, for a young brother and sister who look upon me as mother and guardian. So long as they have need of me I shall always keep for them the one spot where home ties may reign supreme. In the next place, I shall doubtless horrify you by saying that I do not believe in charity."

A look of wide-eyed dismay went around the little circle.

" But let me qualify the ruggedness of so bare a statement," said Margaret as a look of quiet amusement crept over her face. " I have reference only to the charity which is practised under present conditions. In the first place, I think we have heathen enough to convert at home; in the second, if there were more of the genuine charity which was taught by our great Preceptor, there would be scant need of the various forms of associated charity. Modern charity belittles and robs men of the God-given sense of independent manhood which should be cultivated and respected in every one. The helping hand that is given by associated charity fosters a national laziness and sloth which grows every year more wide-spread and disgraceful."

"That is a most astounding statement," cried her hearers.

"I think you will find it true," replied Margaret quietly. "Charity that is bestowed with the air of patronage which such organizations can scarcely fail to exhibit, must make its wards feel that independent effort is not respected as it should be. We do not give any more from a fraternal desire to see our fallen brother rise to his feet and work steadily toward the goal which we have reached or are nearing; but we give perhaps from a desire to display our importance, or from a philanthropy which expects to find its way into the newspapers and be talked about, or because it is fashionable to 'assume a virtue if we have it not.' If we gave from the standpoint of humanity and a desire to see all men on an equal footing before the law, do you suppose it would be necessary to announce such themes from the pulpits of elegant and exclusive churches as 'How to reach the masses?' The masses would be there to be reached. They would not be outside, because an exclusive sexton had found that he must look to the best interests of his patrons. The church is every day growing richer and more influential. How is it with the heaven-born principles of

Him who toiled at the carpenter's bench and proved
to the fishermen of Galilee that a common bond of
divine and human love held them together? What is
the church to-day in a great measure but a business
institution? How much of the old faith clings to the
embroidered garment that has displaced the simple
white robe of the Messiah of all men? It is useless to
offer charity to a man whose rights you have denied,
and expect thereby to build up a prosperous and God-
fearing commonwealth. Ladies, I must forego the
generous offer you make me, for the bread would be bitter in my mouth which I earned by upholding a belief
that I felt to be fundamentally wrong. I ask nothing
more than to be given strength to help wherever I can
in the humblest way and with the sincerest love."

It was a silent and crestfallen committee that bowed
itself from Margaret's presence and whispered "quixotic," "cranky," "absurd," when it reached the sidewalk. Margaret sank into a chair, after the committee had left her, with a feeling of vague discomfort
and unrest. Did this invasion of her private work
bear any occult meaning? Was there really a broader
field of action awaiting her helping hand wherein she
could better fulfill the principles she loved to dissemi-
nate? Suddenly, as if in revelation, she saw Gilbert's
impassioned face as he pleaded so eloquently for his
brother toilers at the anarchist meeting. Here was
work for Gilbert, stretching out into an indefinite and
glowing future. A society of universal brotherhood!
She remembered that once a stranger had preached in
her father's pulpit on that very topic, and she had

never forgotten the five great principles he had enunciated. She had jotted them down in her note-book as truths worth remembering, and now they came back to her with the vividness and force with which a thinking brain is often overtaken by the ideas of the great minds of the world.

1. "A society of universal brotherhood must be founded on eternal truth."

2. "It must permit full and free development to every member of the human race."

3. "There must be perfect harmony between all its members."

4. "It must attempt to secure happiness in this world. Here, now, on this planet, in this day and generation, it must give justice to all mankind."

5. "It must make not only men, but nations, free." *

She well remembered how the eloquent clergyman had enlarged upon this declaration of principles in glowing words.

"Tell me," he had said, "would not such a society meet your desires? Yet such was the organization founded by Jesus Christ. Men have found occasion to depart a long way from it, but not till they retrace their steps and take up the work as He planned it, can they enjoy the fruits of the wisest law-giver the world ever beheld. "He was the true leader of men. He was born in a manger and brought up in poverty. He preached the purest and truest democracy the world has ever listened to. The tramp, the outcast,

---

* These principles were recently enunciated by Father Huntington.

the beggar were with Him the equals before the law
of the richest man on the face of the earth.   There
was nothing narrow in His creed.   But how shall men
establish the new order?   We must take the kingdom
of heaven by storm; we must convert the boodlers
and the aristocrats who now dominate the church.
Let me tell you the rich are getting tired of the life
they are living.   They are beginning to see its falsity,
and many of them are anxious to see some means
adopted by which greater justice can be rendered to
all.   Work, then, my brothers, in behalf of the rich as
well as the poor, and make the society of universal
brotherhood the grand factor in a new civilization."

These impassioned words had burned themselves on
Margaret's memory, and in the light of later events
seemed to have a peculiar force and significance.   A
society of universal brotherhood!   How beautiful it
seemed in theory; how easily, even on the basis of an
eighteen-hundred-years-old truth, the theory might be
evolved into established fact.   Yet that mighty and
eternal truth had been all these years, through innumerable persecutions and conflicts, vainly seeking its
perfect flower and fruit.   Where lay the difficulty?
Why were its life-giving branches so persistently
lopped, its trunk gashed and riven, its healing leaves
stripped and torn, and its fruition hindered and ob-
structed?   Margaret pondered long over the puzzling
questions.   It was a fundamental truth that mankind
was seeking happiness and had the same general nature and desires.   What, then, made the great diver-
gence?   The casusist and sophist might find deep within

the logic of history and the philosophy of man a more
lofty reason; but Margaret's primitive nature saw only
the main truth that men had departed from the underlying principle on which Christ had founded His church
of the living gospel. Primitive ideas had been ignored, scoffed at, trampled in the dust, and yet the
great Master had made those ideas the whole sum and
substance of life when He enjoined upon man to love
God and his neighbor, live soberly and righteously,
visit the fatherless and widows in affliction, and keep
himself unspotted from the world. Setting aside the
divine emanation of such laws, they were the truest in-
terpretation of natural law, for what is vicious is inju-
rious. The divine virtues of truth and equity are the
bulwarks of society; if they are transgressed, the whole
body politic suffers, even as the transgression of natural law causes disease and dissolution. Surely, here
"the steps are not straightened and he that runneth
stumbleth not."

To Gilbert, Margaret communicated all her doubts
and fears as well as hopes upon this theme, and with
the eagerness with which an awakened spirit seizes
upon ideas, he followed her reasoning to a conclusion
which would have been remarkable in one so young, if
it had not been the logical result of Margaret's training and practice.

"I can only work on the plan you outline by first
finding out how those I desire to reach are striving
for the happiness that is their aim. It will be a long
and laborious effort, for I must truly prove myself the
friend of every man. No thief, thug, criminal, outcast,

or harlot must be too vile and degraded to receive
the warm clasp of my hand and the hearty utterance
of my good-will. Am I equal to it?" Gilbert buried
his head in his hands with a sob that was wrung from
the consciousness of a lifelong sacrifice. Margaret
knelt beside his chair and softly slipped an arm around
his neck.

"A second Jean Valjean!" she whispered.

"It is at most an experiment," said Gilbert later,
"and even in the event of failure must do more good
than harm. I will try it."

The loss of Elsie's abundant wages had been a trying matter to the little household. Gilbert's attendance at the manual-training school had been perforce
curtailed, and the question of subsistence became a
serious one. Herbert had begged to be allowed to
supply their needs, since his indiscretion had been the
cause of their loss, but the ingrained independence of
both sisters rebelled at the suggestion.

"No," exclaimed Elsie emphatically, "not until I
say 'yes' at the altar—and that day is still so remote
as to be almost nebulous—shall I permit any expendi-
ture of your money on my behalf."

"Not even for this?" and Herbert drew from his
pocket a small velvet case and flashed a brilliant diamond ring before Elsie's eyes. She took it, flushing
with pleasure over its beauty, and held it up over her
head to watch the play of translucent light on its polished surface.

"Oh, what beautiful things God makes in His labor-
atory!" she cried, "and how I do love beauty! But

take it back, Herbert; it would be out of place on the hand of a working girl."

" I'm tempted to quarrel with you all the time," said Herbert petulantly. " What shall I get you—an iron ring ?"

"'You might have it silver-plated," suggested Elsie soberly, " so that, like the majority of my sex, I would not know it was iron until after marriage."

" You are incorrigible! But what are you going to do with yourself, anyway, while you are waiting for that haughty sister of mine to come under my soothing ministrations ? "

" Something new—work!"

" At what ? "

" Slop-work, like Margaret. I've already bought a new sewing-machine—on part payments, of course— and I am going to break the record on hickory shirts and blue jeans overalls."

"Absurd! quixotic! outrageous!" exclaimed Herbert, springing to his feet and pacing the room with an excited air. "I tell you, Elsie, you and Margaret will kill yourselves in endeavoring to uphold the dignity of woman or labor or some other foolish notion."

" Herbert!" Elsie's eyes flashed ominously. " If the whole world were like you—Supreme Sultans of Gilded Leisure—you might make your uncomplimentary classifications; but under existing conditions, I think—well, I think you ought to be ashamed of yourself; so there!"

" I am," said Herbert contritely, as he took her in his arms. " I don't in the least question the nobility of

motive that inspires all this heroism, but I do question
its result.   Do you think the fate of the world is hang-
ing on the struggles of two such admittedly unselfish
and uplifted slips of girls?"

"You're just like the old heathen masters of morality!" ejaculated Elsie.   "They gave such excellent
rules for other men's guidance, but they hadn't the
courage to try their arguments on themselves.   Of
course Margaret and I are *very* heroic in trying to live
up to our principles—but *very* silly!"

Herbert's laugh was so contagious that even Elsie
joined in it.

"I am afraid I'm a heathen," he said dubiously, "if
in this day and age, when the air is blue with reforms,
I object to seeing the girl I love wearing her life away
for a mere chimera."

"Herbert Lynn!" exclaimed Elsie impetuously as
she drew away from his embrace and looked him earnestly in the face.   "Do you look upon the question
of the day, the question that occupies all tongues and
speaks a heart-rending language in every half-starved
wretch that walks the street, as a chimera?"

"It is a phantom that has been chased a good many
thousand years," he answered, "and the end is not
yet."

"Have you no interest in the question?"

"Specifically, yes; generally, no."

"Then you have no heart!" exclaimed Elsie warmly.

"I confess that it has left me and is in the keeping
of a fierce little radical."

"Who wishes your judgment was with it, for I think

such conservatism as yours is dangerous and—yes, positively wicked !"

"You are charming when you wear that look," said Herbert critically.

"Just wait till I find you are as obstinate as you are evasive, and I shall not look so charming. But really I wish you would go away. Do you see that pile of blue jeans? Every moment wasted on you is just so much stolen from my beauty sleep, and of course you care more for that than for any purpose of mine."

"Well, then, if you'll remember that all I shall ask of you at our next meeting will be to look pretty and talk nonsense I'll go." Suiting the action to the word, he left the room.

"Elsie," he called a moment later as he put his head in the open door, "may I send you a violet if it's a very small and stingy one?"

Herbert dodged just in time to escape the pin-cushion Elsie threw at his head, but the supper-table that night was graced with a generous bouquet of Parmesan violets, and they nestled lovingly in Elsie's dark locks, under her plump chin, and in the cincture of her slender waist.

CHAPTER XX.

FOR some weeks Gilbert had been perfecting a number of handsomely finished medicine cabinets (which were furnished with racks for bottles and drawers for boxes, sponges, and all the various healing paraphernalia which every well-regulated household keeps at hand for emergencies), and now that the question of subsistence was so seriously confronting them once more, he determined to canvass from house to house and endeavor to sell them. Knowing that the homes of the rich would be closed against him, he could only hope to gain access to those of the middle and poorer classes, among whom he meant to provoke what thought and inquiry he could regarding the establishment of a society of universal brotherhood. Beyond the five great principles enunciated by the eloquent clergyman, all ideas were as yet in a nebulous state. Having established the fact of a desire for the proposed reform, the three instigators—for Elsie was already heart and hand in the projected work—believed that wisdom would be given them for the rounding and perfecting of details. "There is one thing to be remembered," said Margaret, "that to-day no less than yesterday a tree is known by its fruit, and love to God can only be reached in the minds of the oppressed through love to man. First prove to men that

17

you love their souls because you love the God that created them, and you will then be able to convey to them some of the greater truths of a divine and spiritual love."

"Is not that material doctrine?" asked Elsie.

"No, I do not think so. The world has been mystified too long. The plain and simple doctrine of a human, interested, generous love even a child can understand, and God does not despise the day of small things."

"How otherwise can you reach a material nature than by material symbols?" asked Gilbert.

"Even as a child learns to rely upon love and gradually reaches back to the motive and inspiration of that love, so back of this earthly brotherhood men will come to see the radiance and truth of divinity overshadowing it."

"Ah, if mankind can only be made to look at it in that light! But what are we going to do, Gilbert, in this new order with the besotted and brutish natures that live only for self?"

"Give them all the personal friendliness we can and help them to outgrow their evil natures."

"It will take generations of refining influences to do that, I am afraid. So much clings to the flesh that is bred in the bone."

"True; but we are to-day only small factors in the great scheme of human civilization. What we leave unfinished other hands may take up. In any event, whether of failure or success, we three, weird fates maybe," said Gilbert with a smile, " we know that for us happiness lies in doing what we can to lighten the heavy load of oppression and injustice under which our brothers are groaning."

"Amen!" exclaimed Elsie, printing a resounding kiss upon Gilbert's cheek. "You look like another Savonarola, only a trifle handsomer, I must admit."

"Give me the inspiration of his genius and the force of his eloquence, and I'll will you my good looks."

"Thanks! Herbert says I'll do as I am," she exclaimed, drawing herself up to her full height and flushing and dimpling as roguishly as a mischievous child.

"By the way, Elsie, how are you and your millionaire lover going to reconcile the very opposite views you hold on various vital questions?"

Elsie's face grew sober instantly. "I don't like to think about it, Gilbert. I'm so happy now that I'm only waiting. Perhaps—some time—God knows!" and tears routed the smiles on the volatile face.

"There! don't worry about it," said Gilbert. "He's a jolly good fellow, anyhow, and we wouldn't be any worse than a number of well-known personages of history if we let conscience succumb to the narcotizing influence of his pieces of silver."

There was an unusual twinkle in the eyes of the sober Gilbert, which provoked Elsie to say: "Go to, thou reformer! What need hast thou of any man's silver?"

With Elsie's return home, her faculty for turning off work, and her fund of good-humor, the circumference of the Busy Fingers Club was constantly increasing.

Now that Gilbert was away so much, she took his place at the bench on the Saturdays allotted to the Club, and if she did not exhibit his dexterity in direct-ing and executing work, she yet preserved order and made fast friends of the boys under her charge. She was so fertile in suggestion that a good many new ideas took shape in inventive heads and found expres-sion in beautiful and useful things in wood. "Some day," said Elsie sagely, "we'll have a bazaar and sell these things, and oh, won't we be rich!"

"What'll we do with our money?" cried the boys.

"Put it in the bank until we can find some great and glorious need for it."

"Like buying me a bicycle!" shouted one of the lads.

"And me a base-ball outfit!"

"And me a fiddle!"

"And me a musical top!"

"And me a white elephant!" cried Elsie. But the laugh did not rout the idea of doing something in the way of a bazaar. It spread among the girls and in-cited them to renewed effort; and it grew to be an open secret in the neighborhood that in the glowing but indefinite sometime, great things were to be achieved by the now well-known Busy Fingers Club.

It was the last of November and Antoine had re-turned from the hospital, able to walk with the aid of one crutch and the promise of discarding that when exercise and development had perfected the cure. A happier woman than Lizzette Minaud seldom walked the earth. All her dreams and anticipations of good fortune seemed to be winging their way to realization. Antoine was getting well; for now that the lad had been lifted to his full stature, the deformed shoulders seemed to be straightening, the color came and went in the once pale cheeks, and the laughter in his heart made a constant music for her.

"Oh, eet ees all von blessed Providence, mon Herbeart," she cried as he sat at her right hand, the honored guest at the little banquet she had prepared at Idlewild to welcome Antoine's home-coming. "Surely le bon Dieu direct ze noble heart to help my boy, and——"

"Fall in love with Elsie," suggested Herbert, who felt a little fearful of a lachrymose scene in which he might be called upon to play actor.

"Certainement!" laughed Lizzette. "Eet ees ze match made in heaven."

"Occasional sulphurous fumes about it when I scold, eh, Herbert?" cried Elsie.

"Oh, just enough as yet to light the flame of a ready wit. Whether there'll ever be any greater combustion remains to be seen."

"Well, I couldn't be any happier over it if I stood in Herbert's place," ejaculated Antoine, which grave announcement, in view of his twelve years of maturity, was met with marked hilarity by the little circle. "And I'm sure," added Antoine, in no way abashed, "if Herbert is never blown up until Elsie lights the fuse he'll walk the earth a good while; for I don't believe she knows how to scold."

"Antoine, my lad, six months of seclusion have

made you singularly trustful. Elsie has scolded me ever since I knew her, and I've grown so used to it in the last few weeks that I regard it in the light of a tonic—like quinine or any other excellent bitter."

"Antoine," said Elsie in a stage whisper, "have you noticed how improved in health and appearance our mutual friend Mr. Lynn seems to be? It is all the result of the exercise induced by trying to ward off some home truths I've been thrusting at him."

"Ze fumes of sulphur!" cried Lizzette. "I protest zey rise no higher. I fear ze combustion."

"They are a somewhat singular pair of lovers," interposed Margaret. "It is a rare thing when they are not sparring, but as they seem to enjoy it and Herbert has not yet asked for a body-guard, I seldom interpose an objection."

"Which, in view of the young man's unprotected situation, is very considerate of you," said Elsie with a defiant toss of her head. "It is my opinion, however, that there are more entertaining themes than the peculiarities of a couple of commonplace individuals. Mr. Lynn, will you please give us a lecture on good manners?"

"I shall be most happy to do so when my audience narrows to one listener."

"And he is before the mirror," retorted Elsie.

"Hush!" said Antoine; "stop that quarrelling! I'm going to sing." And closing his eyes and crossing his hands before him, he began to croon, in well-portrayed negro accent and intonation, the lines of a little dialect song:

" De way is dark an' rough an' long,
    Go slow, hol' hard, chillun !
Doan't git too deep in de slew ob wrong,
    Go slow, hol' hard, chillun !

" Dey's cross-roads heah an' cross-roads dar,
    Go slow, hol' hard, chillun !
But hope is de sign-board shinin' like a star,
    Go slow, hol' hard, chillun !

" Jes' keep a-joggin' tru' de san' an' clay,
    Go slow, hol' hard, chillun !
Dar's lub at de eend ob de 'arthly way,
    Go slow, hol' hard, chillun !

" De eyes some time mighty full ob teahs,
    Go slow, hol' hard, chillun !
But lub is de lawd ob de slabe ob feahs,
    Go slow, hol' hard, chillun !

" So jes' keep smilin' in de face ob woe,
    Go slow, hol' hard, chillun !
Dar's a happy lan' whar de good shall go,
    Go slow, hol' hard, chillun !"

The clear soprano voice rolled out the words and notes with the abandon of his Ethiopian prototype, and Elsie turned and laid an arm around the lad's neck as she exclaimed: "Antoine Minaud! Where in the world did you find that song?"

"In here," said Antoine, significantly tapping his temple.

"An improvisator!" cried Elsie ecstatically. "Herbert, we're in the presence of genius."

"So I perceive. Where did you discover the faculty, Antoine?"

"At the hospital."

"Can you improvise instantly?"

"Give me a theme and see."

"Well, take my lady's eyes," said Herbert with a low bow to Elsie.

"Her nose rather! That would be more in keeping," retorted Elsie.

"All right," laughed Antoine, and scarcely a moment later he was carolling a rollicking Irish jig to words that seemed to follow the tune as if they had been fitted with the utmost carefulness.

> "My lady's nose—
>   You wouldn't suppose
> A poet could rave about it,
>   But as it lies
>   Between her eyes,
> She wouldn't look well without it!
>
> "An 'ornery' nose
>   Can smell a rose,
> But hers has more to do, sir!
>   It scornful tips
>   Above her lips,
> At follies she finds in you, sir!"

"Bravo, Antoine!" cried Elsie, jumping up and bringing his violin. "Now play it."

And as the violin dashed into the abandon of the melody, she grasped Gilbert by the shoulders and the two went whirling off into a jig.

"That's inspiring," cried Herbert, catching up Lizzette and dashing after them. The dishes rattled, the pictures shook, the stove trembled, the floors creaked, but on they danced, madder and merrier as the violin actually shrieked in glee, until Margaret cried aghast:

"Ho! 'Tom the Piper's Son!' Stop! Stop! I beg. It is a veritable witches' dance."

"Come on, my solemn sister," and Elsie caught

Margaret around the waist and dragged her into the merry scramble.

"My poor old bones!" cried Lizzette, sinking into a chair. "Antoine's a necromancer! I almost grow young again." The fiddle stopped, but only for a moment, for by a sudden transition it swept away into an old-time melody:

> "Sleep on thy pillow,
>   Happy and light,
> As the moon on the billow
>   Reposes at night."

The old fiddle seemed to have awakened to new life under the touch of the new Antoine, and Herbert could scarcely repress a glow of satisfaction as he looked at the lad. "Specific kindness does vastly more for the world than general good-will. If I might be permitted to spend the better part of my income on this little circle, I should feel that I had done enough for humanity; but the worst part of it is, this little circle has such exalted ideas of independence, and Elsie—bless her and bother her!—shuts the door in my face continually. I don't more than half like the muddle, anyway!"

The winter wore away with but few radical changes. Mrs. Mason's opposition to Herbert's marriage to Elsie showed no diminution, and after numberless and fruitless intercessions on his part he finally took up his quarters at a hotel, and Mrs. Mason closed her house and went to Europe. His sister's opposition and Elsie's persistent refusal to marry him as long as the present bitterness remained between them, kept

Herbert in a constant state of dissatisfaction. The world was quite too much upside down with the conflict of ideas, and men no longer seemed to be permitted to work out their own lines of happiness with out treading on somebody's toes. Helen's sole objection to Elsie had been the capacity in which she had served them, and the consequent fear of society's verdict. He didn't care a bit more for Helen's narrow world, than he did for Elsie's quixotic schemes for a regenerated humanity. He wanted simply to be happy in his own way and according to his highest light. Helen and Elsie had both called him selfish, and both from opposite standpoints. As to the truth of their judgments, he didn't care. He only knew that an overmastering love for Elsie as the sweetest-natured, most piquant, and original woman he had ever met held him fast in an irrevocable bondage, and but for an obstinacy on Elsie's part, as settled as it was difficult to understand, he would have cut the Gordian knot by an immediate marriage and absolute defiance of Helen. Lizzette had been right when she told Herbert he did not know Elsie's nature. It was developing a faculty for self-abnegation that alarmed him. There were times when the sweetest and most sacred love shone in her eyes, and the barriers of restraint were broken down by the utmost sympathy of thought and feeling; at others the spirit of a martyr looked out from their translucent depths and an invisible yet conscious wall seemed to separate them. Herbert trembled in vague alarm whenever he encountered this look, lying but thinly veiled beneath the mobile face. But with a man's blindness he could not see that the love which he arrogated to himself and which shut out the world as of little moment, was only broadening her sympathies and making divine revelations of its beauty and value. Love with all its sacredness and possibilities, holding close to the one dear image enshrined in the holy of holies of her heart, had opened wide its door to suffering mankind. So vividly burned the fire on the altar of her love that she turned as if with out-stretched arms, crying: "O ye who are cold and hungry! Here ye will find warmth and shelter."

It is rarely that a man understands either the motive or development of a love like this, and he is quite apt through ignorance or jealousy to quarrel with any of its various manifestations. To Herbert many of Elsie's ideas on the great and vexed social questions of the day seemed the acme of absurdity, and he cherished the fond hope that when she was once trans-planted to regions of luxurious ease, they would die from inanition. He looked upon them as the natural outgrowth of a circumscribed horizon and constant association with the seamy side of life. "When she sees what art, science, culture, and wealth can do for those she loves, her sympathies will not wander so far, but will narrow down to an area wherein we can walk hand in hand."

Thus Herbert often assured himself as he became daily more conscious of the undercurrent of feeling and belief that was gradually widening in her nature.

The winter had been an unusually long and severe one, and the resources of the little family had often been severely taxed to keep the wolf from the door. Herbert's alert eyes had discovered this fact, and he had taken to leaving sundry packages of groceries and provisions of various kinds in the most unheard-of places, trusting to time to discover them and good sense to appropriate and say nothing Margaret had found them stuffed under the cushions of the chairs, behind pictures, tucked under the book-rack, and impelled by a need sharper than even Elsie had guessed, since into Margaret's hands had been transferred the domestic machinery, had, as Herbert hoped, used them without inquiry. "It is one of God's balances," she said to herself, "that may one day even up. It is a delicate and generous act for which I can only be thankful and keep silent."

To Gilbert the winter had been a revelation of suffering and vice that had only stirred deeper the pool of the living faith within his heart. In his vocation as peddler he had found access to much of the hidden life of poverty and crime which escapes even the most far-sighted general observers. Wherever he had been able to pierce the strata of callousness which the severest forms of poverty invariably create, he had found the same helpless appeal that has for so many generations sounded down the aisles of time—give us something to hope for, believe in, trust in! Something palpable that we can touch, feel, and know. Inquiry as to churches surrounding them usually elicited a shrug of the shoulders and the reply: "They are not for such as me. If I dares to go, they talks about a far-off God that I doesn't understand, and hitches their fine clothes away from me as if my rags would pisen 'em!"

The more that Gilbert came to know the impulses stirring in these benumbed hearts, the more he and Margaret felt the need of establishing a ground of inter-communication between them. To be able to meet these wretched mortals upon their own plane and lead them along, by paths they could understand, up to the great truths of time and eternity, and to make palpable to them that God's love is not a mere abstraction, but a revivifying, humanizing influence—what dearer work could one ask? And yet how was it possible in their straightened circumstances to make even a beginning of this work? Elsie's fertility of resource solved the problem.

" Make the Busy Fingers Club a factor in the case. Let them hold their long-talked-of bazaar, rent the necessary room, and christen the project 'The Children's Home Meeting.' Then let Gilbert go among his poor, tell them of the wonderful violinist and improvisator, Antoine Minaud, and promise them a free concert on some Sunday night. After the concert, have a few moments for social intercourse, in which all four of the principal instigators and abettors in the scheme endeavor to make the acquaintance of those in the room, and then let Gilbert or Margaret give them a few—only a few—of the simple truths of every-day living and learning. It is a very simple beginning," added Elsie dubiously.

"And for that reason the best," said Margaret decidedly.

The members of the little club were enthusiastic abettors of the scheme as outlined to them by Mar-

garet and Elsie. The name which Elsie had so hap-
pily bestowed upon the project instantly won upon
their regard and made them noisy advertisers of their
work throughout the neighborhood. The rooms of a
member occupying the lower floor of the tenement-
house were secured for the use of the bazaar, and
what audience the handiwork of the little folks did
not attract, the music of Antoine's violin succeeded in
catching and holding. Altogether the bazaar was
pronounced a success by its delighted originators, and
at its close there was money enough to pay the rent
of the hall for one night and possibly two. Then
came the work of training the children for the concert.
Elsie took especial care that every song should breathe
the tenderness, the mercy, the helpfulness of divine
love, and the sweet, clear voices of the children, trained
to the subtile sympathy of expression by her innate
appreciation, made many of the songs long to be remembered.

It was a curious and motley throng that assem-
bled in the hall one Sunday night in response to Gilbert's invitation, as he stood at the door and took
every comer by the hand. Women with shawls over
their heads, with babies asleep on their breasts, men
with hats pulled low over eyes that cast furtive glances
of unrest and suspicion, brazen-faced and gaudily-
dressed creatures with their calling stamped upon their
countenances, ragged and barefooted children, pale-
faced and distorted cripples, came slowly and half-
reluctantly into the room. It was something so new,
so unlike anything they had ever been offered, that

they were more than half afraid it was a trap, and
that it would end in their being preached at, told how
vile they were, and warned to flee from the wrath of
an angry and a jealous God. They had heard these
words so many times and had felt, deep within dis-
quieted and tumultuous bosoms, the wide gulf between
the prosperous promulgators of the church and their
own degraded and unhappy condition. Yet somehow
they all trusted Gilbert; there was something in the
clear, earnest, boyish face that won the most suspi-
cious nature, and it was because they had felt that he
was truly their friend that they had ventured to come.
The hall was a barren, smoke-begrimed, illy-ventilated
room, but Elsie and the children had made what effort
they could with meagreness of material to brighten it
up. Above the platform, where stood Elsie's organ
and where the semicircle of children was ranged,
those in the audience who could read beheld in large
letters, "Whatsoever ye would that men should do to
you, do ye even so unto them." Over the windows
hung gay cotton banners bearing such inscriptions as
"Love is lord of all." "A cup of cold water to the
thirsty." "A kind word maketh the heart glad." "A
true heart is one of earth's jewels." "A little child
shall lead them."

Antoine's violin caught the inspiration of the hour
and spoke in almost human tones the pathos, the
prayer, and the hope of each bosom. The airs were
those of simple, well-known hymns, many of them so
familiar as to be almost household words, and when
in response to Gilbert's invitation the audience arose

and sang the choruses, there were not many lips that
remained motionless.   They had doubtless heretofore
been hummed many times by the same careless, unthinking voices; now they seemed to strike deep into
some inner fibre of feeling, and many a furtive tear
rolled from beneath quivering and down-cast lashes.
The children sang, as Elsie declared, "like little
angels;" but the crowning event of the evening was
Antoine's improvisation.   Advancing to the center of
the platform on his one crutch, he began in a low,
plaintive, and touchingly-sweet voice:

"My heart is sair wi' muckle woe,
   God knows! God knows!
I ken nae mair the way to go,
      God knows!

"My feet are cut, my shoon are gane,
   God knows! God knows!
And every step is hurt wi' pain,
      God knows!

"Nae light is roun' aboot my way,
   God knows! God knows!
I canna see the sun of day,
      God knows!

I faint and fall in sairest need,
   God knows! God knows!
And men go by wi' little heed,
      God knows!

"Sae little costs the kindly word,
   God knows! God knows!
Sae sad it is sae seldom heard,
      God knows!

"Sae bitter is the thirsting lip,
   God knows! God knows!
Some time mayhap love's cup we'll sip,
      God knows!"

Before Antoine had finished, men and women were rocking back and forth and sobbing like children, and when the last strains of the song died away, it seemed minutes before any one spoke, and then a woman, who an hour before had entered the room with a brazen face and a foul-mouthed ejaculation, cried out in heart-broken tones: "Oh, sing it again—God knows! God knows!"

Softly, as if taken up and echoed by angel voices, Antoine sang once more the last stanza, and before the lingering notes were lost on the air, he was at the woman's side clasping her hand in his.

Instantly Gilbert, with Margaret and Elsie on either side and Lizzette and the children following, left the platform to mingle with and take the hands of those present. They passed among them with words of cheer and good-will, and when order was again called, there was an unmistakable look of eager expectancy upon the faces that was balm to the watchful eyes of Margaret and Gilbert. Advancing to the front of the platform, the latter said simply:

"My friends: I am glad you trusted me sufficiently to come here to-night. We hope to have many more such nights together, and I only ask you in going away to remember that, sad as is the pathway of life for many of us, there is light ahead. The soul of man through which God seeks to work the salvation of the world is not dead but sleepeth. Slowly it is awaking, and love that abides in the world shall some time teach men that its universal practice must be "Whatsoever ye would that men should do to you, do ye even so unto them.'"

18

CHAPTER XXI.

As the winter grew into early spring, the fame of the Children's Home Meetings spread so rapidly that a larger audience-room became an imperative necessity. The churches began to inquire into the matter, and Margaret and Gilbert were beset with questions as to their creed and purpose. To all such they gave answer, "Our only creed is love, and our only purpose to help each other."

"Too vague and indefinite; the structure will fall for lack of proper support. You ought at least to have a set of rules."

"So we have," replied Margaret, "but they spring from the need of the hour. We have order at our meetings because even disorderly natures find that to keep the peace best subserves the interest they feel in the all-pervading friendship we are seeking to establish. Beyond this we keep in sight, although not obtrusively, the axiom, if such it may be called, that the interest of one is the interest of all, and transversely, that the interest of all is the interest of one. When these simple truths have become the bone and sinew of belief and practice, then we may go a few steps farther as the way opens and light dawns."

"You must have an ultimate line of procedure

marked out—some plan as to its religious aspect, have you not ?"

"We teach no so-called system of theology. Since atheists, infidels, deists, and trinitarians all meet upon the common ground that the civilized world has never beheld a grander epitome of what is called 'living' than that afforded by Jesus of Nazareth, we are content to forego modern complications of creeds and isms and establish among ourselves the fundamental truths taught by Jesus and, better yet, practised by Him. In doing this we think we shall better both man's desires and surroundings. This idea, carried to its logical conclusion, is so far-reaching that inequalities of opportunity will fall away as if by magic and the now unceasing mutterings of discontent and strife will be one day relegated to a past age of unconscionable greed and injustice."

"The church has been striving to accomplish this for eighteen hundred years. How can you expect, with no trained organization, to reach so beatific a state of society ?"

"Because we shall not do as the church does and partition the goats from the sheep. We shall practice no exclusion, no worship of mammon, and shall acknowledge no caste except that of heart and brain. Personally I do not look beyond the good of the present hour; if that is rightfully spent the future will take care of itself. Indeed, our effort is much like guiding the first steps of the child; development must come with years and growth."

"Well, you have a good motive and are an earnest

advocate. We shall watch your progress with interest and wish you God-speed."

These words were but a type of the interest the movement aroused among cultured and progressive thinkers who came to watch and listen and went away to ponder. Margaret and Gilbert, ever watchful of the trend of current thought, smiled hopefully at each other when, in the columns of their daily paper, they read the announcement of sermons on such topics as " The Era of Religious Harmony: What Signs of its Approach? What can we do to Hasten it?' " The Co-operative Principle in Morals." " The Ethics of the Eight-hour Movement." " Religious Communism."

" The way is clearing for us," said Margaret eagerly. " Thought is awake and we are only followers in the march of progress; we are not even forerunners."

"And yet we are looked upon with suspicion by a great many well-meaning people. The conservative element in the church regards our ideas as subversive and dangerous."

" So thought the money-changers in the temple when Jesus drove them out. What are we attempting to do, indeed, but re-establish the line of faith on which the church has built itself? And if in doing this we brush some of our plebeian, homespun ideas against a shocked silken-coated aristocratic culture, we may advance the price of homespun in the market, if nothing more. I am not afraid for our cause, since it is identical with everlasting truth."

" Yes, and walks hand in hand with the heart-hun-

- gry and soul-begging mortal! Margaret, every time
I stretch out my hand to one who has need of a
friend, I feel that the grandeur of that *Life* which is
enthroned in my conscience and teaches me to aspire
to the highest development, is something infinitely
greater than the same truth could have been as a mere
abstraction. Jesus, the Nazarene, a man among men,
makes possible all that is highest in human endeavor.
A philosophy as old as the earliest time and as fundamentally true as God himself, that 'Nobility arises
from individual virtue and not from Abraham's blood,'
and which Jesus made so potent when He walked the
earth, needs now, as then, apostles who fear not to
preach the truth. It underlies in all its simplicity
every system of religion and statecraft, and yet it is
ignored, brow-beaten, trampled under foot, and sneered
at by those who seek power at the expense of all that
is noblest in man. Oh, had I a thousand tongues I
could not hurl these old truths at the world fast
enough!"

Flushed and tremulous with feeling, Gilbert walked
up and down the room, pouring out the flood of ideas
which his work called into activity.

"Social well-being, industrial thrift, active con-
sciences—let us place these in the corner-stone of the
new structure. Religion has been 'set apart' too
long; so long, indeed, that within its doors have crept
the monsters of greed, gold-worship, and place-hunting, until its higher and holier meanings have been
well-nigh crowded out. What, indeed, does man want
of a religion that does not permeate every hope, de-

sire, and action of life? We must bring it down from its idealized height and make it common as the air we breathe and the bread we eat. Then indeed may man, glancing upward, behold the dawn of a new and happier day!"

It was a day or two later that Herbert and Elsie were at the organ trying a new piece of music, which accidentally slipping from its rack fell behind the organ as it stood diagonally across the room. In rolling the organ out Elsie discovered a market basket full of groceries hidden in the corner.

"Where in the world did that basket come from, and what a strange place to put it!" cried Elsie in amazement. As she glanced at Herbert his flushed, uneasy face told the whole story.

"I am exceedingly obliged to your estimate of us as objects of charity!" she exclaimed, placing the basket in the middle of the room, and standing over it with the air of a queen of tragedy.

Herbert could not forbear a laugh, and there was a trifle of malice in the tone with which he said: "It seems to me there is a striking conflict of ideas between the democracy you preach and practice at the Children's Home Meetings I hear so much about, and the aristocracy of pride you practice at home and toward those whom you ought to trust."

Elsie winced under the home thrust, and with the quickness with which she could judge herself, answered contritely: "I know I am proud, Herbert; but I think it is an honorable pride. At least so I have always considered pride of character, and it always *did* hurt when anything struck at my independence. It isn't as if I were sick, or incapable, or——"

"Exhibited a proper humility of spirit, instead of an obstinate and irritating pride," interrupted Herbert.

"Am I irritating?" asked Elsie simply. "In what way?"

"In ever so many ways," answered Herbert, evidently bent on fault-finding. "I seem to count but a cipher in your estimation beside some of these over-mastering ideas of yours. If I exhibit a generous motive toward you, you smother it——"

"In kisses," she cried, throwing her arms around his neck and proceeding to stop further explanation. "Herbert Lynn," she added, drawing a long breath after the bit of violent exercise above recorded, "you're a most ungrateful man! Now don't bluster, for it won't do one bit of good. I'm going to tell you something new. I love you more than any man in the world—that is, any I've met so far! Keep still! and I'm going to do an exceedingly generous action; I'm going to keep the groceries, and drop you a courtesy of the properly humble kind, and say, 'Thank you kindly, sir! May heaven's blessings shower——' Why, what is the matter? You won't even wait for the proper ending of the performance."

Herbert shook himself loose from her detaining arm and walked to the window with a highly-offended air.

The laugh on Elsie's lips and in her eyes died away, and after a moment's pondering she followed him and said penitently: "Forgive me, Herbert; you know I love you more than——"

"What?" asked Herbert suspiciously.

"Money," said Elsie sententiously.

"Bah!" exclaimed Herbert, angrily.

"Be calm, my friend! Now look me squarely in the eyes and behold your image reflected there as—I'm in earnest now—truly it is engraven on my heart, never to be erased as long as I live."

Herbert's reply was that speech of silence so eloquent to the ears of all lovers, and for the time being it bridged over the tide of their differences.

"Herbert," said Elsie, when the silence had been effectively disposed of, "why do you never come to the Children's Home Meetings?"

"In the first place, because I've never been asked, and in the second place, I'm not altogether in sympathy with the movement."

A sudden pang shot through Elsie's heart. "Please explain," she said quietly.

"Well, probably my reasons are selfish and personal. I believe you know that I am somewhat generous at heart, that I am in the main humanity's well-wisher, and that I am ever ready to relieve a specific case of distress; but I do not feel as if I wanted the girl who is to be my wife hand in glove with the riff-raff of society."

"The riff-raff of society!" repeated Elsie wonderingly. "Who are they? How am I hand in glove with them?"

"Well, from what I hear," answered Herbert uneasily, "you not only talk the gospel of love in its broadest sense to women of the vilest stamp, but you take their hands when it is pollution to touch them, you sit beside them and try to teach them truths they are too dulled and besotted to learn, and while you are, I must admit, an angel of light, you are but a mock for their vile tongues, and make, I fear, only questionable progress."

"Go on," said Elsie faintly as Herbert paused.

"There is a spirit of unrest and dissatisfaction abroad which I think your efforts will do much to incite instead of quell. I do not question your motives, but I do question your methods. Let them alone, Elsie, darling, and be content to shine at the hearth-stone of those who love you. Intensify your light for me, instead of diffusing it until it is as thin and almost as cold as moonshine."

There was no fire of playful fancy in the eyes that met Herbert's as Elsie raised her head from his shoulder. He started as he saw the dull, cold hopelessness beneath the heavily-fringed eyelids.

"O Herbert! Herbert!" she cried despairingly. "Why do you ask this? Why did you ever learn to love me? I told you it was a mistake! I am one of these common people whom you despise. I can no more shut out my aspirations, hopes, dreams, and efforts for them than I can cut off my right hand. I have fed on these thoughts until they have become bone and sinew. You knew us, you knew our methods —why, oh, why did you learn to love me?"

"For the very reason that you are not one of the common people. I have, I think, told you several times before that I am not so blind I cannot tell a jewel regardless of its environment. I loved you de-

spite education, surroundings, social pride, everything.
I swept away every obstacle to call you mine, and I
care nothing for the world's verdict.   I only want you
for myself, queen of my heart and home, adored as its
sovereign light, surrounded by all that the eye delights
in or the heart can ask."

"No, not all," said Elsie quietly.

"What else?" asked Herbert eagerly.   "You shall
have everything that love or wealth can procure."

"Can they buy a quiet conscience?"

Herbert shrank back.   "I think you exaggerate the
matter," he said hastily.   "I cannot see that the conscience is called into question."

"I can," said Elsie decidedly.   "I had a heritage
left me, here," and she placed her hand upon her breast
as she spoke, "and daily and hourly it tells me that if
I selfishly lock up my God-given sympathies and turn
away from the impulses of my better nature, I am
committing a crime whose punishment is no less
severe because eternity shall judge it."

"Elsie! Elsie!" cried Herbert, awed into a great fear
by the solemnity of her words, "you shall be the
dispenser of charity as bounteous as you desire."

"And yet be forbidden to soil my hands by contact
with poverty or crime.   No, we have too much of that
sort of charity already.   Besides, do you not see, Herbert, that there could be no happiness for us holding
such opposite views as we do?   Marriage is too holy
to admit a division of sentiment and endeavor between
husband and wife.   Ah, I have been so weak to permit a love that I knew could only bring disaster!"

"It is only a few moments ago that you assured me you loved me for all time."

"I do."

"And yet you can throw me over for a disordered society that never will appreciate an iota of your sacrifice."

"You are mistaken! The sacrifice appeases a deeper and holier feeling."

"You have a very strange way of reasoning, it seems to me," said Herbert bitterly. "You rob Peter to pay Paul with surprising alacrity."

The look that Elsie turned upon him was so filled with agony that he cried remorsefully as he caught her hand and endeavored to draw her toward him: "Forgive me, Elsie, darling! I am not worthy of your love, I know; but I hunger so for it—I can't give it up!"

Elsie drew back with the despairing cry, "We are so wide apart, Herbert."

"We needn't be if you would trust more to me and less to that hypersensitive soul of yours."

A look of scorn not usual to Elsie's face met Herbert's appealing gaze. She rose to her feet and stood stiffly before him.

"You are centuries too late. My hypersensitive soul has a right to its own distinct existence. Your prescience should have told you how little I could strike palms with you in utter self-annihilation."

A faint smile crossed Herbert's face at Elsie's grandiloquent words and air, but it died quickly away as she swept haughtily from the room and would not

come back, though he called her repeatedly. Angrily
he snatched his hat and left the house. Abused, insulted, hurt, misunderstood, he felt himself to be, and
the more he reviewed the situation the more he felt
that Elsie's obstinacy, as he termed it, had raised an
impassible barrier between them. Still his heart would
not be stifled, and it was not till after dispatching a
note to her and despairingly reading her answer—that
marriage between people so distinctly at variance could
never bring happiness—that he wholly lost hope. It
was but the work of a few hours to make arrange-
ments to join his sister abroad. At the last moment
he dispatched a note to Elsie containing these words:
" I have placed the sum of five thousand dollars in the
C—— National Bank, subject to your call. If you
love me as devotedly as I can assure you I shall ever
cherish your memory, you cannot do less than make me
happy by using it. You owe me this small recompense for the suffering that will be mine to the day of
my death."

CHAPTER XXII.

To Margaret alone Elsie opened the flood-gates of
her heart, and it was only after days of overwhelming
grief that she could again take up the burden of life.
Margaret's tears of sisterly sympathy and words of
counsel could not at first still the torrent of heart-
broken tears with which she mourned her lost love.
Not even Herbert had known how precious it had been
to her—how everything high and holy had seemed to
be the offspring of that vitalizing force in her heart.
Now, because having lived up to its highest revelations and endeavored to be true to its holiest purposes, she had crossed a counter-current of thought
and will, this love had been taken from her. Had she
been wrong, opinionated, obstinate, as Herbert called
her? Had she forgotten the sweet submission of the
weaker unto the stronger in that natural order of divine and human love which popular clamor voices as
the proper sphere of woman? Often as she asked herself these questions—and with the not unnatural hope
of finding herself in the wrong, since her heart prompted
the slave-like humility of a perfect love—just so often
conscience answered, "No!" Stronger still, as she
reasoned, grew the feeling that her soul had a right to
its own individuality, and that whatever it cost her,
she had no right to bind its wings, even though the

fetters were silken and lightly held by the hand of
love. Neither Margaret, Lizzette, Antoine, nor Gilbert
dared offer a verbal sympathy to the sore heart behind
the white, set face that confronted them when Elsie
had fought her battle alone. The sparkle was irre-
trievably gone from the dark eyes, and the curved lips
drooped pitifully at times; but in all the earnestness
of purpose, the kindliness of spirit, she was still the
same Elsie.

The work of the Children's Home Meetings grew
almost hourly under her efforts; for now that she had
sacrificed her heart on the altar of this work, she meant
to make the sacrifice acceptable in its good results.
Every hour that she and Margaret could snatch from
the demands of their daily work, they spent in forming
what they called "Conscience Classes." The system of
ethics taught was as simple as the minds with which
they came in contact, and bore the stamp of the ever-
living truth. The magnetic presence of the four chief
workers grew to be a living delight to all who came
from motives of curiosity or interest within its circle.
Beginning at first only with what Herbert had been
pleased to term "the riff-raff of society," the circumference of the circle had gradually widened until a
better-educated and more self-respecting class had
found its way among them. Yet even with intelligence gaining upon them, the one great need of basing
all reform, all happiness, all prosperity upon the code
of ethics which, while it demands the highest development of the individual, yet takes its inspiration from
the thought of a common welfare, was never lost sight

of. Earnestness is the great lever of the world, and while there were many to oppose the idea as of disproportionate value to the need and development of the times, the effort still found many adherents. To be called cranks, laughed at by unbelievers, and derided by the class for which nothing is holy but success, came to be, as Elsie said, "normal as the air they breathed;" but after the first sharp sting these shafts remained unnoticed, and the one or two perishing ones uplifted, helped into the light and warmed by the sunshine of human kindliness into a knowledge of the great inspirer of their work, was balm enough to heal all the wounds of a scoffing world.

Margaret had also formed a Mother's Class, in which everything pertaining to motherhood and its duties, was thoughtfully discussed. This class came in time to be presided over by Mrs. Carson, who, partially recovered, found no greater delight than in seconding the good work which had saved her in her hour of need. The Daughters of the Carpenter was a class headed by Elsie and especially devoted to helpfulness wherever it was needed. A list of the regular attendants of the meeting was kept, and if a mother was found to be sick or overworked, some one of the Daughters was appointed to render the needed assistance. Among the men and elder boys Gilbert formed a reading class, in which history and the science of government were brought down to the comprehension of the illiterate, and men were shown that if they were dissatisfied with existing social conditions, the remedy lay in their own hands in a rightful use of the ballot, and that if they sold that ballot to a ring or combination they only forged new links in the chains that bound them to a slavery against which they were constantly rebelling. Nor were the children forgotten in this work. Every original "Busy Fingers" boy and girl had a new class, in which were resown the good seeds implanted by Margaret and Gilbert. Thought and action were growing slowly but surely in the little community; but already a serious question was confronting them. The rental of the hall had easily been effected by the subscription of a few cents from every regular attendant; but the work, especially among the mothers' and children's classes, required money to prosecute it. They were all poor, living from hand to mouth, and while the work was growing there was no money to help the growth.

"O Margaret," moaned Elsie, "if the money Herbert left me had only been left to our beloved work, how gladly I would use it! Now, knowing how he feels about it, I can never touch it."

It was nearing midsummer, and the work among their members was increasing fast, by reason of sickness brought on by living in noisome atmospheres and without proper food and care. Gilbert had come home from his daily rounds one evening, the most of his cases unsold, and with an unusual dejection of face and manner.

"I am comfortless," he said, "for lack of the dross of earth. I have seen such realization of human suffering to-day without the power to alleviate that I am in despair. I gained admittance to one room, where a mother and her new-born babe lay dead for lack of care, while a couple of little ones were begging her to give them something to eat. I had but ten cents in my pocket that I had saved for street car-fare; but I rushed out, got the children some buns, and aroused the other inmates of the house, who were themselves too poor to do more than care for the children temporarily, while I called in the authorities and had the body disposed of in the potter's field. How are we going to make this work of ours reach such cases without money? I shall have to go begging to-morrow. I had hoped that our work would so speak for itself that we would not need to beg; but to-morrow I must endeavor to start a fund of some kind."

As Gilbert ceased speaking, the open door was darkened by the form of a tall, handsome woman dressed in deep mourning, whom Elsie at once recognized as Alice Houghton. She turned with outstretched hand to Elsie. "There is no need of introducing myself to you," she said, smiling, "but as I came to see your sister, will you make me known to her, and your brother also?"

The introductions over, Miss Houghton at once entered upon the object of her visit. "I have come to you, Miss Murchison, for help. I have recently been sadly bereaved in the loss of one I loved, and life has very nearly lost its charms for me. I have been hearing a good deal of your work lately, and I want you to teach me to find forgetfulness in what is evidently very great happiness to you."

"Do you mean that you wish to become one of us?"

19

"That is my meaning. I shall gladly be your ser
vant in any work you may have for me."

"To have a servant would be something new in my
experience," said Margaret, smiling; "but we shall all
be glad of help. Have you any knowledge of our
work? It is not agreeable only from one standpoint.
There isn't the least æstheticism, superficially speaking, about it."

"I do not believe I shall be afraid to try it. I know
you three alone, unaided, without money or friends,
have been doing a work that is already forcing its way
into notice by reason of its unselfishness. I have
money, much beyond my needs, and as I learn of the
help you have given to many sufferers, I feel sure that
I can abet your efforts, with money if not judgment."

Elsie sprang from her chair and impulsively held out
her hand to Miss Houghton. "We have such need of
money," she cried, "and you seem like a providence of
God."

"You are more willing to accept money from me
now than you were once before," laughed Miss Houghton."

"That was unearned; this is for the bettering of
God's poor."

"Your pride struck me as strange then. I understand it better now."

"And appreciate its motive, I hope," said Elsie wistfully.

"Indeed I do, my dear child; and if the pride of the
world had a similar foundation there would not be
such a war of caste as afflicts society to-day."

Fearful from Elsie's flushed face and her knowledge of Helen Mason's opposition to Herbert's marriage that in her last words she had unwittingly trenched upon delicate ground, she slipped an arm around Elsie's waist, saying: "Tell me, my dear, why did you send Herbert away?"

It was a difficult matter for Elsie to summon self-command enough to reply; but with a face from which the color quickly receded she faltered: "We differed so much in our views that there was no reconciling them."

"Then Helen was not wholly responsible?"

"No, she was not responsible at all. Mr. Lynn's education and mine had been from such widely-different standpoints that the wonder is our ideas ever came into conflict. It has always been a mystery to me why Mr. Lynn ever chose to think——"

"It is a wonder," interrupted Alice Houghton dryly as she bent down and kissed Elsie's cheek. "I wouldn't mourn, my dear, for a man who couldn't pocket a few whims to make me happy."

"But you don't know," said Elsie seriously; "it was no whim on my part, for I seemed to belong here to this work. I could not give it up and be happy."

"Ah, well, Herbert Lynn has lost the best of his life, and yet it is only a few months ago that I looked through his spectacles. It is strange how contact with sorrow opens our eyes to the true value of qualities we did not notice before. Elsie, you must let me work beside you, under the guidance of this wise sister of yours, and try to find the same peace you are seeking.

We seem to have met here from widely-different paths. I gave up all for love—you, dear child, gave up love for all humanity, and now we join hands in the same search for the peace that passeth understanding. Will you show me the way, my little girl?"

It needed no words from Elsie, Margaret, or Gilbert to prove how heartily and gladly they welcomed the proffered aid, even as they strove to recompense in some measure the faltering and hungering spirit of their benefactress. With intuitive quickness she became one of them in the earnestness of her efforts, and the line of distinction so often made apparent in the manner of those who seek the welfare of the oppressed was entirely absent. Side by side with Margaret and Elsie she walked among that class of women whose hands Herbert had said it was pollution to touch; but when she saw the glow of appreciation lighting up the dulled, imbruted faces, and heard the wails of penitence from sore hearts, and the promises to gather up the remnants of shattered lives and dedicate them henceforth to righteous living, she felt something of the joy of the Master who thought it no disgrace to eat with publicans and sinners. She was not long in following Gilbert from door to door and inspecting the homes where, Gilbert said, a self-respecting man would be ashamed to house his cattle. The absolute disregard of sanitation in many of these herding places —for they were little else—shamed with a burning blush the boasted nineteenth-century civilization. The names of the owners of these tenement hovels were listed by Alice Houghton and found in the majority

of cases to be those of men of wealth and prom-
inence in the community, who never gave any thought
to their property except as regarded its monthly income.   Ordering her carriage and horses and dressing
herself in her finest raiment, Alice presented herself
at the doors of these men.   Without any preliminaries
she told them of her discoveries, the deplorable condition of their tenants, and begged that something be
done to improve their condition.   Her handsome presence, her dress, equipage, all bespeaking her a person
of consequence, she met with the usual courtesy which
such externals command; but in the majority of cases
she was listened to with that air of constraint betokened by elevated eyebrows and idly drumming fingers.
More than once she was given to understand, sometimes broadly and sometimes indirectly, that she might
better be minding her own business.   For all such she
had a parting shot in saying: " I am preparing for publication in the city press a series of articles on the condition of our poor.   I really hope, sir, I shall not be
compelled to include your name in the list of inhuman
landlords."

The stroke told, and invariably elicited a promise
of looking into the matter, supplemented with at least
some slight attempt at repairs. With Alice Houghton
conspicuous in such work, society became at once
interested.   It might be a delightful fad to investigate
this labor question and exploit one's charity in behalf
of these poor dear creatures.   But whenever this desire was submitted, it met ignominious and instant
death.   Only those who felt the earnestness of the

work were permitted any share in it. It soon became apparent, however, that the latent impulses of human nature, veneered as they may be by false ideas as to wealth and social position, are in the main generous and humane ones. Under the influence of Alice Houghton wealth came to the succor of the newly-formed and still chaotic society. Gilbert's reading class became possessed of a room for its exclusive use, where all the current periodicals and papers and some of the best books could be found and read by any one. It became a sort of poor man's club-room where living topics were discussed, and where twice a year a banquet was given at which the speeches and toasts emanated from the growing minds of those who had risen from the ranks.

The parlors of several well-known society ladies were also thrown open once a week to the orchestra formed by Antoine, but now placed under the tutelage of a more proficient master. The Mother's Class, the Daughters of the Carpenter, and the Busy Fingers Club had each a fund from which to draw in emergencies, and better than all else, it seemed to Gilbert, the five great principles lying back of all these efforts had been submitted to a council and a code of rules drawn up under the general plan, which bade fair to make the society cohesive and enduring. Yet it was by no means free from turbulent elements, nor had it come to its present prosperity without encountering many well-nigh overwhelming obstacles. As long as human nature is content to remain on the low plane of self-indulgence, just so long will every good and unselfish impulse find a bitter warfare waged against it, and not every one of those who were to be most benefited by the movement was in favor of it. There seems to exist in some natures a wolfish opposition to everything high and holy, and Gilbert had long been aware, without in the least understanding the reason, that he had incurred the enmity of one of their number known as "Red Handed Mike." If the fellow possessed any patronymic it had long since passed into oblivion, and he was known only by his sobriquet, and feared accordingly. Gilbert had been warned that Mike was only waiting an opportunity to "make it hot for him"; but thinking the threat, for lack of cause, merely the idle boast of a bully, he passed it unnoticed.

It was the morning of a day in early autumn. Margaret was made glad by the sight of Aunt Liza and Eph, who, climbing to her sky-parlor with many "oh's" and "ah's" and rheumatic squeaks of the joints, had greeted her with the old-time effusion and affection which absence had not dulled.

"I was jes longin' so fer de sight ob your face, Miss Margaret, I couldn't stay away no longer, and Eph heah has been a heap wuss'n me," exclaimed Aunt Liza.

"Sho!" said Eph, fumbling with his hat and trying to hide his feet under the rounds of his chair. "I only jes wanted to tell yer we'uns has done a heap ob savin' this heah summer. Mammy heah's got a new red gown, an' I's got a whole suit of store clothes, and besides, Ma'am Minaud's banked money fo' us, too."

"Well done!" cried Margaret. "I couldn't hear better news."

"I knowed you'd be tickled!" exclaimed Eph, delightedly displaying a couple of rows of ivory teeth. "I done tol' mammy dar wa'n't no use backslidin' in this yere business when all you'uns had got to be jes perfeck angels."

"Angels?" queried Margaret.

"Why, don't yer know we'uns has hearn tell all 'bout de society out to Idlewild? And eberybody done says you'uns is saints and no mistake," exclaimed Aunt Liza.

"Everybody is very kind," said Margaret soberly, "but we are far from saints. We are only trying to find the best side of human nature."

"Yo' done it—yo' done it fo' shuah, Miss Margaret!" exclaimed Eph excitedly. "Yo' jest took us po' trash and made us 'sponsible bein's, and showed us how to be 'spectable if we is brack."

"Deed yo' did, Miss Margaret," chimed in Aunt Liza. "And de bestest part ob it is, as Eph's a-sayin', dar wa'n't no ornery mission 'bout it."

"I's jes been wonderin', Miss Margaret," interrupted Eph, "eber since I hearn 'bout Antoine's singin' and de way de home meetin's is callin' de po' sinners, ef dar's any reason why mammy an' me couldn't come jes once, anyway. It's white folkses' meetin', I know, but I jes like mighty well ter heah some ob Antoine's singin'. Day do say he jes 'lectrify de aujience."

"Come and welcome," said Margaret, who could not forbear a smile at Eph's rendering of popular phraseology. "We have room always for those who are trying to find the way up."

"Deed'n I's so glad, Miss Margaret," said Aunt Liza effusively. "'Pears like sometimes dey's a dreffle prejice 'gainst folks jes cause de Lawd made deir skin brack."

That evening, as Aunt Liza and Eph mounted the stairs of the Home Hall, as it had come to be called, Red Handed Mike stood in the doorway and blurted out as they passed: "We don't want none o' them d——d niggers here. If Brother Gib 'lows 'em to stay I'll break up the meetin'!"

Just then Gilbert, accompanied by his sisters and Alice Houghton, entered the hall.

"Say," called Mike, "do you see them niggers? Goin' to let 'em stay?"

"Certainly," answered Gilbert. "They are friends of ours."

"No, they hain't," growled Mike. "I hain't got no such devilish taste as that."

Gilbert paused for a second, and said quietly as he faced the offender with a steady glance: "I hope your good taste will prevent your making any disturbance."

"Hush, Mike!" "Keep still, for God's sake!" whispered several of his companions as he turned to Gilbert threateningly.

"Never fear, men," said Gilbert reassuringly. "Mike knows this isn't any place for a mill," and without saying anything further he passed on to the platform.

Under the entreaties of his companions the bully sank into a corner and sulkily watched the proceedings. A little later Antoine stepped to the front of the platform and began one of his inimitable improvisations. Catching sight of Eph's interested face in the audience, the impulse to give a song in negro dialect came over him with irresistible force. With scarcely a moment's waiting the clear young voice rang out in a lively carol.

> " What if some troubles yo' do know ?
> Jes doan min' 'em, let 'em go !
> It only makes de bigger hill,
> A-pilin' up ob ebery ill,
>   So jes let trouble go !

> Chorus.

> ' Git a lil' sunshine in yo' heart,
> Whateber grief yo's knowin',
> Git a lil' sunshine in yo' heart,
>   An' set de smiles a-growin'.

> " De stranges' thing is when yo' smile,
> Yo' done forgit yo'sef a while !
> Yo' doan' no mo' remember pain,
> Till yo' forgits to smile again,
>   So jes let trouble go !

Eph s feet had been strangely uneasy during the rendering of the preceding stanzas, and Aunt Liza had pulled at his coat and whispered warningly : "Doan yo' forgit, Eph, dis yere's white folkses' meetin'. Dey doan 'low no shuffle heah."

"Cain't help it, mammy," returned Eph. " It do jes go clar through my toes."

> " Dar's mighty lil' dat we fin'
> Dat's like a nice contented min' ;
> It makes de worl' de fines' place
> To lib dis side ob heabenly grace ;
>   So jes let trouble go !"

> " ' Git a lil' sunshine in yo' heart

"Yes do!" responded Eph fervently.

"'Whateber grief yo's knowin'!'"

"Neber min' it! Neber min' it!" interposed Eph, growing more and more excited.

"'Git a lil' sunshine in yo' heart!'"

"Send it, Lawd! Send it, Lawd!" cried Eph, rocking to and fro, heedless of the wondering glances bestowed upon him and Aunt Liza's frantic clutches at his coat.

"An' set de smiles a-growin',"

sang Antoine's clear voice.

"Yes, Lawd, we needs 'em! 'Deed we does," groaned Eph half-aloud. A wave of applause greeted the singer as he turned to leave the platform. It swelled louder and louder and would not be stilled. In the midst of the excitement Eph half-rose to his feet and called out: "Come back, Antoine, honey! It's jes like hearin' ob de angels sing!"

Only Antoine's instant compliance quelled the rising flood of laughter and hisses. Clasping his hands before him and half drooping on his crutch in the pathetic attitude of old age and decrepitude, Antoine began in a broken voice:

"What ef my face is old an' brack,
 An' hard my han's, an' bent my back,
 An' mos'ly shadows on de way
 Hab followed dis yere form ob clay?
 What ef, despised by brudder man,
 I jes works on de bes' I can,
 An' toilin' airly, toilin' late,
 For arthly joys I's long to wait?

I knows some time dis face ob min'
As white as Jesus' robe will shine,
   For He, oh, He's my Mahstah !

"O Jesus, my Mahstah !
  De frien' ob de poah,
Deah Jesus, my Mahstah,
  Yo' sorrows will cuah;
O Jesus, my Mahstah,
  He's callin', I come !
O brudder, my brudder,
  Why stan' yo' dar dumb ?"

There was an unsurpassed tenderness and sweetness
in Antoine's rendition of the words, and an unusual
hush fell upon the audience, which was broken now
and then by the audible sighs and incoherent ejaculations of Eph, and when, as it seemed to Eph's
agitated bosom, Antoine's voice soared, in its freshness and simplicity, to the very verge of the eternal,
he could no longer restrain himself, but threw up
his arms in an ecstasy of self-abandonment and
shouted : "I's comin', Lawd ! I's comin'! I's heah !
Take me, po' mis'able sinnah, take me home to
glory!"

Instantly all was confusion. Men, women, and children craned their necks for a view of the excited African whom Aunt Liza's frantic efforts could not calm.
Eph had become possessed of the "power," and was
deaf to his mother's intercessions. "I's knowed it
long, Lawd," he moaned. "I's been a dreffle sinnah.
Jesus, my Mahstah, de fr'en' ob de poah! O Jesus, my
Mahstah, yo' sorrows will cuah——"

"Come, Eph," said Gilbert, who had quickly left the
platform. Eph rose at once, whispering as he did so:

"I neber mean no harm, Mars Gilbert. I's jes a feel-in' de force ob conviction."

"I know," answered Gilbert soothingly. "Antoine's singing was evidently too much for you. You'll feel better in the open air."

"'Deed I'll neber feel any bettah till I knows de Lawd's forgiben de mis'ble sinnah Eph Blackburn! I's jes got to be convarted, Mars Gilbert."

Eph was growing excited again as they neared the door where Red Handed Mike stood among a knot of his fellows. As Gilbert and Eph passed them, Mike exclaimed in a tone loud enough to be heard through-out the hall: "I told Brother Gib he'd better not let them d——d niggers in here."

Gilbert turned and faced him. "That is not fit language for this place, and I don't want any more of it."

"You don't, eh?" cried Mike with a sneer. "I rather guess I've as good a right to say what I please as any d——d nigger."

"Leave the room at once, or I shall be compelled to have you put out."

"You will? Take a little of that first, won't you?" and drawing back the bully, flaming with passion, sent a heavy blow of his fist into Gilbert's face. With a panther-like leap Gilbert evaded the blow, and in-stantly closed his fingers in a vise-like grip around his opponent's throat. Struggling and clutching with the fierceness of a tiger at the long, lithe fingers closing in upon his throat like bands of steel, with his tongue lolling on his chin, his face growing black, and his eyes starting from their sockets, Mike was forced by Gilbert against the wall, who held him there as he cried, " Call the cops, boys!"

"Hold him fast!" "Bully for you, Brother Gib!" "Make him ax yer parding!" yelled the crowd.

"I shall some other day," answered Gilbert. "Just now I'll keep my fingers on him till the cops get him."

A moment later "Red Handed Mike," crest-fallen and sulky, was passed over to the care of a couple of policemen, and Gilbert turned to the men who had gathered around him and said, with a grim appreciation of its underlying humor:

"Boys, I am going to talk to you to-night on the beauty of peace."

He walked quietly and quickly up the aisle, but had not yet mounted the platform when a tremendous cheer broke from the audience. Men threw their hats in the air, and women waved their handkerchiefs as the story of "the fighting parson," as they then and there dubbed him, passed from lip to lip.

CHAPTER XXIII.

Two years passed by; years that brought increasing strength and prosperity to the Society of Universal Brotherhood, and gave it a recognized standing as an important factor in the structure of social reform. Dealing primarily with the fundamental truth of human relationship, and resolutely adhering to the application of those principles to all the conduct of life, it soon established a method of reason which, if primitive, still satisfied the highest aspirations of the heart. In Red Handed Mike Gilbert had won, after long proof of the value of brotherly kindness and forbearance, one of his most earnest co-workers, and it was no uncommon sight to behold the two side by side at political, social, and semi-religious gatherings, endeavoring to promulgate in quiet ways the truths which had become inherent parts of their daily thought and work. To Antoine alone, of all the members of the little circle, the years had brought apparent change. Increasing stature and added health had given him greater comeliness of form, while the once pale, thoughtful face was now enlivened by the glow of color and sparkle of happiness. The parting of Herbert and Elsie had been a great grief to the lad, for love and gratitude to both had built in fancy a glowing future for them. In numberless little ways

he had enoeavored to show his sympathy and appreciation, and to Herbert he had taken to writing long
letters descriptive of the lives and pursuits of the old
circle; but avoiding with intuitive delicacy any direct
reference to Elsie. The progress of the society was
therefore an open book to Herbert, who, wandering
restlessly over the continent of Europe, hungrily
awaited the coming of Antoine's letters in the fond
hope of gleaning even in imagination some news of
Elsie. The two years of his wanderings had been but
a record of growing discontent. His prosperous life
had never before known a serious rebuff, and his love
for Elsie had been the one and only love of his life.
Try as he might in his anger and disapproval, he
could never shut out the memory of the dark eyes and
the piquant face, now sparkling with gayety or quivering with the pathos of grief. All her little crudities of
speech, her high-tragedy airs, her inimitable mimicry,
and her tender flower-like caresses, dwelt so deep within his heart that they were constant companions of his
waking and sleeping hours. He grew old and irritable
under the pressure of grief and disappointment, and
Helen Mason declared that "a mummy from the Cata-
combs couldn't be more unsociable." They wandered
together up the Nile, Herbert declaring his intention
of tracing it to its source and joining Stanley in the
heart of the Dark Continent.

"I'm tired," he said, "of civilization, and think of
returning to savagery, where 'labor strikes' and
'bloated capitalists' are unknown quantities."

"I think you've already reached that state," Helen

retorted, "for I live in almost constant fear of having my head snapped off."

"Well, since I'm so nearly on the confines of cannibalism, I think, to insure your safety, we will go back to Paris."

To Paris they accordingly directed their steps, but the gay capital had no attractions for Herbert. Indeed, he was more at peace lazily dreaming in the land of the Pharaohs, for in the new republic he could not altogether shut his ears to the cry of the people. Thought seemed to be teeming, even in the effete monarchies of the Old World, and when he and Helen, in despair of enjoyment fled to the Russian capital, even there nihilism and nationalism, dogged by the visions of Siberian prisons and infuriated with the cry of slaves in mine and factory, were in the very air they breathed. It was in Russia that Herbert first set himself to studying the conditions so productive of upheaval as well as the worst forms of human cruelty. To Helen's intense fear he took to mingling with the common people, and learning the reason for the scarcely breathed, but only too apparent discontent and rebellion.

"The people! The people! Away with the divine right of kings!" This was the whispered shibboleth of nihilists and nationalists alike in the courts and wilds of Russia, and it swelled into a modulated but well-defined chorus along the banks of the Rhine, until it rang resonant and clear in the heart of the new republic. At home, abroad, wherever he journeyed, the echo of the world's suffering and despair was sure to reach him. But after all what was it to him more than an episode of history, interesting as a study of the conflict of ideas, the upheavals by revolution and evolution? What part had he in forming history, only as one of the many on whom the mantle of existing orders must inevitably fall? With a good deal of impatience he shook off the obtrusive question. Every man must be his own savior and avenger in the battle of existence. Elsie herself had preached the independence of the individual. "True," said Conscience, "but did she preach that alone? Did she not also believe in the fullest co-operation as a prop and encouragement to individual effort? Was not her life an epitome of the highest personal development, morally at least, combined with the most unselfish desire for the prosperity of others?"

It was a long battle between a selfishness born of his environment, as well as what he considered the inherent rights of individuals and classes, and conscience and conviction. But the latter finally won the day, and with an eagerness out of all proportion to his former weariness and disgust with life, he set out for Paris and London with the determination to investigate this industrial question to its farthest limit. He was in London on that great first of May, when over two millions of men throughout the world laid down their tools and quietly awaited the declaration of advancing reason. He began to see that the principle of co-operation, based, as it must ever be, on the simple lines of equal opportunity and equal footing before the law, held within its embracing bosom the solution of many of the vexed and complex problems of sociology. It was while in Paris, however, that he made the vital discovery which gave direction and concentration to his study of the industrial question. While rambling with Helen in the purlieus of the great city, he chanced upon a small community of neat flower-enveloped cottages contiguous to an immense factory, and of which they were evidently a part. Inquiry developed the fact that the little village belonged to a manufacturer, who had organized a colony of workingmen on an entirely original plan, in which their comfort was co-ordinate with the profits to be gained. The cottages were rented to men with families at from one dollar and a half to three dollars per month, with the result that after long service they finally fell into the hands of the occupants. The workingmen were insured against accident, and their savings invested in the works at a guaranteed six per cent per annum. Work was paid for by the piece at remunerative wages, thus giving the skilled workman the opportunity to realize on his ability, and stimulating the unskilled to greater activity. Imperfect work was rigidly rejected at the expense of the employee, thereby insuring the greatest carefulness and exactness. The streets of the little village were handsomely paved, an ornate concert hall and good school-houses adding to the attractiveness of the picture. The unmarried workmen were able to secure comfortable lodgings at three cents per day, and a restaurant provided meals at prices just paying expenses. Discontent was an unknown quantity, while rosy-cheeked children and plump matrons were living proof of the beneficence of the system. In fact,

situations were eagerly sought after and rarely va-
cated save by death or disaster. The profits of the
establishment were not, of course, enormous, like so
many similar institutions where human lives are sacrificed on the altar of greed; but being moderate yet
afforded a safe permanent investment, which was never
affected by strikes or lockouts, and which in the zeal
and affection of the community for its employer relieved the burden of care and anxiety under which
capital so often groans in less favored circles. After
weeks of investigation, Herbert concluded that here
was the middle ground on which capital and labor
must meet before either can achieve an unbroken line
of progress. Making himself and Helen acquainted
with the owner and promulgator of all this thrift and
contentment, and beholding him in his charming home,
surrounded by luxuries, and with his daily comings
and goings lighted by the smiles and affection of his
people, Herbert found his own ambition fired to be
the originator and center of a similar community. He
realized that the outlay at first would be enormous,
involving his whole fortune, and that the most arduous
and exacting labor would be demanded of him in its
execution. But here under the balmy skies of France
was the living prosperous proof that business and sentiment, so universally divorced by popular clamor, may
be united in a harmonious and prolific marriage. For
the first time within the last two years, Herbert
dropped his taciturnity and discussed the project with
Helen, who strangely enough had become as infatu-
ated with the little community as had Herbert himself.

"After all, Herbert," she said plaintively one day, "I believe having your own way all the time is like living on honey—it palls on the appetite very soon."

Herbert glanced up quickly. "Are you turning philanthropist too?" he asked with a touch of satire in his tone

"Well, it is in the air," she answered resignedly, "and I don't see how one can help being infected."

"Bravo! Helen, you take the disease charmingly! Shall we go back to America to establish a new Eden?"

"On one condition, and that is—to take me in as equal parter."

"My sweet sister!" cried Herbert ecstatically as he sprang from his chair and caught her around the waist. "Do you really mean it?"

"Truly; and, Herbert," and with tears in the eyes upraised to his she added brokenly, "if—if that little saint, Elsie, Alice Houghton writes me about, can be induced——"

"There!" Herbert's face hardened as he placed his hand on his sister's lips. "Say no more on that subject. I appreciate your generosity, but hope died long ago."

Two days later they were on the ocean homeward bound, and with the zeal of new-born ambition were deep in their project almost before they returned the greeting of their friends. Some two weeks after their arrival the C—— *Sunday Herald* contained a notice of the purchase of a large tract of land in the northwestern part of the city, including the subdivision known as "Idlewild," by Herbert Lynn, Esq., who proposed

the erection of a mammoth shoe factory to be managed
after a method which he had investigated abroad, and
believed to be not only the safest investment for capi
tal, but one yielding the largest returns from the
standpoint of the philanthropist.

"Mr. Lynn," the article went on to say, "is the
pioneer in this form of enterprise, and feeling that
there is no reason other than inexcusable greed for
the occurrence of so much idleness, suffering, destitu-
tion, vice, ignorance, and penury in so many depart-
ments of American labor, he proposes a plan of co-
operation, now working harmoniously and profitably
in France, which will no doubt do much toward solving some vexed industrial conflicts."

Following this was a short history of the colony on
the edge of Paris and its plan of operations. Elsie
read the article with swimming eyes, and impulsively
kissed the insensate bearer of such good news. She
had not seen Herbert since his return, and this was
the first intimation of his project which she had received from any one. How beautiful the world grew
all at once! How much there was in life to hope for,
work for, enjoy! Suffering humanity under Herbert's
fostering care—ah, how could it be other than happy?
To live in the light of those sunny blue eyes—how she
envied the prospective inhabitants of that social para-
dise. But the weeks grew into months, and Herbert
made no effort to renew his old standing in the little
circle. His name was rarely mentioned to Elsie, although she learned from Lizzette that he had appro-
priated one of the handsomest residences included in

his purchase of Idlewild, and had taken Lizzette from her market gardening to preside over his bachelor establishment. Voluble as Lizzette had always been, she was now suspiciously silent, unless she had a bit of gossip to offer regarding the interest taken in the proposed work by Alice Houghton. Antoine, happy as a bird in the new home and the exceptional progress he was making in music, took especial care to avoid the mention of Herbert's name, although Elsie often intercepted a wistful glance of commiseration in his dark eyes. Why were they all so silent? she often asked her longing heart. Did they think she had no courage? Did they fancy her a Lily Maid of Astolat who needs must die for love? Well, they should see she could be brave and work on through a long life, and make no sign of heart-break! So with renewed earnestness, never sparing a moment for much-needed rest, she toiled on, earning her daily bread and giving the helping hand to all who needed it. Margaret's watchful eyes noted with pain how thin and transparent the once rounded face was growing, what an intent light burned within the old laughter-loving eyes, and how feverish was her application to her work.

It was a year before the great co-operative shoe factory was in running order, and on the evening of the first day of regular work, Herbert, flushed and elated over the promised success of his plan, was driving hurriedly along the street, on his way to visit Helen and report progress. Glancing up suddenly he encountered the gaze of Elsie's eyes as she paused for a second on the crossing. Heavens! How white and frail she looked! What caverns those great dark eyes had grown to be! Was she dying and nobody to tell him?

So preoccupied was he with these hurried thoughts that he passed on, failing to return the slight salutation she had made. A moment later he drew rein, but Elsie had disppeared from view. He turned and followed in the direction she had taken, but she was no-where to be seen. He had been working of late like the traditional galley-slave, curbing his impatience in the thought of the offering he could one day lay at her feet, and now, like a phantom of her old blithe, rosy-cheeked self, she had crossed his path, and the dark eyes had seemed to speak the despairing words, "Too late! Too late!"

Lashing his horse into a white foam, in absolute de-fiance of the ordinance against fast driving, he rushed a few moments later in upon Margaret with the frightened question:

"Where is Elsie? Why has nobody told me she was dying?"

The question seemed almost brutal in its abruptness, and Margaret staggered as if struck by a blow.

"Forgive me, Margaret," cried Herbert piteously. "I passed her just now, but lost her again, looking so frail and wan—did you not know? Have you not seen?"

"Ah, yes," moaned Margaret. "But I had no medicine for a breaking heart. A spirit like hers soon burns out the fires of a frail body."

It was some time later that the door opened suddenly and Elsie, pale, trembling with the exertion of climbing the stairs, and with eyes veiled in the shadow of utter despair, stood on the threshold.

Herbert was at her side in an instant. "Elsie! Elsie!" he cried. "Love is master. I've come back to you, strengthened, purified, ennobled at your hands. Do not scorn the gift now. It is richer than all else I ever offered you."

But Elsie had no answer to make. For the first time in her life she fainted, and lay a veritable picture of death in Herbert's arms. "Dear God," he cried, "not this! Not now with our work all before us! Let me keep her lest I grow slothful in the service of her dear Master!"

Down on his knees beside the frail form, chafing the thin hands and with the tears chasing each other in torrents over his face, Herbert knelt, too frightened, too heart-broken to be of any service in Margaret's hasty efforts at resuscitation.

Joy seldom kills, and Elsie slowly came back to life and love with the shadow of the old smile on her lips.

"Herbert," she whispered as, still faint, but supremely happy, she rested her head on his shoulder, "the old wilful, independent Elsie is dead, and I want to prove to you hereafter how patient and submissive I can be."

"Well, then," said Herbert, after one of those eloquent silences which "the world that dearly loves a lover" can readily interpret—"well, then, I'm going to take you at your word; for to-morrow at high noon, in society vernacular, I shall be here with license, priest, Helen, and all the rest of us, prepared to hear a very meek 'I will' from those white lips."

"But I have no wedding-gown!"

"Put on your best calico," said Herbert composedly. "So long as I can see you wear that glad light in your eyes and the old happy smile on your lips, I shall always feel that you are clothed in radiant attire."

One evening several days after the wedding, Gilbert came home to Margaret with an inscrutable smile on his face. "Margaret," he said composedly, "I have come to the conclusion that your occupation as home-maker is about gone."

"What do you mean?" she cried aghast.

"Well, Herbert has given me a place in the factory, and he and Elsie insist that I make my future home with them. It rather strikes me that you are left out in the cold in consequence."

Tears sprang to Margaret's eyes, and with a heart-breaking sob she buried her head in her arms as she leaned against the table.

"My dear sister," cried Gilbert quickly. "My joke is rather rough I'll admit; but I've a little excuse for it." And stepping to the hall door, he beckoned mysteriously to some one standing there. Margaret raised her head apprehensively, and saw Dr. Ely with smiling face standing upon the threshold.

"Here is a gentleman," said Gilbert soberly, "who thinks he would like to have a home made for him." And with an ostentatious bang to the door he slipped away.

CONCLUSION.

Of the remaining members of the little circle there are but few words to speak. In Alice Houghton and Helen Mason the Society of Universal Brotherhood finds able coadjutors. Life becomes broader and fairer to them as they realize the existence of a common bond in humanity and a universal creed of brotherly love.

Slowly, but surely, the seed sown in doubt, darkness, and tribulation has begun to bear fruit, and Gilbert, the powerful leader of the new movement, often blesses the memory of the hours of sorrow and trial which have made these helping influences spring from a soil watered by tears and harrowed by privation. Antoine's violin and marvellous gift of improvisation are the delight of an enthusiastic public, and Lizzette's brown face, with the wrinkles growing a little deeper as the years go by, wears a look of supreme pride and contentment as she comtemplates his progress. A cherished member of Herbert's home, she is at once housekeeper, friend, and companion.

The marriage of Herbert and Elsie is one of those perfect unions in which oneness of spirit, heart, and effort keep an unbroken bond. They have seen their endeavors paying them a tenfold increase in the growing tide of thought and prosperity overtaking the workingmen and women and widening out into an irresistible current of human kindness. Children have come to them, endowed with the same warm, generous natures, who are never so happy as when smoothing a wrinkle out of papa's tired brow, or making a dimple come in mamma's pretty cheek. Elsie, the idol of her home, and beloved alike by the prosperous circle of universal brotherhood, and the thrifty, contented colony at Idlewild, often delights, with children clinging to her skirts, and a crowing baby perched on Herbert's shoulder, half-laughingly, half-earnestly, to proclaim him the founder and father of America's New Aristocracy of heart and brain.

THE END.